THE REDDENING PATH

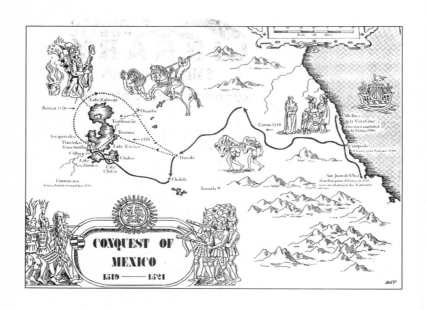

CONQUEST OF
MEXICO
1519 — 1521

THE
SEA ROUTE
OF CORTES

THE REDDENING PATH

AMANDA HALE

thistledown press

Library and Archives Canada Cataloguing in Publication

Hale, Amanda
The reddening path / Amanda Hale.

ISBN 978-1-897235-26-3

I. Title.

PS8565.A4313R44 2007   C813'.6   C2007-900653-1

Cover painting by Pedro Rafael Gonzalez Chavajay
Cover and book design by Jackie Forrie
Typeset by Thistledown Press
Printed and bound in Canada by Marquis Book Printing Inc.

Thistledown Press Ltd.
633 Main Street
Saskatoon, Saskatchewan, S7H 0J8
www.thistledownpress.com

Thistledown Press gratefully acknowledges the financial assistance of the Canada Council for the Arts, the Saskatchewan Arts Board, and the Government of Canada through the Book Publishing Industry Development Program for its publishing program.

 Canada Council **Conseil des Arts**
for the Arts du Canada

 Canadian   Patrimoine
Heritage   canadien

For Alejandro, Zoila, Byron, Alex, Juana, Tijax,
Joel and Marco:
my Mayan family

ACKNOWLEDGEMENTS

Thanks to all the generous people who have helped me in varying degrees, especially those in Guatemala City who provided me with invaluable information and who, for the sake of discretion, must remain nameless. Special thanks for information, encouragement and ideas to Zoila Ramírez, Alejandro Ruiz, Aija Mara, Mariana Trucco, Tom Knott, Lorenne Clark, George Buvyer, Nancy Goldhar, Louise Jarvis, Ana Miriam Leigh, Sara De Rose; to Basil du Plessis and Tom Lownie for computer rescue; and to Anna Lanyon for her wonderful books on Malinche and Martín Cortés. Thanks also to the other writers and scholars, living and dead, whose works have inspired me and are cited in the text. Thanks to my readers: Susan Cole, Nery Espinoza, Rosemary Sullivan, Alan Twigg, and George Szanto, all so generous with their time. Thanks to Thistledown Press, my publisher, and to my skillful editor, John Lent, for their vision in supporting this book; and to all the talented people at Thistledown Press. Finally and most importantly, thanks to my friend, Joy Gugeler, who has so generously given of her time and expertise in the development of this novel.

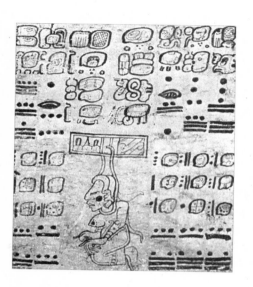

PROLOGUE

•

Madrid, 2003

My face is broad and pitted like stone. My forehead slopes steeply into the thin bridge of a parrot nose, curved like my back, flaring into the fullness of nostrils. My eyes are downcast, dark as a storm brewing, lips closed over jade-studded teeth. Above me rises an elaborate head-dress, like a veil over the world, bejewelled with jade and turquoise. I'm an angry old woman, wrinkled and bent, my sweetness fermented by what I have seen, and what I have done to survive. But it wasn't always so. I drank cacao, elixir of the Gods, with my husband, Itzámná, and all the Gods were progeny of our pleasure, all from my body..

I've been silent for centuries. Now I must speak.

Listen.

The place where my shrine stood is grassed over. My shadow stands on the hillside of that small island off the coast of what they call Yucatán. Waves crash on the shore beneath, plumes of spray rising in the blue air. Arms folded across my breast, I watch corn growing in the blood of my people, watch the faces of the Maya emerge from silken husks. My skirt flutters in the wind; along the cliffs ghosts of proud temples perch on the edge of the land, my own temple ransacked by the one they called Tonatiuh, the blonde Captain of the Spanish God, Cortés.

My body, turned to stone, has sailed east, rocking amidst the golden plunder of the temples. And from my stony interior, imprisoned behind glass in this museum, I have learned to spread my consciousness throughout the world, beyond time and place.

I see the faces of my people, their tattoos obscured by the branding iron, their skin palimpsests of power, branding over branding imprinting their bodies, obliterating them. My spirit travels back to the green skin of the mountains; I know they are alive because I feel them tremble as the rivers run with blood. I hear their breath and see the exhalation of mist that veils the horrors. La selva esta respirando. *I don't weep, I cannot. I've woven a hammock which stretches across the oceans, spanning the worlds, old and new, and I've hoisted it high where I lay in the Heavens, my hand trailing to touch the stars. Here I've lain for centuries, my back curved into the moon, illuminating the Earth, while my body is displayed in Madrid as a curiosity. I've seen mighty ships rising and crashing, rolling with waves of conquerors. I've seen the lands of the Maya, the Aztecs, the Culhua-Mexica, springing afresh with white corn, red and yellow corn, from the burnt and blooded earth. I see myself imprisoned, people paying to see the plunder, the spoils of war. They peer at me through the glass, they lean in close and when the alarm shrills, they jump back, guilty. Listen to them.*

"What a strange creature. Her back's bent double. What is she, a medicine woman?"

"*Ix Chak Chel, the Old Goddess of weaving, water, medicine and childbirth. Wife of Itzámná, God of Creation.*"

"Here she is again, "*Lady Rainbow.*" And look there, she's sitting in the moon holding a rabbit."

"Here's another.""That's not her. The hair's a mass of serpents, clawed hands and feet, crossbones embroidered on the skirt . . . "

"It's written here — "*Ixchel . . . proves she's the equivalent of Coatlicue, Great Mother of the Aztecs.*"

I see the devout Christian, Cristóbal Colón, hoist his sails.

"We must spread the word," he cries, but his men are moonstruck, dreams of gold glinting in their eyes. A fleet of galleons sets sail on a Friday, blessed by Isabel la Catolica, Queen of Spain, galleons loaded with barrels of wine and olives, priests holding relics over the water, pointing the way.

1492, a watershed year for Spain, a renaissance of the weakened, medieval Inquisition. A tide sweeps across the red Spanish earth as the Moors are herded out of Granada, Córdoba, Sevilla, and the Jews are expelled by Royal Edict of Ferdinand and Isabel, who strive for religious orthodoxy and racial purity. They are driven south across the parched earth, into cold salt water. The tide sweeps on across the ocean, across the lands of a New World as the Spaniards, led by Hernández de Córdoba, wade from their ships in 1517, through warm aquamarine waves frothed with spume. As the hooves of the first Spanish horses bite into the earth of Mexico, a metal-clad standard-bearer gallops ahead, bearing the cross aloft, and my people run before him in terror of the four-legged man-beast.

"¿Donde estamos, Donde estamos?" the Spaniards shout.

*"Ma c'ubah than, Ma c'ubah than," chant my people, for they do not understand the bearded ones who, in turn, do not know where they stand, on golden sands fringed with stone-carved pyramids. Desperate for an answer, a swarthy fellow makes his own interpretation of our language. "*Yucatán!*" he*

shouts and so they locate themselves, tumbling onto the beach, heavy boots imprinting the shifting sands.

I see old Martín Cortés working in his vineyard in Medellín in the province of Estremadura. He pulls back the vine and prunes it deftly, his fingers thick and work-worn. Martín fought to drive the Moors from Granada in the final stages of La Reconquista. Spain had been conquered by the Romans, the Visigoths and finally the Arabs who had reshaped the country with their Great Mosque at Córdoba, the palace at Medina Azáhara, the Alhambra whose walls were inscribed with tales that could not be told in images, because the Koran forbids representation of the human body. The tide has turned and the Spaniards are overcoming centuries of subjugation. But the ousting of the Moors has been a bloody business and Martín wants something different for his son; an education, a profession outside of the military. With the wine of his vineyard, with the honey of his wife's hives, with the proceeds from their flour mill, they have scrimped to send Hernándo to the University of Salamanca, where he listens open-mouthed to fabulous tales of the discovery of a New World. He reads the great chivalric romances of the day — Tales of Amadis and Ballad of Montesinos. So engrossed is he in the world of imagination that he fails at his studies, but oh, he is inspired at the gaming tables, in the bedroom and astride his horse. Dismounting one moonlit night outside the window of Doña Carmen, wife of his aging philosophy professor, the young Hernándo is surprised by Don Arguelles.

"What is your business at my wife's bedroom window, Cortés?"

"I am taking instruction from her in the fine arts of pleasure, sir. And may I inform you that I have already learned more

*from your wife in only one night of instruction than I have
learned from you in an entire three-month."*

*I see Hernándo leap at the wall, grasp a thick vine and begin
his rapid ascent to the open window. He disarms everyone in
his path and dreams nightly of the new lands discovered by
Cristóbal Colón. At nineteen he bids farewell to his country
and sets sail for the Indies, landing at Santo Domingo on the
island of Hispaniola in 1504.*

*I see him standing, hands on hips, before the Spanish
governor of Hispaniola. Where people have stood they
sometimes remain, shadows, like me, and Cortés stands yet,
looking at an elegant mansion furnished with tapestries and
paintings from Spain, his brown eyes shining as he remembers
his beginning.*

*"I will grant you a plot of land," says the governor, "And
in time you will acquire Indians to serve you."*

*"But I came to get gold, not to till the soil like a peasant!
Are there no expeditions I can join?"*

*"To get gold you must have gold. You must first apply
yourself, Cortés."*

*Soon his lands are tall with sugar cane. He quadruples
his profits at the gaming tables and gains a reputation as a
dueller who'll go to any lengths to maintain his favour with
the ladies. Only once is he blooded, by Miguel Gutiérrez
who, infuriated by Hernándo's seduction of his wife and his
arrogant lip — "I'm plowing your furrow for you, Gutiérrez.
You are guilty, I believe, of neglecting your land. You owe me
for my labour," — slices him neatly below that same lip, a
bloody line which matures into a thin white scar. Fearless, he
is in the arms of Señora Gutiérrez that very night, receiving
the solace of her kisses upon his injury.*

1511: I see him join Diego Velasquez in the conquest of Cuba and prove himself so valiant that Velasquez, governor of the new colony, rewards him with a rich plantation and slaves. But Cortés, twenty-six years old and swollen with ambition, is not a good follower. Their relationship sours and Velasquez clamps him in leg-irons. Cortés escapes and wins over Velasquez by agreeing to marry Catalina Suarez, a beauty whose reputation has been jeopardized by Cortés' long dalliance with her. The Spanish hold great score by chivalry. Velasquez rewards Cortés by naming him alcalde *of Santiago.*

I know about slavery and entrapment, but I have learned my escape. I stand in many places; I see everything. I see myself reflected, a golden orb floating in the red wetness of my land as the blood of seventy million Indians soaks into the earth. I who gave birth to all the Gods, see my belly swell into a great circle, pulling light from the stars, illuminating the darkness as the Heavens heave with lost souls. This is only the beginning of an endless river of blood. This is the history of the Earth, the foundation of a New World.

Cortés is not a settling man. When Pedro de Alvarado, the one they call Tonatiuh, comes with news of a golden land to the west, his appetite for adventure sharpens. Alvarado is blonde as Cortés is dark. They are spirit twins, sun and moon, both cursed with a ruthless energy to conquer.

"The place is called Yucatán and the Mayan Indians live there," says Alvarado. "They have roads and reservoirs of stone, and ornaments made of silver and gold with precious stones." I see him watching Hernándo's eyes. He knows he has him.

When Velasquez sends an expedition to Yucatán in search of Juan de Grijálva, an explorer who has not returned after more than a year, he chooses Cortés as commanding officer. "Officially you go in search of Grijálva," he says, "But between you and me, Hernándo, you're free to trade with the Indians for whatever you can get." Velasquez pauses a moment, his steely gaze fixed on Hernándo. "On my behalf of course," he adds.

At table that night Catalina pales when Cortés broaches the subject of his departure. She takes several breaths before laying down her knife and fork carefully.

"Hernándo, what about the plantation? I can't manage it without you."

"I'm not a farmer, Cata. Do you think I want to spend my life cutting cane to sweeten the lips of King Carlos?"

"But we have slaves," she replies, "Your hands are clean."

"You knew when you married me that I was not a lap dog, my dear."

Catalina's hands fly to her neck. I see this gesture over and over, her moment of panic circling the earth. She plays nervously with the pearls that ring her white throat. Hernándo gave them to her on their wedding night. Her head jerks. "Hernándo, I want a child."

"Indeed. And aren't I doing my duty as I vowed before the priest?"

"But if you go away . . . "

"I shall return, and if not I shall send for you, rest assured."

"But Hernándo . . . I will miss you." Her face is flushed now, her voice filled with pleading, her fingers twisting the pearls. As Hernándo watches her from the end of the long table a muscle twitches in his jaw. He finishes his meal and leaves the dining table to begin preparations for his voyage.

On the day of departure Velasquez follows Cortés up the gangplank of the lead ship with a bundle under his arm wrapped in goldspun cloth. Safely within the confines of the Captain's cabin Velasquez unwraps the cloth. "The Virgin of Socorro to guide you on your journey," he says, placing the painted wooden figure in Cortés' hands. "I brought her with me from Spain. She has given me great good fortune. Now she's yours."

Cortés presses his scarred lip against the hooded blonde hair of the Virgin. A dark cloak covers all but a red slash of her dress, streaking down the centre of her body as she succours her child. "You have blessed me, Don Diego. Now you must go ashore."

I see him set sail in the spring of 1519, Captain-General of an armada of 11 ships with 100 sailors, 508 soldiers, 10 cannon, 16 horses and many Indian servants from the island of Cuba. As the sails swell, pulling his galleon out to sea, Cortés turns his back on the port of Santiago and walks to the prow of the ship. The wind in his face, he holds the Virgin of Socorro out over the waters, blessing his path towards a New World.

I see the fleet anchored in stormy seas off the coast of Tabasco. Chief Taabscoob sees them and prepares his warriors to fight. He knows the Spanish; he's already dispensed with Grijálva and his expedition. Cortés meets with his officers, Pedro de Alvarado, Cristóbal de Olíd, Alonso de Puertocarrero, and Gonzalo de Sandoval.

Alvarado paces the cabin. "We must get ashore," he says. "The first move always wins."

"Let us first send Jerónimo de Aguilar to tell them that we come in peace," says Sandoval.

Cortés took Aguilar on board at Cozumel, a priest who was stranded on an earlier expedition to Yucatán. He's lived with my people for eight years and speaks our language, Chontol Maya.

"Let us send Aguilar immediately, mi capitán, while we prepare our men and horses for disembarcation," says Puertocarrero.

Cortés slaps his shoulder. "Of course," he says, "We're looking for Grijálva. And those golden treasures Alvarado promised us. You'd better not disappoint me, Pedro!"

His laughter fills the cabin, and Alvarado ducks his golden head under the low doorway and vaults up on deck. Cortés turns to the Virgin's niche, sinks to his knees, crosses himself. His lips move in silent prayer, his eyes never leaving hers, then he touches his lips to the crown of her head, and is out of the cabin in four strides.

Cortés leaves 800 dead, with only two of his own men lost. They seal the wounds of the injured with fat melted down from the flesh of our dead. Taabscoob sends gifts to the victors to placate them; gourds full of fruit, and brightly coloured birds, each tied to a stick with a long vine so they can flutter in the air but never escape. They receive golden cups and bracelets. They receive twenty Indian girls, slaves passed on by Taabscoob. The thirteenth in line is Malintzín, the girl who will come to be known as Malinche. Cortés does not recognize her at first, a thin, dark-skinned slave girl. He is preoccupied. He gives her to Puertocarrero, but he himself is a marked man from her first glance. I see Malintzín leave her body that night as the young Spaniard enters her. Quetzalcoatl is testing me, she thinks, and she watches from the night sky as Puertocarrero rolls off her body and falls into a deep sleep. I see her come to earth, hunker in the shadows of the firelight, reach across his body and cram her mouth with meat and bread. She will have a full belly and she will never be sold again.

Now it is time to tell the story. You thought this was it? Oh no. I squat to water the Earth and the sun catches my golden stream and arcs a rainbow across the Heavens. Here I pick my threads; blue of the ocean, golden sun, bright blood-red and yellow corn, magenta and jade, the green Earth studded with turquoise. I weave a story, beyond time as stories always are, my shuttle passing back and forth, weft over warp, each thread disappearing, becoming part of the pattern. I spread my story. I am everywhere; watch for me.

PART ONE

Mestizo means not solely a mixture of blood, a child born of parents of different races, but also the irrevocable mixture of cultures that lies at the heart of Latin American history. Mestizo is as much a historical as biological quality.

— Ana Mendieta:
The Rupestrian Sculptures

Toronto, 2003.

Paméla's bare feet slapped the kitchen linoleum as she padded from refrigerator to stove. She frowned, trying to remember her dream as she spooned chocolate into a large blue cup. Milk sizzled at the edges of a pot and she waited a few seconds for the liquid to foam to the top before scooping it off the element and into the cup. She was still in her nightgown, her black hair falling heavily on her shoulders, swinging with the motion of her body as she walked into the living room of the rambling three-storey house she shared with her mothers, a stone's throw from Withrow Park. The house had a dark lush atmosphere, shaded by leafy maples and chestnuts in summer.

She had been adopted by Hannah and Fern in November 1982 when she was nine months old. They had travelled to Guatemala to get her and adored her from the first moment, Hannah's face aching with smiles and Fern weeping as the young girl from the orphanage carried Paméla into the receiving room of the adoption agency. Hannah and Fern were pillars of the Toronto lesbian-feminist community, Hannah an immigration lawyer and Fern a professor at the Ontario Institute for Studies in Education at the University of Toronto. They'd brought her up bilingual and attended Spanish classes themselves to keep up with her quick tongue. In the early days they'd taken her to annual reunions with her fellow adoptees in Montréal and Ottawa. They took her to Cuba, to the Dominican Republic, and to Mexico. They had discussed taking her back to Guatemala, but had decided it might be somewhere she would want to visit later, as she matured. They'd done everything right, but lately Paméla had been troubled by dreams, waking in the night crying for something she couldn't remember, left with a heavy feeling all day.

She leaned back and sipped the thick sweet drink. "*Que rica,*" she murmured. She'd woken with a longing for chocolate on her tongue. The rich taste comforted her and blended with the darkness of her dream. A pale winter light stole through the window. She closed her eyes and tried again to remember. Her eyes moved back and forth as she traversed the edges of her dream, a border flaring with a strange luminosity, then suddenly she was inside it, out of her own skin, in another place, and the images began tumbling in.

She's crouched in the corner of the schoolroom with Mamá and all the children. Sweat trickles down her temples. She sees Mamá's lips trembling. They're all crowded in, all the women and children.

"*Why are we here? Why do we have to be quiet*"
"*Shhhh!*" *Mamá's finger to her lips.*

She whimpers and Mamá pulls her face to her breast, covering her head, stroking, stroking. A single gunshot jolts her body and Mamá grips her so hard she thinks she'll die. Then the air is filled with cries and shots, one after another, bam bam bam, *like ten thunderstorms. When it stops the air has turned white, the women's faces are white. One of them looks through a crack in the wall and doubles over, sobbing. She trembles like a corn stalk when the wind comes up with a warning smell of summer rain. Then the door bursts open and she hears loud voices, feels the vibration of boots hitting the ground, the tightening of Mamá's hands on her shoulders, around her hips. She's lifted into the air, she's flying through the screams, across the schoolroom,* thunk *in the corner. She crouches there, curled like a caracol, eyes shut tight.*

When she uncurls her body it's almost dark and everyone is gone. A terrible silence hangs in the darkened air. She walks across the earthen floor, her bare feet raising little clouds of dust. The blackboard is empty, their slates are clean. Outside the earth is dark with blood. She hears the earth gulping; it drinks and drinks, darkening with each gulp. All the Papás are lying in a heap, their mouths open in surprise. She keeps walking, the soles of her feet turning red, walking on the gulping earth. By the time she reaches her house she's empty. There's no one, no one left, only the disembodied limbs of her mother, a brightly woven cloth still grasped in one hand, all the women and children, hacked to pieces with machetes, the blood of the massacre mixed with the blood of babies swinging in circles, their heads splitting open on the white plaster fashioned by the hands of their fathers, their brothers, their uncles. She sees hands everywhere, holding, patting, smoothing, picking, swinging, stroking — she cannot tell one from another. She starts walking, ankle deep in blood now, out of the village, past the mountain of Papás, past the smoking milpas, all the cornstalks burned like discarded limbs, into the jungle. She sees herself disappearing down a reddening path, and she wakes sobbing.

Paméla wiped her eyes with the sleeve of her nightgown and gulped the rest of her chocolate. She had classes to attend; she was a second year student at the University of Toronto, doing a joint major in History and Political Science. As she showered and dressed she tried to shake the feeling of grief sitting in her. *It's only a dream. It has nothing to do with me. I wasn't even walking when I left Guatemala.* As she brushed her hair, staring sadly into the mirror, the card caught her eye — a print of Georgia O'Keefe's shamelessly petalled orchid. It looked to her somehow predatory. She opened the thick white card yet again.

My Mayan beauty . . . I'll never forget you.
The river flows on, don't be sad, Talya

She should have listened to Hannah and Fern. Of course she had thought they would be thrilled that she'd fallen in love with a woman. It had all happened so fast. She had barely heard their warnings.

"Take care of your heart, darling. She's got a reputation," Hannah had said. And when Paméla protested, Fern had cut in quickly, "I know this is different, but we don't want to see you hurt."

She had opened like the flower on Talya's goodbye card; three months of bliss, then it was over with no explanation. Just another affair for Talya, but it had shattered Paméla; her first experience of loss, the first that she could remember. In those final days she had phoned

Talya three or four times a day and left messages. She had walked over to her apartment between classes and left a note — *Come on, Tal, call me! I'm so worried. Where are you?* She had fought the sinking feeling in her gut, until the card arrived with its message shooting through her like an electric shock. Paméla lost her confidence, but within her dwelt a fierce, unrelenting spirit which seemed to come out of the darkness. It came from the same place as her dreams and pushed her forward into the world. Three torturous days after receiving the card, days of waking with swollen eyes and an aching throat, filled with longing for someone who was no longer there, she had started searching for her birth mother, looking up references for Guatemalan adoption agencies on the internet. The information was quite revealing. Although she had come no closer to tracing her own origins she'd learned that third world adoption was a booming business. She hadn't yet told her parents about the search. She was hunkered down, curled in on herself, nursing the humiliation of her rejection. She couldn't bear the thought of Hannah and Fern's well-meaning sympathy. She didn't want to lose it with them; they were too good. And she'd thought all the world was like them, at least everyone in her immediate world of downtown Toronto.

Paméla realized that she was caressing the creamy textured paper of the card, the surface like braille under her fingers. She folded it abruptly and was going to tear it in half and throw it in the garbage, but changed her mind and placed it instead at the back of her underwear drawer.

Paméla perused the shelves of the Robarts Library, gathering books until her arms were full. She had to write a paper for her Latin American history course which spanned pre-Colombian through the colonial period to the wars of independence. She'd been procrastinating, but now she was grateful for a focus to keep her mind off the dream and off the fruitless search for her birth mother. She staggered to a carrel to begin her research, her pile of books wobbling as she plunked them down on the desk. William H. Prescott, *History of the Conquest of Mexico*; Hugh Thomas, *Conquest: Montezuma, Cortés and the Fall of Old Mexico*; W.J. Jacobs, *Hernándo Cortés*; John Wilkes, *Hernándo Cortés — Conquest of Mexico*; Gloria Durán, *Malinche, Slave Princess*; Bernal Diaz del Castillo, *True History of the Conquest of Mexico*; Ronald Wright, *Stolen Continents*; Oakland Ross, *The Dark Virgin*.

Paméla leaned back, overwhelmed. She rummaged in her pack and found the handout from History 291.

Discuss the circumstances that enabled Cortés to conquer the Aztec peoples of Mexico. It is suggested that the student begin his/her research with a character study of Hernándo Cortés, discussing the affairs of the time, both in Spain and in the Americas, giving special attention to the separate groupings within the Aztec nation, such as the Culhua-Mexica of Tenochtitlan. Discuss the clash of cultures between Old and New Worlds, European and Primitive, using examples from the Spanish Conquest.

She closed her eyes and ran her fingers down the tower of books, leaning in to smell the musty pages. When she opened her eyes and found Gloria Durán's book in her hands she laughed and began reading.

∾

Darkness closed in on Malintzín until she couldn't breathe. She swallowed, gulping for sustenance in the swampy Gulf air. She woke with her mouth full of blood and spat on the earthen floor. "Where are you, Tonantzin? Where are you hiding, Mother Moon? Is it blood you want?" Malintzín had heard that the Mother Goddess had her own altar atop the great pyramid of Tenochtitlan next to Huitzilopochtli, the Sun God. Her father had told her about his journey to the great city of the Culhua-Mexica and had described the temples there. Seven years ago, after her father's death, she had been sold into slavery, into the house of the wealthy *cacique*, Taabscoob, chief of the town of Potonchan. At first she'd slept with the other servant girls in the house and had learned to weave the fine fabrics of the region. But as she'd ripened her master eyed her, then he picked her and she fought like a wild cat and was banished to this hut on the edge of the swampland. She was given the most menial tasks; washing, cleaning, lifting heavy sacks of corn and flour, and her food rations were quartered. Malintzín had prayed to Tonantzin and to Chicomecoatl, Goddess of the ripened *maíz*, to help her in her hunger. She dreamed of warm tortillas, steaming tamales, rich atole and pinole. "Is this my punishment," she whispered into the darkness, "for refusing my master? Or is it because I am born under the sign of trouble and strife?" The birth of a son had been predicted by the priestess, one who would rule over an empire, but never over his own heart. Malintzín's father, *cacique* of the town of Paynala in the Gulf region of Coatzacoalcos, had raised her accordingly, despite her surprising gender. Coatzacoalcos lay on the Gulf side of the Tehuantepec Isthmus, the narrowest part of Mexico.

"She will know great victories and defeats. Death and destruction will follow in her wake," the priestess had said, "But Quetzalcoatl will guide her journey on Earth and give her a place beside him in the Heavens."

When Malintzín was born at the turn of the European century, nineteen years before the predicted return of Quetzalcoatl, on the day *Ce Acatl*, Day of the Reed, in the year 2-Rabbit of the Aztec calendar, the omens had not yet begun. But soon, from Tenochtitlan to the Gulf, people began to hear again the sound of a wailing woman in the night.

"Cihuacoatl," they said, "For what does she weep? Still for the loss of her children?"

Cihuacoatl was worshipped by the Culhua-Mexica, but she had not originated with them. When the conquering tribe had moved south and established the city of Tenochtitlan they appropriated Cihuacoatl, Serpent Goddess of the vanquished inhabitants of the Valley of Mexico. After the conquest Cihuacoatl was said to wander in the night, wailing for the violation of herself and her lost children. She struck terror into the hearts of those who heard her and remembered the bloody stories of massacre. Malintzín, too, had heard the wailing and seen streaks of light flashing through the sky and flames springing from the earth.

A dog howled with the first light of dawn and soon all the dogs in her master's compound were howling.

Malintzín left the slaves' hut, tucking a small pouch, dark and damp, into the belt of her tunic, and splashed her face with water from the gourd that stood outside. She remembered that Quetzalcoatl had discovered the first grain of *maíz* with the help of an ant, when the world was still in darkness — an eternal night in which all the Gods assembled to dream the kings, priests and warriors who would people the Aztec empire. She ran down the narrow path to the shrine of Quetzalcoatl, who was called Kukulcán by her Mayan lords, the Tabascans. They had their own Gods and sometimes Malintzín prayed to the Mayan Goddess, Ixchel, as well as to her own Mother Moon Goddess, Tonantzin.

The blackened stone God stood in a grotto amid scattered petals and offerings of food. Smoke hung in the air with the smell of copal. Circles of fire patterned the earth, strewn with red, yellow, white flowers, their petals trailing in the ashes. Malintzín ran to Quetzalcoatl, scraping her knees as she slithered to the ground. She stared into the stony face. "Give me food, oh Father, give me *maíz* to fill my belly." Tears ran down her face and into her salty mouth. Moisture welled in all her dark places and she softened as light surrounded her and her hungry belly filled with cobs of *maíz* tumbling from the hands of Quetzalcoatl. The Serpent God wound himself tightly around her and she surrendered, caressed by his feathered body. As the serpent's jaws gaped, under its fangs appeared a human face, open-mouthed, about to speak. Then it was gone and the face of Chicomecoatl appeared, resplendent in her head-dress framed with sticks covered in amacalli paper strips. "Oh Goddess of the ripened *maíz*," Malintzín prayed, "Something is going to happen. You're warning me, but I don't understand." She was afraid for her soul. Her people believed that a child taken from her village is separated from her soul, which remains in her birthplace, waiting faithfully. And if she dies and is buried far from her village, then her soul will wander forever, exiled from the world of her ancestors. Malintzín pulled the damp pouch from her belt, opened it and pinched a morsel of dark earth with her fingers. She placed the earth on her tongue and let it melt inside her mouth. Every time she ate the earth of her homeland, grabbed and secreted as she'd been dragged away, her desire to go home was renewed.

The face of the God was stony and Malintzín felt scorned. He hadn't spoken after all. She jumped to her feet and ran into the bush, but she stumbled on the root of a giant ceiba and fell, sprawling, her belly hugging the earth, clenched tight in a fist of hunger. She ran back to the compound as the smell of tortillas floated in the swampy air, and she lurked by the kitchen hut and snatched a tortilla when the cook turned to scoop up the *masa*. Her teeth tore into the hot corn, thin like a wafer on her tongue, teasing her. "I will never be hungry again. Whatever happens, this is my desire, never, never again."

Malintzín slapped wet cloth on a stone, rocking back and forth, bending and straightening until her back throbbed. She leaned back with her hands on her hips, arching away from the pain.

"Are you all right?" Zaachila asked. She moved slowly, her face pale and dreamy as she crouched by the water, scrubbing a pile of clothes.

"I'm tired. The Weeping One woke me again last night. Did you hear her?"

"I was so frightened. What does it mean, Malintzín?"

"They say the land is filled with portents. She is heard weeping and wailing in the streets at night. In Tenochtitlan the temple of Huitzilopochtli burst into flames and all the wooden columns burned. And people tell of towering waves in the Gulf, bigger than anything we've seen before."

"I heard something yesterday," the girl whispered. "My master came from Taabscoob's house. He said a messenger has been sent to Tenochtitlan to report to the Emperor. They've seen floating houses in the Gulf and men who make lightning and smoke in the sky."

"Shhh!" Malintzín clamped her hand over the girl's mouth. "You mustn't say such things."

"I'm frightened." Zaachila began to cry. She flung her arms around Malintzín's waist and sobbed.

"What is it? What's wrong?" Malintzín knelt and held Zaachila's face, forcing her to look at her.

"My . . . my blood has stopped."

"Your master?"

"Yes." She cast her eyes down and her shoulders began to shake. "His hand was at my throat. I thought he was going to kill me!"

"Shh. I know what to do. I'll give you some herbs to get rid of it."

"Will it hurt?"

"Your belly will cramp and you'll vomit, but when the blood flows you'll be free."

"He comes often and surprises me, in the bathhouse, on the path to the shrine . . ."

"You mustn't let him near you, Zaachila."

"How can I stop him?"

"Stay close to your mistress. Make sure you're never alone. You must be very strong."

"Like you."

"I'm tired. I wasn't born to live like a dog skulking in the shadows."

"Did it happen to you?"

Malintzín shook her head. "I learned the herbs from the priestess at my first blood, just before my father died. She taught me how to look after myself." She tossed her head proudly and walked over to the boulder where the wet clothes lay. "I must finish the washing. My mistress will be looking for me."

As she stood in the water, working cloth on stone, slapping and rinsing, wringing and spreading the clothes on the bushes, her mind raced back to the shock of her father's death, her disbelief when only that morning they'd walked together, his strong arm around her shoulders. Her heart swelled with love for him. Her mother had soon remarried and borne a son. After the birth, Malintzín's step-father had started touching her; he wouldn't leave her alone. She hated him because he made her feel like a traitor. Eventually she lost her temper and lashed out, bloodying his cheek, and the next day Malintzín's mother left her infant son and took her daughter to the river. It was Malintzín's favourite place. She loved the water and she was happy to be alone with her mother finally. She was standing at the edge, dipping her toes, when the merchants came, men from Xicalango, a famous trading centre along the sheltered banks of a lagoon, east of Potonchan. She watched the richly dressed Mayan merchants come in silent procession through the bush, marking the way with their black staves, emblems of their profession. A line of servants followed, carrying bolts of cloth and rabbit fur, copper tools, jade and turquoise, bundled in their arms and on their backs. Malintzín's mother took hold of her arms and before she knew what was happening she was bundled onto the back of one of the servants. He grasped her wrists firmly and held her there. One of the merchants, a man with a broad smooth face, handed her mother a purse of money. Malintzín heard the clinking. She couldn't cry out; she was mute with disbelief.

When they were far enough from the river the servant tossed her from his back and was shaking out a coil of sisal to tie her hands when she bolted into the bush, shouting for her mother. She felt the ground pulsing with the footfalls of the servants as they pursued her. When she stopped screaming for her mother, who was on her way home to tell the household that her daughter had drowned, she heard the angry shouts of the merchants, but she couldn't understand what they said, because they spoke a foreign tongue — Chontol Maya. She was almost at the river bank, ready to plunge in and swim through the reedy depths to an underwater cave she knew, which came up into a sinkhole on the other side of the river, when she tripped and they were on her. Malintzín had time to grab a handful of damp earth from the river bank and knot it into the hem of her tunic before they tied her hands and led her on the sisal rope, away from her homeland. They took her far away, to Xicalango and sold her to Taabscoob, but first the servants pleasured themselves on her, two of them, there by the river, pressing her body into the soft earth. When her blood stopped she didn't know whose seed was planted in her, only that she must rid herself of it.

"Will you bring it tomorrow?"

Malintzín turned, startled.

"The herbs, Malintzín. You will help me, won't you?"

"Of course. I'll collect them at dawn and dry them in the morning sun. Come at mid-day."

Zaachila wiped her hands down the front of her belly, pushing as though she could force the child out of her. "I'm so hungry all the time," she whined.

"I can't help you with that. Better get used to it."

∾

The air shimmered with the prophecies of Chilam Balam. The mountains trembled with the voice of the Mayan priest, mouth of the Gods, as he recorded his prescient knowledge in a codex of mystical texts.

Prepare yourselves, oh my little brothers, for the white twin of heaven has come,

and he will castrate the sun, bringing the night, and sadness, and the weight of pain.

∾

Malintzín tossed in her sleep, smoke drifting across her face. Smell of copal, blood incense, moan of the priestess, heart ripped out, a sharp scream, ringing louder until she was deafened and woke in terror of what was to come. She ran into the night, down the path to the shrine. Quetzalcoatl was invisible in the darkness, but she knew him, her fingers touching his rough stone as she knelt at his feet, praying. Her eyes rolled until she was a blind girl filled with the spirit of what was to come and she began to understand there would be no order to it. Her spirit nosed its way through a labyrinth, searching for a safe route. Her body knew and prepared itself for the conquerors. Lights flared in the sky, illuminating her eyes, firing the inside of her skull. The roaring inside her was like the ocean and she fell to the ground and slept where she lay, a deep sleep.

In her dream she saw eleven great birds, their white wings puffed, flying across the sky. Her eyes were filled with their whiteness. Quetzalcoatl crept up behind her as she watched the galleons drop from the sky one by one, floating towards her. He placed his hands over hers, cradling her hips. His breath was warm as he leaned down, nuzzling her neck, and slid his tongue into the shell of her ear. An aching bloomed in her throat as tears rose in her, tears for her father and for her hunger, tears for the loss of her life. "How can you want me like this?" she wept, her hands on her own skinny body, arms hugging her ribs, his hands covering hers, then hunger woke her, growling, and there she was, rooted again, her soaring spirit anchored.

∾

"How's the history paper coming?" Fern asked.

"It's not. I'm still researching," Paméla said. "There's so much material on the conquest."

"Don't neglect your other courses," Fern said, moving quickly around the kitchen, gathering glass, plastics and cans. "It's not as if that's the only paper you have to write."

"Don't worry, I can handle it. The only problem is there's a ton of books on Cortés, but hardly anything on Malinche."

"Surprise, surprise!" Fern laughed. "An indigenous woman living in that time — what do you expect?"

"But she was crucial to the conquest."

"Was she?" Fern raised her eyebrows. "Malinche the traitor? Isn't that a cliché?"

"Of course it is. In fact I don't believe she was considered a traitor by her own people. From what I've read so far it looks like a rewriting of history. Malinche was labelled traitor 300 years after the conquest, by the leaders of the Mexican Revolution who were all of Spanish ancestry."

"Don't the boys love to blame a woman," Fern quipped. "But why do you say that Malinche was crucial to the conquest?" She began filling plastic crates with recyclables.

"Because the massacre at Cholula was pivotal and she engineered it. She was Cortés' translator. Without her he wouldn't have known about the Cholulan conspiracy. Of course there are other arguments, such as the superior military strategy of the Spanish, and the desperation factor, because they were stranded after Cortés scuttled the fleet at Veracruz; and they were fighting against a divided nation . . .

"Now *those* are good academic arguments which can be backed up with solid research. Don't get yourself stuck on the horns of an ethical-historical dilemma, Pam. It's just a paper, one of many. Have you looked at Prescott and Hugh Thomas?"

"Oh yes," Paméla said impatiently, "And Wilkes, Jacobs, Carlos Fuentes, Salvador de Madariaga . . . but the most inspiring are the fictionalized accounts — Oakland Ross, Gloria Durán, Graciela Limón — they take you there and put you in the setting so you can imagine what might have actually happened."

"Not exactly an academic approach, honey."

"What I've learned so far in academia is that when something becomes history it turns into a fiction, so why not include historical fiction in my research? At least it doesn't pretend to be the only version."

"What source materials are you using?"

"*Broken Spears* — voices of the Aztecs themselves, taken from preserved manuscripts."

"Where? Where are they preserved?"

"Oh, the National Library in Paris, the Laurenziana Library in Florence . . .

"What about the the Museum of Anthroplogy in Mexico City? We took you there, remember?"

"Yes, there too, some written as early as 1528."

"Good to have both sides of the story."

"The Aztec accounts are so poetic. They talk about 'the eight bad omens,' or 'wonders,' that preceded the coming of the Spanish. And the voice of Cihuacoatl, a kind of Goddess-seer who predicts disaster. You can see the cultural clash in the first battle. The Aztecs always started battle with a ritual warning — shields, arrows and cloaks sent to the enemy as a formal declaration. They were shocked by the sudden attack of the Spanish."

"Help me out to the car with the recycling, honey."

Paméla lifted a crate of plastic bottles and followed Fern down the back steps. "I've read Cortes' letters to King Carlos, and I'm just starting on Bernal Diaz. It's so exciting to know that Diaz was actually there, witnessing the whole process. It's like the difference between reading a newspaper report, trying to read between the lines and interpret someone's slant, and listening to a real live witness. Like the demo outside the American Embassy last month. Remember how they downplayed it in the media and minimized the entire event? But we were there! We know how huge that protest was. We were part of it!"

"I don't want to dampen your enthusiasm, Pam," Fern said, plunking her crate of glass bottles in the driveway and opening up the hatchback, "But remember that all these sources have been translated and a translation is only an interpretation. Take it all with a pinch of salt."

"Don't worry, I do. But I feel inspired by this story. I'm even beginning to dream about it. When people write things down they send out a communication which goes on forever. In the oral tradition stories grow and evolve with cultural change, but the written word remains, even if it is an interpretation. I can *feel* the difference between an historical investigation and a source account, Fern."

"And then there's your imaginative fictional accounts," Fern teased. She was beginning to weary of student enthusiasm. How many eager young women had she supported through their discoveries?

"Which inspire my own imagination. And what is imagination? Perhaps it's not as fictional as we think." Paméla heaved her crate of bottles into the vehicle.

"You may be onto something here, but just remember, Pam, this is an academic paper. It will be judged on its logical arguments and factual veracity. I don't want to see you disappointed with something less than an A."

Fern picked up a soda bottle that had rolled onto the driveway and threw it into the vehicle.

∾

. . . we fell on the Indians with such energy that with us on one side and the horsemen on the other, they soon turned tail. The Indians thought that the horse and its rider was all one animal, for they had never seen horses up to this time . . . As it was Lady-day we gave to the town which was afterwards founded here the name of Santa Maria de la Victoria . . . This was the first battle that we fought under Cortés in New Spain . . . we bound up the hurts of the wounded with cloths . . . and we doctored the horses by searing their wounds with the fat from the body of a dead Indian which we cut up to get out the fat, and we went to look at the dead lying on the plain and there were more than eight hundred of them, the greater number killed by thrusts, the others by the cannon, muskets and crossbows, and many were stretched on the ground half dead . . . The battle lasted over an hour, and the Indians fought all the time like brave warriors, until the horsemen came up."

— Bernal Diaz del Castillo,
The Discovery and Conquest of Mexico

They came to get her in the early morning. She went willingly, her body full of knowledge. She was changing hands again, but this time it would be different. Her eyes were downcast until she stood before him, then she looked up and she knew. "The God has come." She saw the feathered serpent on his face, covering his mouth and chin. She saw his long hair and fine white hands, his armoured body, his muscular legs. He had emerged from the serpent's mouth finally and come to her.

∾

"They brought him, in cup-shaped vessels of pure gold, a certain drink made from cacao, and the women served this drink to him with great reverence."

— Bernal Diaz del Castillo,
The Discovery and Conquest of Mexico.

Emperor Moctezuma was filled with forboding as *Ce Acatl* in the year 2-Rabbit approached, the day Quetzalcoatl, the great Aztec God, part bird, part water serpent, was to return. Quetzalcoatl had created the Fifth Sun and given it movement. He'd founded a civilization, centred in Tula, then disappeared, some said to the east, to Chichen Itzá, where the Mayans called him Kukulcán. His rival, Tezcatlipoca, God of the Smoking Mirror, had revealed to Quetzalcoatl his earthly form reflected in the mirror, and tempted him with pulque. Quetzalcoatl took five drinks of the fermented cactus and lay with his sister, Xochiquetzal, the beautiful Goddess of love. Afterwards he repented and built a great fire and cast himself into it. As his heart rose into the sky Quetzalcoatl travelled to the Land of the Dead, accompanied by his twin, Prince Xolotl, Lord of Darkness, in the form of a dog. After many trials in the underworld he rose triumphant as Venus, the Morning Star, Lord of the Dawn, and at night he appeared in the west as the Evening Star.

Moctezuma knew the science of omens and prediction. He had been a priest in the temple of Tenochtitlan until his accession to Emperor in 1502. He had torn living hearts from the bodies of slaves, feeding their blood to Huitzilopochtli. Now he was torn by the conflicting words of his advisors, the priests and seers who surrounded him at the temple, and by the appearance in the night of Cihuacoatl wailing her blood-curdling cry of warning. He was a slight, fine-boned man with grey eyes and a thin, sensitive nose. His people were a tribe from the north, from Aztlan, the place of the white-feathered heron. During the twelfth European century they had migrated south to the central valley of Mexico where they had displaced the people living around the shores of Lake Texcoco and established their own city of Tenochtitlan. They had been mocked by the vanquished people as Azteca, people of humble origins, but as Moctezuma's ancestors marched south from Tula to build their own city, they had called themselves the Culhua-Mexica and they called their capital Tenochtitlan. It was a magnificent city, built in the middle of Lake Texcoco with many canals and waterways for transportation, and a causeway to the mainland. They built temples to their Gods, the principal of whom was Huitzilopochtli. They conquered the surrounding territories, appropriated their deities and drew tribute from the people in the form of taxes and slaves for sacrifice to Huitzilopochtli. The Culhua-Mexica believed that living, beating, human hearts must be offered to their God to ensure his rising each day. He was the Sun; he was the God of War. Tenochtitlan became a place of blood tribute and the air was filled with swarms of jade-backed flies and the metalic smell of blood.

Moctezuma stood on the bloodied steps of the temple and pondered. For the first time in his life he felt unsure. He recalled the annual sacrifice in honor of Quetzalcoatl. In spring when the earth was bursting with new life, shoots breaking through green skin, a young man was sacrificed in the image of Tezcatlipoca, the Smoking Mirror. The youth was chosen with care and, dressed in fine robes and garlanded with flowers, he walked through the streets of Tenochtitlan playing his flute. Eight pages accompanied him and he was honored by all he met. He took four virgin wives, and many feasts and banquets were held for him, the chosen one. When time came for the sacrifice he mounted the temple-pyramid and lay in submission as he was bound on the belly of the Chacmool. The reclining stone figure stared into the distance as the priest opened the boy's breast with his obsidian blade and lifted his beating heart free of his body, lifting it to the sky.

Moctezuma stroked his downy cheek and ran a finger across his full lower lip. He'd sent runners to the Gulf with gifts: a serpent mask inlaid with turquoise, a breastplate of quetzal feathers, a woven collar with a gold disc at the centre, a shield decorated with gold and mother-of-pearl, bordered with quetzal feathers — the treasure of Quetzalcoatl. Now he awaited news of the prodigal God as the Spanish fleet sailed westward along the Gulf coast, guided by Aguilar who'd learned from

Chief Taabscoob that Moctezuma's messengers awaited them up the coast.

∞

On Good Friday, April 21, 1519, Cortés waded ashore a second time and knelt to pray. The sand clung to his wet hose as he advanced slowly upshore on his knees. He closed his eyes and felt the embrace of the warm air, thick with an undefinable mix of scents and feelings. He heard the plop of mamaya fruit dropping further upshore where sand turned to earth. "Our Lady is with me," he murmured. "She has blessed my enterprise." His body surged suddenly and he clasped his hands to heaven as he saw the Virgin's face, wet and contorted as she gazed up at her Son on the cross. He grasped that moment and named the enchanted place Villa Rica de la Veracruz and claimed it in the name of Carlos, King of Spain and Emperor of the Holy Roman Empire.

∞

"Doña Marina knew the language of Coatzacoalcos, which is that common to Mexico, and she knew the language of Tabasco, as did also Jerónimo de Aguilar, who spoke the language of Yucatán and Tabasco, which is one and the same. So that these two could understand one another clearly, and Aguilar translated into Castilian for Cortés. This was the beginning of our conquests and thus, thanks be to God, things prospered with us. I have made a point of explaining this matter,

*because without the help of Doña Marina we could
not have understood the language of New Spain and
Mexico."*

— Bernal Diaz del Castillo,
The Discovery and Conquest of Mexico.

Moctezuma's messengers were waiting. Their gifts were
taken and they were dismissed, but they refused to go.
They spoke, repeating over and over, words that no one
understood.

"They're speaking Nahuatl," Aguilar said. "I know
only Chontol Maya, *mi capitán.*"

"They want to know what Lord Quetzalcoatl wishes
in our country."

Aguilar whirled around to stare at the slave girl who'd
spoken to him in Chontol Maya. "You speak Nahuatl?"
he asked.

"I learned from my father. I am from Paynala where
we speak our own language, Popoluca. My father was
the *cacique* and I was to be his successor, but when he
died I was sold into slavery under Taabscoob. I have
learned to speak the language of my master."

"The girl is God-sent, *mi capitán!* She speaks both
tongues! And she's well-born. Her father was a Chief."

Cortés looked at Malintzín and saw her for the first
time, a skinny Indian girl with full lips and burning
eyes. He summoned her with a toss of his head, but she
stood firm. A smile spread across his bearded face as he
walked over to her. "What is her name?"

"Malintzín," she replied, before Aguilar could
speak.

Cortés raised his eyebrows. "We will call you . . . Marina," he said. "Come." He extended his hand and, after a moment's hesitation, she took it and allowed herself to be led to where Aguilar stood with Moctezuma's messengers.

And so Malintzín was christened with a Spanish name and her new life began. With her gift of tongues she interpreted the New World for Hernándo Cortés and she was translated into flesh, feeding voraciously off the Spanish supplies, her body filling and rounding, a lush landscape rising from the stony earth. As questions and answers travelled from Cortés to Aguilar, to Malintzín, to the messengers and back again, she learned the power of interpretation, the first power she'd held in her short life, given to her by Cortés, who had no choice, and she listened carefully to the Spaniards and determined to split her tongue a third way, to increase her value to Lord Quetzalcoatl.

He wants me to translate the world for him. I will do it and I will learn his tongue and my belly will be full.

∾

"The White God wants to enter our city of Tenochtitlan. He speaks through the Feathered Serpent and the woman, Malintzín, changes his words to our Nahuatl."

Moctezuma turned his head, his index finger in the hollow of his smooth cheek. After a moment of reflection he dismissed the panting messengers and summoned new runners. They left the city laden with more gifts of gold and fine textiles for the adventurers, and a request that they return to their land in the sky.

But Cortés had no intention of returning. "We will advance at all costs," he declared, "Under the True Cross, gathering souls for God." He formed a colony at Veracruz in the name of the king and, kneeling before the Virgin of Socorro, he remembered the governor awaiting him in Cuba. Before Velasquez could learn of his betrayal, Cortés put one of his ships under the command of Alonso Puertocarrero and commanded the young captain return to Spain. The ship set sail, fluttering with rainbowed birds, loaded with nuggets of New World history trapped inside translucent chunks of amber, its decks filled with dark-skinned men struggling under the weight of golden discs and ornaments; all Moctezuma's gifts. They picked baskets of avocado and mamaya fruit for the journey and plucked birds of paradise, wild and fresh on their day of departure. The exotic flowers died a week out on the long voyage.

Many of his followers wanted to return to Cuba, so Cortés scuttled the rest of his fleet to ensure the loyalty of his men. The only way was forward, to discover the fabulous wealth of Tenochtitlan, he told them. Cortés led with the Virgin of Socorro in one hand and his sword in the other.

∞

Malintzín shivered on the edge of the fire circle, her pouch of earth dangling between her breasts. When she touched herself she hardly recognized the swelling shapes of her body. Her fingers traced the new landscape in wonder and she was aroused. The Spaniards sat around the fire drinking and eating, grease and wine dripping into their beards. They were camped thirty miles outside Tlaxcala, a settlement of 50,000 brave warriors. They had already traversed almost 200 miles of hostile land, from insect-infested swamp, through thick forest inhabited by jaguars and rattlesnakes, to numbing mountains that ripped the breath from their bodies. The Tlaxcalans were the only barrier now between the 400 strong Spanish expedition and the golden city of Tenochtitlan. Cortés sat in the flickering firelight, unaware of the girl who watched him from the edge, concealed by the darkness, free now that Puertocarrero was gone. Cortés plotted his strategy with Alvarado and Sandoval, the men leaning into each other, hands grasping shoulders, slapping thighs, their deep voices and rich laughter ringing into the darkness from the feathered circles of their mouths. Malintzín absorbed the Spanish tongue like music as her quick eyes darted from mouth to mouth. Each sound bore a colour and a gesture, which she memorized and matched, leaping and vaulting as she discerned patterns in the Castilian tongue, which was to become for her the language of love. She knew he would be hers, the pale, dark-eyed chief. She traced his shoulders with her eyes, followed the muscles of his back as they snaked down the curve of his spine and flared into powerful buttocks.

"I will not be sold again. I will never be hungry again. The Spanish *cacique* will be mine." She chanted her spell over and over, in Nahuatl and Popoluca, branding it into her belly, searing herself with the words. She called on Tonantzin, Chicomecoatl and Ixchel, all the deities she had prayed to in her misery, and she thanked them for her sudden good fortune. Lord Quetzalcoatl was come;

the Feathered Serpent had returned and she would give her body in devout prayer to him. She laid her dark head on the ground and filmed her eyes like a sleeping cat, listening, watching until the last moment when she crossed the border into sleep.

She dreamed she was speaking in tongues, her body a great temple, Lord Quetzalcoatl entering. As he ascended she was filled with light and her body and soul resounded with Castilian, Nahuatl, Chontol Maya, Popoluca, four tongues of fire flaring from her mouth.

Cortés yawned and stretched his arms into the night sky. "We must sleep. We march on the Tlaxcalans at dawn." He stretched out on the ground where he sat, his face turned to the fire. He watched the dying flames leap, little tongues caressing the air, and in the fire as he began to drift he saw Malintzín's cat eyes and he stirred as though the earth itself were opening to receive him. "*Mi lengua,*" he mouthed silently as he descended into sleep, flaring and fading like hot coals fanned.

∞

Malintzín skilfully translated an alliance with the Tlaxcalans after Cortés had overcome them with his cannons and cavalry. "He will be Emperor," she said. "He is the God we have awaited to restore order to our land. He will keep his word."

It was not difficult to persuade the Tlaxcalans to join with the Spanish and march on Tenochtitlan. They hated Moctezuma. He taxed them heavily and sacrificed their people in the temple of Huitzilopochtli.

"Malinche, Malinche, pardon us for having attacked you," the *cacique* said, bowing to Cortés.

. . . in all the towns we passed through Cortés was called Malinche . . . The reason is that Doña Marina, our interpreter, was always in his company, particularly when any Ambassadors arrived, and she spoke to them in the Mexican language. So that they gave Cortés the name of 'Marina's Captain' and for short Malinche."

— Bernal Diaz del Castillo,
The Discovery and Conquest of Mexico

∽

Cortés fell ill with the swamp fever that had taken three of his men on the journey west. His body burned and fear smoldered in him like fire without air to ignite it. In his delirium he felt cool fingers on his brow.

"Tlacopatli," he heard a familiar voice say. "The root of this herb will make him sweat and will restore his strength." He felt her packing the cool, slimy root around his throat and on his chest. The fire leapt out of his body and burst into flames which licked his skin through the night. He called her name as his fever broke. By morning he was dry and clear.

∽

Moctezuma had a mysterious change of mind. He sent messengers inviting Cortés to Tenochtitlan.

"But first he must stop in the famed city of Cholula where the Emperor's subjects will refresh him after his long journey," Malintzín told Aguilar, who translated the message into Castilian.

Cortés listened, but his eyes were on Malintzín. That night he took her. She was not the first Indian girl he'd had but she was the first he valued. His hunger was voracious. He wanted to know everything embedded in the customs of her people, the secrets of the earth, the trees, the soaring sky. He desired her body, trussed with the poetry and myths of her people, blood-bright threads he extracted and bound her with; but in so doing he felt his own hands tied. He needed her over and over, and again by his side as he slept, so he could wake to take her again. His desire for her was not separate from his ambition. "Marina, *mi corazón*," he whispered, and she surrendered, speaking her first stumbling words of Spanish into his ear. In his embrace she received visions pulsing with brilliant colour; strange music deafened her with the roaring of blood in her ears; it was another world, a New World they shared, beyond language. She had him and she would keep him.

Before they left Tlaxcala, Cortés knelt before the Virgin of Socorro and prayed for her blessing. But it was a half-hearted prayer; he didn't need her now that he had Malintzín at his side. As they entered the city of Cholula people crowded the streets, welcoming the Spaniards and the Tlaxcalans. They were fed lavishly and lodged in the best houses, but Malintzín read the shapes swirling in the *caciques'* minds and she saw blood running in the gutters around the great pyramid of Cholula; she saw severed limbs and people running, their mouths open in silent screams. She tried to find her place in the vision, but she could not. She whispered to Cortés in the darkness that night and the next day she went to the house of a *cacique's* wife. When the woman stared at her with cold eyes she whispered, "He beats me, look," and showed her bruised thighs, the dark welts of his bites in her soft flesh. "I'm a prisoner," she wept, "a slave. How can I ever escape?"

The *cacique's* wife softened. "Poor child," she said, "You are one of us, of noble birth like my own family. I will help you. Come." She put her arm around Malintzín and led her into the house. "No one must hear what I have to tell you," she said and she whispered in her ear, quieter than a breeze, the Cholulan conspiracy. "Moctezuma says he will reduce our taxes and free the Cholulan prisoners held in Tenochtitlan. They are our sons and brothers, our husbands and fathers. We cannot refuse his request. Tomorrow we are to assault the Spanish as they march out of the city. They will never reach the capital."

Malintzín clasped the woman's hands. "Is it true?"

The woman nodded solemnly. "You must come here for refuge," she said, then her eyes lit up. "My son will be returned! You will marry him and live in our house, my child. You will be safe."

When Malintzín left, slipping through the narrow door, her steps were hurried, seeking the shadows.

In the light of dawn, as the massacre began, she closed her ears and heard a running river. She felt a stealthy presence creeping up behind her, felt her body bundled, her wrists grasped; she heard the clinking of coins. Malintzín stood dry-eyed as the blood of the *caciques* flowed from the pyramid of Cholula and the screams of their wives circled her silent ears. By noon the sun was obliterated by murders of crows, by vultures, flocking and plunging, plucking the eyes from fresh corpses. The slaughter continued for two days until 8,000 Cholulans lay dead.

∾

Fern lay with her head in that sweet hollow, the tender place between her lover's shoulder and neck, drifting between sleep and waking. "Mmmm," she sighed, "This is heaven. Just when I think I know you completely, my darling, you surprise me with another layer. You're an endless wonder." Fern reached up, her elfin face flushed with pleasure, and kissed Hannah's soft mouth. She barely knew herself as a separate being in that moment, then, all her senses alert, she felt the ruffled surface of Hannah's calmness. "What is it, Hannah? There's something."

Hannah hesitated a moment, not wanting to break the spell, but she couldn't hide anything from Fern. "Paméla told me she's searching for her birth mother."

Fern's body tensed. "Really? She didn't tell me."

"I went up to her room this evening to get her laundry and she was on the computer. There it was, a Google search on Guatemalan adoption agencies. I couldn't help seeing. It's nothing to worry about. We knew it would happen eventually."

"But you are worried, aren't you?"

"No." Hannah took a deep breath. "If I could just get her to do her own laundry . . . "

"Don't hide from me," Fern teased. "More than twenty years, Hannah. We're a family. There's nothing to worry about." She took Hannah in her arms and stroked her hair. It was springy with coppery curls that glinted in the candlelight of their bedroom. Like her brilliant mind,

Fern thought, fiery and alive, full of twists and turns. Her own mind was on alert now, her senses receding. "What did she say?"

"She was casual. Said she was just curious. But she's secretive. Our Pam never used to be like that."

"She's had her heart broken for the first time. Don't you remember those puppy love days?"

"Maybe I should've had a biological child," Hannah whispered.

"How could you possibly imagine our lives without Paméla?"

"As well as her, that's what I meant. It might have been a way of bringing Bubby and Zaideh back, keeping the genetic line alive. I still feel guilty, Fern. I can't help it."

Fern pulled Hannah closer and stroked her back, trying to calm her. She was always worried beneath that deceptively calm exterior, always trying to prove herself, to justify her existence.

"But it would have been selfish, wouldn't it, to bring yet another child into this crazy world?"

"Not to mention the hassle of dealing with the sperm donor and the turkey baster. And what if it'd been a boy?" Fern teased, trying to get a smile out of her.

"That would've been OK."

"Not for me, honey. I grew up with three brothers, remember?" Pregnancy hadn't been an option for Fern, sterile at twenty-two from a massive infection caused by an IUD. She'd grown up Catholic with a phobia about getting pregnant, because she knew her parents would never let her have an abortion. Her first female lover had been the nurse who'd looked after her in the hospital as she recovered from the infection which had almost killed her. She hadn't called herself a lesbian at first, preferring 'bi-sexual,' but it hadn't taken her long to realize that she'd moved into a sub-culture and that her new way of life with its altered perspective was what determined her identity as a lesbian more than the much-touted tag of 'sexual preference.' She'd met Hannah when she was finishing law school at Osgoode Hall. Fern had her PhD and was already teaching Women's Studies. It was 1980, first year of the Sandinista government in Nicaragua and the crippling US blockade. They were both working with Canadian Action for Nicaragua and met at a demonstration in front of the American Embassy. Fern had fallen in love right away; nothing had ever been so clear to her. Hannah was twenty-four, a year younger than Fern, and she was working like a fiend, driven by chronic guilt, as though she could never do enough to make up for what had been lost. They went through a lot together; the eventual defeat of the Sandinista government, attacks on the abortion clinic, the burning of the Women's Bookstore, and a lot of painful encounters with their families before their relationship was taken seriously and finally accepted. Hannah's mother had been the only child of German Jews who had died in Dachau. They had been in hiding and were already frail and sick when they were captured, because they'd been giving all their food rations to their child. She was in good health and survived while Bubby and Zaideh were worked to death within weeks. When the allies liberated Europe Hannah's mother had been sent to New York. She was nine. At twenty she had married a New York Jew, a sweet and gentle man who never trespassed on her pain, and Hannah was their only child. She'd had to escape the silent pressure to make up for her mother's loss, but she'd brought it with her, to Montréal, then to Toronto. When her father had died suddenly of a heart attack Hannah had asked her mother to come and live in Canada, but she'd refused, elusive as ever, insisting on living alone all these years. And now she had been diagnosed with Altzheimer's, the only survivor, receding further into the silence of her past.

"I think we should help her with the search, Fern."

"We have to let her do this one on her own." Fern reached for a glass of water on the bedside table.

"At least we can encourage her so that she'll know we — "

" — are scared shitless and want to control her every move?"

"That's not fair!" Hannah sat up in bed, two angry dots of colour spreading on her cheeks.

"You realize that if she finds a lead she may want to go to Guatemala."

"Oh, my God," Hannah moaned. "I can't bear it, Fern. I can't bear the thought of losing her!"

"Shhh, it's going to be OK."

"What if she finds her birth mother and rejects us?"

"Are you crazy? That's not going to happen."

"Hold me. Please hold me." Hannah began to sob, her breath coming in huge noisy gusts.

"Come on, honey." Fern gathered her in her arms. "Whatever happens we have each other."

"Nobody else sees me like this," Hannah sobbed.

"It's how I most love you," Fern said, stroking her wet face.

∽

As her fascination with the history of Mexico and Guatemala grew Paméla began to skip classes, losing track of time as she sat at her library carrel surrounded by stacks of books. She read about the Mayans, about their spiritual beliefs and practices; she read about the Aztecs, about their wars and sacrificial rites; she read about the Spanish and their advance on the city of Tenochtitlan. She read Eduardo Galeano, Frank Waters, Tzvetan Todorov, Michael D. Coe, and Dennis Tedlock. They filled her head and kept her from thinking about Talya's betrayal and her recurring nightmare. But her body remembered and it took her there in the night, to the massacred village. She woke sobbing and shaking, craving to be held. She read that 440 villages had been wiped off the map of Guatemala.

"Any luck with your search?" Hannah asked, reaching for the marmalade.

Paméla shook her head sadly. The slight downturn at the outer corners of her eyes gave her a tragic look that only her dimpled smile could transform. "The adoption agency no longer exists. I guess organizations don't last long in Guatemala with the political instability."

"But I thought things had settled down since the peace treaty was signed," Hannah said, her brow furrowing. "When was it . . . ?"

"Ninety-six," Fern interjected. "I suspect we just don't hear about the conflict any more. Media's full of the Middle East and the big oil grab now."

"The people have to plant their corn and coffee practically on their doorsteps, because eighty percent of the land is owned by American corporations," Paméla said indignantly. "Do you know which village my mother was from? I found a webpage for a government agency that deals with registration of births, but they need a name at least, and preferably an address."

"They didn't tell us anything at the adoption agency," Hannah said, "except that your mother had left you in an orphanage, which I think was run by nuns. The girl who brought Pam to the agency was a nun, wasn't she, Fern?"

"She was only a kid really . . . fourteen, fifteen? How old do they have to be to take the veil?"

"They don't wear veils any more."

"You know what I mean . . . vows," Fern laughed.

"Oh, it's hopeless!" Paméla said impatiently.

"No, it's not," Hannah said, "What about trying — "

"I'm never going to find her. When I phoned the Montréal and Ottawa families who adopted at the same time they said they don't know anything. Why didn't somebody get details?"

"The LaPierres?" Hannah exclaimed. "Did you talk to them?"

"Sure. Madame LaPierre said to say hello."

"We haven't seen them for years. How are they?"

Paméla sighed. "Oh everything's fine," she began in a sing-song voice with a Quebecois accent, "She's so glad to hear from me, Michel's in engineering at Université de Montréal — "

"Cut it out, Pam. I don't like your attitude," Fern said sharply.

"And I don't like this whole scene! Mrs. Lozano doesn't even care. She says Peter pretends he's not adopted. His dad is Colombian so he fits into their family perfectly."

"When you were little, people always thought Fern was your mom, with her dark hair and — "

"You know what Mrs. Lozano said? 'Why stir up trouble? Be grateful to your parents for saving you.'"

"But you always called me 'Mama', and you'd run and — "

"Pam, you're taking this much too seriously," Fern snapped.

"What a waste of time talking to those 'happy families.' And I wasted my time doing computer searches when I could have been researching my paper. Well, of course I've got nothing better to do since Talya dumped me."

Paméla burst into tears. She laid her head on the table and sobbed. Fern reached over and clasped her hand while Hannah, her face flushed with concern, jumped up and crouched beside Paméla. "So what's this really about?" she asked gently, wrapping her arms around her, her soft bosom muffling Paméla's sobs. The girl's body shuddered and her outburst subsided as suddenly as it had begun, like a summer storm.

"I'm sorry," she said, raising her head.

"Look, you have butter in your beautiful hair," Fern said, offering her a napkin. Paméla wiped her hair, then she caught Fern's eye and they both began to laugh.

Soon she was hiccoughing and Hannah rushed for a glass of water. Paméla gulped several mouthfuls, then gasped, "I feel so stupid."

"Oh darling, you're the smartest kid in the world," Hannah said.

"I remember when we first saw you," Fern pulled her chair closer to Paméla. "Remember, Hannah, how excited we were?"

"Oh, when that girl walked into the room carrying you in her arms . . . I fell in love with you in a heartbeat. And Fern was crying she was so happy!"

"We'd waited so long for you and suddenly there you were, a real little person, nine months old. I couldn't believe it."

"You reached your arms out to me. You weren't the least bit scared. And when I took you, you nuzzled into my neck."

"The girl was crying," Fern said. "I felt sorry for her, but we were so thrilled to have you."

"Why didn't you get my mother's name? Didn't you realize I'd need to find her one day?"

Fern ruffled her hair, "I never thought — "

"In all fairness," Hannah said, her green eyes troubled in her flustered face, "It was a long time ago and — "

"But it's *not* fair! Nothing about this situation is fair. I have nightmares every night. I don't know who I am. And I feel so ungrateful. I don't mean to hurt you, but you don't understand what it's like. I have to wait for the million to one chance that my birth mother is going to come looking for me, and that she'll contact one of the agencies I've registered with. What if she's forgotten I exist? What if she's dead?"

"Calm down, honey." Fern got up from her chair and stood behind Paméla, kneading her shoulders. "You've been through a tough time. Things will get better, I promise."

"I'm so sorry, darling. I didn't realize you felt this strongly about it," Hannah said. "What will you do if you don't find her?"

Paméla stared at the table, gathering into herself, stranded and alone in that familiar, alien place which was all she knew. Before her watery eyes the table became a shining sea with a flotilla of white-sailed ships rimmed with gold, and the smell of ripe bananas and mangoes filled her senses.

"You could . . . go to Guatemala . . . to your home country to see what it's like," Hannah said, gripping Fern's hand.

"No I can't," she snapped. "What about school? I have to write this paper. Besides, I'm afraid of flying. And *this* is my home!" She ran from the room, almost knocking her chair over, and took the stairs two at a time until she reached the haven of her third floor bedroom.

∾

"When we saw so many cities and villages built in the waters of the lake and other great towns on dry land and that straight and level Causeway going towards Mexico, we were amazed and said that it was like the enchantments they tell of in the legend of Amadis, on

*account of the great towers and temples and buildings
rising from the water, and all built of masonry. And
some of our soldiers even asked whether the things that
we saw were not a dream."*

— Bernal Diaz del Castillo,
The Discovery and Conquest of Mexico

On November 8, 1519 the Spanish entered the enchanted
city of Tenochtitlan, accompanied by some 6,000
Tlaxcalan allies. They saw channels of sparkling water,
a lake embedded with temples and palaces, causeways
alive with brown people carrying baskets of fruit,
flowers, dried corn; their ankles and wrists rattling with
tiny gourds and conch shells, their heads plumed with
irridescent feathers.

Malintzín stood close to Cortés before the temple
rising at the eastern end of Lake Texcoco. A statue of
Huitzilopochtli stood at the top of the steps, the mouth
smeared with blood offered daily from the still beating
hearts of silent slaves. The skulls of honored victims
were displayed on the *tzompantli,* a rack at the foot of
the temple pyramid. She watched Cortés, his scarred
lip curled in disgust, and her womb trembled as she
remembered his face floating above her, his cry as he
came into her. She watched him every moment; the
curve of his mouth, his feathered beard and mustache
rippling around his lips like a moving serpent; and she
looked up again at Huitzilopochtli, the mighty War God,
and remembered what her father had told her about the
Culhua-Mexica coming from the north to conquer the
people of the valley. Their empire had grown, reaching
across the land, but they had never gained control

over her father's people, the people of the Isthmus surrounding the Gulf city of Coatzacoalcos; they had kept their language, Popoluca, and their autonomy. Now that Quetzalcoatl had come Malintzín didn't know where she belonged, with him or with the people of her land. She felt the earth moving under her bare feet, the shifting layers of sand and grit under the swampy terrain of Tenochtitlan.

Cortés watched as Moctezuma approached, sitting aloft a litter carried by six slaves. The Emperor's steady gaze met Cortés as he descended and walked on the cloth spread for him. Cortés moved forward to embrace him, but immediately the slaves surrounded their Emperor. He was not to be touched. But Malintzín and Aguilar were at Cortés' side and, as he began to speak through them to the untouchable Emperor, Malintzín stole his words, pulling them from his mouth, a scarlet thread thickening as she interpreted for Moctezuma almost before Aguilar had a chance to complete his own translation. The Emperor raised a finely drawn eyebrow when he realized Malintzín's role. He was unaccustomed to dealing with women in matters of state business.

The Spaniards were led down the causeway to a palace where they were quartered in luxury, far from the stench of the bloody temples. Gifts of gold arrived daily with fresh clothing, finely prepared foods and female slaves to serve the men. Cortés relaxed for the first time since he'd set foot in the New World. Malintzín was always at his side and he spoke with Moctezuma through her. Together they charmed the Emperor, but when she tried to talk with the slave women who had been sent to serve the Spanish they shunned her. They'd heard whispers about the Cholulan massacre and they were afraid of her. So she kept to herself and marvelled at all the changes in her short life as she watched the Spanish amassing gold.

News came of an attack on Veracruz by an Aztec band. Several Spaniards had been killed. Cortés demanded that Moctezuma bring the leaders to Tenochtitlan and burn them alive. As the people reeled in horror, a Franciscan padré climbed the bloody pyramid and placed an image of the Virgin next to Huitzilopochtli. Before he'd completed his descent the figure was smeared and smashed to pieces.

Velasquez, learning of Cortés' betrayal, had declared him an outlaw and a traitor. He'd sent Pánfilo de Narváez in command of a flotilla of eighteen Spanish ships with instructions to hang Cortés. The galleons had set sail from Cuba, ploughing west through the mighty waves of the Atlantic as Cortés had marched his men out of Cholula, tracking bloody footprints across the earth. When news of the flotilla's arrival at Veracruz reached Cortés in Tenochtitlan he left Pedro de Alvarado in command and marched with Malintzín and his loyal friend, Sandoval, back to the coast. He intended to defeat Narváez before he had a fighting chance.

It was a difficult journey for Malintzín. She had grown up on the Gulf lowlands, always close to the ocean. The mountains stole her breath and shrouded themselves with it, misting the thin air about her. Her nose bled and her head throbbed as she climbed blindly beside the cursing Spanish soldiers. A grudging respect grew into acceptance of the triple-tongued girl. Her skin was welted with bites, her feet swollen with blisters and cuts as she braved the rocks. As they began the descent her womb clenched like a fist and a thin trail of blood marked her path. She left Cortés' son on Mount Orizaba, 15,000 feet above the sea, a scarlet stain on stone. When she rejoined the procession winding down the mountain towards the forested lowlands her face was pale, but her heart beat calmly. "I will grow another," she said. "I will bear him a son."

∾

Cuba, 1519: Catalina Suarez paced her bedchamber. She saw her reflection in the darkened window and she wept at the ravages of her yearning body. She'd grown pale and thin in Hernándo's absence. She threw herself on the bed and lay sleepless through the long night. When she dropped like a stone into sudden sleep she was catapulted awake by terrible visions. She longed for Hernándo as the tortured long for death. She prayed to the Virgin for his safe return, telling the pearls of her necklace like a rosary, all her desire entering the pained circles, penetrating the nacreous grains of sand.

∾

Tanned people smiled down at her from the walls. A woman lay on white sand under a giant palm, in her hand a cocktail glass filled with fruit and a tiny umbrella.

"Can I help you?"

Paméla stared blankly at the bright-eyed travel agent across the desk. She had a million questions. Is it dangerous to go to Guatemala alone? Can I get an open ticket? Where will I stay? How long will it take to find her? What will I say to Hannah and Fern? Will they lend me the money?

"Are you all right?" The woman reached out to touch Paméla's hand.

She jumped as if she'd been stung. "I . . . I want to go to Guatemala," she heard herself say. "I want to go home."

Hannah clapped her hands and grinned nervously, her sparkling eyes almost disappearing. "Of *course* I'll give you the money, of course, of course!

"Really?" Paméla looked doubtful.

"I received a very generous bonus at Christmas and I can't think of a better use for it, darling."

"You're so brave," said Fern, hugging her. "You fly May 1st?"

"How long's your visa for?" Hannah asked.

"Three months. But I'll probably run out of money before then."

"It's really cheap to travel in Guatemala. Hotels, food, buses — they cost next to nothing compared to Canada," Fern said.

"Maybe you'll get up to Mexico. Remember how you loved it when we went to the Yucatán?" Hannah said.

"Of course I remember. I turned ten while we were there. And it was the 500th anniversary of the discovery."

"Oh darling," Hannah said, clasping her hands, "Promise me you'll keep in touch?"

"Course I will. I'll e-mail."

"And call once in a while, just so we can hear your voice," Fern said.

"And send postcards," Hannah said, "We'll be thinking of you every minute."

"Mom, it's still three weeks away."

"But you have a lot to do before you leave," Fern said. "How about that paper on Cortés?"

"I've changed the focus. I'm calling it 'The role of Malinche in the Conquest of the Culhua-Mexica.' It's so complex and so exciting, I can't stop researching."

"Don't overwork it, Pam. I've seen many a brilliant paper aborted through procrastination," Fern cautioned.

"This is not procrastination. I have new information — an entire book on Malinche by Anna Lanyon, *and* a book on Martín Cortés, her child and the first significant mestizo."

"When's it due?"

"End of the month, but I could get an extension. I've done so much research at this point that I can't even distinguish between what I've read and what I've dreamed. It's driving me crazy."

That night she dreamed of a place she barely remembered; the Yucatán, with air close as an embrace and trees rooted in the swamped Earth, holding it there; footsteps resounding through the Earth into limestone caverns filled with water, realm of the Rain God, Chac, the roof fallen in, the sky reflected in a watery cavern, a circular sinkhole, eye of the Earth gazing upward. The sacred cenote of Chichen Itzá . . . Itzá . . . Itzá . . . The Chacmool stared out across the swampland of Yucatán, leaning back on his elbows, belly exposed to receive her heart.

∾

Cortés dreamed he was uprooting trees with his fist, grasping bright birds and throwing them into the Castilian sky. With a single breath he filled the sails of his galleon and sent it speeding across the ocean, the bowels of the vessel crowded with brown-skinned people. Atop the highest mast, on a foot square platform, danced los voladores de Papántla, the flying men of the jungle village inland from Veracruz. The brown bird men danced, oblivious to the heights they commanded, flinging themselves into the limpid air, strong vines clenched between their teeth, circling the mast, round and round in ever-decreasing circles. In his dream Cortés looked into the mirror of Moctezuma's eyes where a feathered serpent lay curled, sultry and dangerous. I am God, it hissed.

Malintzín watched Cortés as he rose from the bed and padded across the room, barefoot in his nightshirt, hair curling from the opening at his throat. She watched him unroll the Virgin of Socorro from her goldspun cloth, placing her carefully in the corner by his desk, then he knelt before her, his back to Malintzín. She heard his whispered words of prayer and saw the swell of his buttocks where his nightshirt caught. She closed her eyes as he rose and turned. She heard the creaking of a chair as he sat, the clearing of his throat, the dipping of his pen into the inkwell. She nestled down in bed, pulled the covers to her chin and opened her eyes, watching as he wrote, she an illegible book invisibly branded with her own story.

Most Royal Highness, Emperor of the Holy Roman Empire, I have burned more than ten towns, of more than three thousand houses, all resisting the Holy Word. Before dawn I fell on two towns, in which I killed many infidels.

Women and children ran naked in the streets. I surprised them unarmed, I fell upon them and caused them some loss and harm.

He did not tell King Carlos about the limbs torn from the people's bodies by savage war dogs, each weighing 200 pounds armoured. He did not write about the fires, sputtering in the night with human fat, about the green bones twisting and screaming in the intense heat, nor about Narváez, felled in his tent by Sandoval, with a lance through his right eye. Cortés had commandeered his forces like pawns in a chess game, promising them a share of the golden riches of the New World. Men without a leader, they'd had no choice, and Cortés was persuasive.

He moved forward to the topic of bounty:

Your Flotilla is much depleted on the High Seas, and the Captain lost. I return to you a galleon replete with treasures from the New World where we continue your missionary work with zeal. Of the gold jewellery and goblets melted down, I send your Royal Fifth, keeping one fifth for myself, and distributing the rest amongst my men according to rank. Plus Ultra . . . yet further. We search for the mines from whence these riches came . . .

When Cortés returned to Tenochtitlan he found the city in silent rebellion.

"They were murdering the slaves!" Alvarado protested. "They ripped their hearts out and shoved them into the mouth of their idol! We had to stop them!"

The Culhua-Mexica called Alvarado *Tonatiuh*, the Sun, for his crown of golden curls. He was tall and handsome, but he was a hothead and had taken advantage of Cortés' absence to provoke the Culhua-Mexica, attacking them during a religious ceremony at the temple of Huitzilopochtli. The slaughter and looting that followed had satisfied the gold-lust of his men, but left the people in shocked silence. That silence broke with an attack on the Spanish, followed by days of fighting. Malintzín thought she had misunderstood when she heard Cortés give the order, and still she could not believe it as she watched his men topple the War God down the steps of the temple pyramid. The God shattered under its own weight at the foot of the steps, and into the terrible silence that followed a roar ripped and echoed across the water. For the first time Cortés regretted his actions. *Plus ultra;* he'd gone too far. He appealed to Moctezuma for a safe retreat, but as the Emperor spoke from his palace balcony a stone struck his brow and bright blood spurted into his eyes. The Spaniards dragged him inside the palace to die, whether of his wound or at their hands none would tell. They began their retreat at midnight on June 30, 1520 when the sun was at mid-heaven, relinquishing the day reluctantly to a bright moon for a brief mid-summer night. But *La Noche Triste* was long enough to kill more than half the Spanish army and their allies; they drowned in the canals, pulled under by their own armour and by their pilfered gold. The fingers of the dead had to be broken to release their grip on the sacks of treasure. Cortés was wounded and Malintzín bound his hand with strips torn from her skirt, packing herbs into his wound to stop the bleeding. The sight of his blood frightened her; he was mortal and in his blood whispered the voice of his soul.

The Culhua-Mexica, inflated with their own visions and prophecies, had fallen under the spell of the Spanish, but now the magical power of the bearded Gods was dispelled. Their horses were fallen, their war-dogs fled whimpering as their masters drowned. The Culhua-Mexica were forever disillusioned with Hernándo Cortés; he was toppled and his translator stood alone amongst the fragments. Cortés' false words and broken promises had earned a particular resonance to his name, Malinche, Malintzín's captain. When people spoke that name it was only by context that they understood which one was spoken of, the translator or the traitor, and so they were joined through history in the fluctuating connotations of language.

Cortés faced threats from his own countrymen as well as from the Indians. Fresh recruits came from Cuba with adventurers from Jamaica, seeking treasure. They were sent to capture Cortés, but he won them over with simple logic. "If you follow me you will have gold, slaves, women, and land of your own. If you kill me you will have nothing and the Indians will kill you. We must stand together under the Cross. It is our only hope."

Malintzín watched the men succumb to his will. She knew this power. Had Cortés not succumbed to her, to the power of her tongue? And now he held her in his wounded palm.

"Quetzalcoatl will guide you through your journey on Earth and give you a place beside him in the Heavens."

As long as she lived she would walk beside him.

Thus Cortés reassembled his army and prepared for another assault on Tenochtitlan. He trained his new army by raiding Indian villages on the long journey back to the capital, demanding surrender or destruction. They gained momentum as they burned, killed and took prisoners, their numbers swelling, and fear of the Spanish growing with their Catholic converts.

Again the Tlaxcalan allies fought with Cortés in great numbers, but the attack on Tenochtitlan was met with fierce resistance. Then smallpox, carried by one of the new recruits, spread like fire through the city. The Spanish, immune to the disease, appeared once again like Gods, but they were regarded with hatred now, not with wonder.

Cuauhtemoc, nephew of Moctezuma, was the new Emperor of Tenochtitlan and he refused to surrender, even though the city had become a charnel ground for the pock-marked corpses.

"Why will they not surrender?" Cortés growled.

Sandoval and Alvarado stood at his side, staring across the devastated waters of Lake Texcoco, remembering the shining city that had greeted them on their first approach. Now it was like a wounded animal refusing to die.

"I do not want to destroy these people, but I will conquer them." When he took Malintzín in his arms and entered her body he was Lord of the New World, filled with triumph and peace. But she was one of them, a savage to be conquered. Her mystery inflamed him and he had grown rough with her. "We'll make a three-pronged attack," he said suddenly.

Alvarado stopped his pacing and caught Sandoval's eye with his own piercing blue eyes.

"Pedro, take the north-west side, Gonzalo the south. I'll attack from the east. Lead your men boldly. Take no prisoners."

They slaughtered until the canals ran red and the steps of the temple were strewn with limbs severed by their broadswords. Yet for three months more the Culhua-Mexica resisted as the Spaniards laid siege, forcing them to eat rats, roots and, finally, tree bark.

On August 13, 1521, in the hot stinking night, Cuauhtemoc and his wife were captured on the water in the royal canoe. Sandoval restrained his men and took them, prisoners, to his captain.

The day on which we laid down our shields and admitted defeat was the day 1-Serpent in the year 3-House. When Cuauhtemoc surrendered, the Spaniards hurried him to Acachinanco at night, but on the following day, just after sunrise, many of them came back again. They were dressed for battle, with their coats of mail and their metal helmets, but they had left their swords and shields behind. They all tied white handkerchiefs over their noses because they were sickened by the stench of the rotting bodies.They came back on foot, dragging Cuauhtemoc . . .

— *The Broken Spears,*
The Aztec Account of the Conquest of Mexico.

∽

"Death and destruction will follow in your wake. You will rule over many people, but never over your own heart."

Malintzín looked down at her body, but she didn't recognize herself. Where was the thin girl filled with a fierce resolve and the dark gritty earth of her homeland? "I am Marina now," she whispered, smoothing her hands over her breasts, circling her belly filled with the serpent's seed. "I have a new body. I belong to him."

Through the nightmare of the long siege, through the hunger and slaughter of her devastated people, through the stench and rot, flesh of her flesh, she'd clung to this. But she couldn't quell the fear that rose in her and bloomed into a splash of pain that threatened to burst her heart. "It belongs to him, I've ripped out my beating heart and given it to Quetzalcoatl. What more can I give? I have nothing more."

She knelt inside the charred circle, her arms raised to the Heavens, eyes half-closed. Her lips moved and a steady moaning drifted on the air. She was hidden by smoke of the burning copal so Cortés didn't see her at first, only heard her low keening and the soft Popoluca sounds.

"Oh Mother Goddess, all-powerful Cihuacoatl, help me now. My people are gone and I'm all alone. Give me a new skin, oh Serpent Skirt, to cover myself so that I can make my way in this new world." She lifted the pouch from between her breasts, pinched the dark earth and laid it on her tongue. She closed her eyes and tilted her face to the sky, earth melting on her extended tongue. She swayed from side to side, arms reaching in a gesture of supplication.

Cortés watched, the muscle in his jaw twitching. Something dark in her, blood and dirt on her tongue. His loins stirred. "Marina!"

Her tongue retracted as she turned, startled. Cortés stood in the pre-dawn light, an eerie figure. *"Mi capitán?"*

He strode towards her, took her by the hand and raised her, pulling her against him roughly. "What are you doing?"

"I am praying for your life, Hernándo. Every day I fear to lose you."

He leaned close to her, smelling the earth in her. "What did you put on your tongue?"

Saliva filled her mouth and she swallowed. "It is . . . the earth of my homeland . . . we have a belief . . . "

He pushed his tongue into her mouth, searching the strange muskiness of her, twisting her copal-scented hair in his hands. Abruptly he pulled back and spat on the ground.

"You have your painted woman," she said accusingly. "I've seen you — "

"The battle is over. Cuauhtemoc is captured. I need you at my side."

A slow smile spread across her face, but underneath the smile her heart was wrung with loss and it beat irregularly like a caged bird alternating between panic and paralysis. *Everything is changed, oh Snake Woman, I have lost my skin and I am naked. Give me protection. Will I ever go home? Help me, Cihuacoatl, help me!*

"Cuauhtemoc is being held at his Palace, such as it is. Why did they resist so fiercely, Marina? I didn't want to destroy this city."

"This is how my people are. We're proud, Hernándo."

"They're not your people. You're from the Gulf, a slave of Taabscoob."

"They are more my people than you are. This is our land, the earth I eat." The words were out before she'd thought them and then it was too late. With her hand thrust in his face, the mud and grit of her earth and saliva smeared in the palm, she said, "If your people had fought fairly, with warning, according to our customs, we would not have had to resist. You were welcomed in our land with gifts and you betrayed us." For a moment she thought he might slap her, but slowly his tongue protruded from his mouth, flicking onto the palm of her hand, light and feathery, arousing her until her lips parted and her eyes were glazed with desire.

"Let us pray, Marina. Come, kneel with me and pray to our Lord God for grace in this victory." He took her hand and forced her slowly to her knees, then he knelt with her, staring into her dark eyes. "You are a baptized Catholic, Marina. You must not eat dirt."

She hesitated a moment, then wiped her hand vigorously on her shawl, placed her hands together in prayer and closed her eyes.

∾

Every house was filled with corpses. There were mountains to burn and the mountains turned into hills of ash and charred bones. Alvarado was in charge of disposal. He paced up and down, holding a handker-chief to his nose, his bloodshot eyes stinging from the billowing smoke. Impatient with the long process, he armed his men with palm branches and instructed them to spread the ashes and collect the bones.

"It's b-b-bad luck to handle the b-b-bones of the dead," a poor man stuttered.

"They'll bewitch us!" another fellow said, crossing himself nervously.

Alvarado brushed an offending ash from the sleeve of his doublet and fixed the men with his red-rimmed eyes. "The first man to uncover anything resembling a human soul will be rewarded," he shouted, "with three pellets of gold. I've heard the soul has a way of hiding under bones," he paused, "and sometimes inside them."

The bone piles grew as the poor Spaniards searched like dogs, crossing themselves assiduously.

PART TWO

● ● ●

Marginality is the site of radical possibility, a space of resistance.

— Bell Hooks

In a small village in the Highlands of Guatemala a woman stands on her doorstep overlooking the rich land of the valley, owned by foreigners. The coffee finca. She and her husband plant their coffee all around the edges of their one-room house. The tiny building rests on a slope, tilted on the edge of the world, breathless in the thin air. One day, she thinks, we will go tumbling down to the bottom of the valley and fly up the other side. She's never been to the other side, although she's been to Canada, far away to the north, and lived as a refugee from the war of genocide against her people. Her name is Chavela. She is the village midwife. She knows about flowers and herbs, animals and birds. Today Sister Guadalupe will come from the city, with Doctor Ramírez, and she will help them at the clinic. But first she has work to do. She's received a dream after waiting so long, and now there's no time to waste. Chavela sets her threads — blue, yellow, red and white, turquoise and gold. She pushes sticks into the ground and stretches the warp threads around them. She ties the ends onto bamboo sticks and secures the threads with another stick placed horizontally through the warp, tightening it so that her shuttle can pass through easily. She is ready to begin her grandmother's journey. In her dream Chavela saw her grandmother lying in a hammock, and the hammock was an arc of light like the new moon and the old woman's body curved into it, becoming light, her long grey hair spread out into the sky. Her arm dropped over the side of the moon and where her hand fell a scattering of stars appeared, piercing the darkness of the night sky. Chavela saw it all in colours — dark blue sky, white stars, bright yellow arcs of light, moon after golden moon, waxing and waning with the tide, her grandmother's body red with life, her head adorned with turquoise as she rested in the bright moon surrounded by darkness. She had wept to see her grandmother and was reaching out to touch her as she woke, her prayers answered. She had left her husband sleeping and knelt on the earth in front of her doorstep and prayed to the Mother-Father, Earth-Sky, to the birds and animals and plants. Now she's ready to begin her work. She runs her fingers along the fine threads, bought from the market in Huehuetenango. She picks up her shuttle and makes the first pass. It weaves back and forth between the coloured threads and slowly, slowly the story begins to appear.

∾

As Paméla entered the terminal building of La Aurora International Airport she inhaled that strange between-worlds smell that lingers in airports, gives them an edge of excitement. Although the airport seemed small after Pearson International, it was lavishly decorated with Mayan glyphs and blow-up photographs of the giant pyramids of Tikal and the ancient sites of Iximché, Quiriguá and Zaculeu. There were grainy pictures of the old capital of Antigua with a volcano smoking in the distance. Paméla's excitement had dissipated during the five hour wait at Houston airport so, even though she'd read about these places and had expected a grand sense of recognition, her mouth tasted of ashes and she felt empty and very tired suddenly. She picked up her backpack from the carousel, hoisted it onto her back and headed for the exit.

"Promise me you'll take a taxi," Hannah had said. "It'll be late when you arrive. We'd better book you into a hotel, at least for the first few days, so you'll know where you're going." They'd picked a budget hotel from the guidebook.

"Chalet Suizo, *por favor*," Paméla said, "Zona Uno, Centro Histórico."

The driver smirked and gave her an appraising look as he swung her pack into the trunk. Soon they were speeding away from the airport, along a dimly lit road lined with tall palm trees, their leaves rustling in the darkness. All the windows were open and the night air felt warm and full of strange smells: exhaust fumes mixed with the sweetness of rotting vegetation, tropical night air tinged with woodsmoke. The radio was crackling, cutting in and out, and the driver leaned down to speak into it, but Paméla was too tired to register what he said. He swerved suddenly and gunned the engine to overtake another car, then they were on the outskirts of the city, buildings springing up on either side, white against the hazy night sky. The driver pointed and said, "*El Torre del*

Reformador," but the tower disappeared and Paméla saw only a broad avenue, deserted except for a car behind them, glimpsed in the rearview mirror. She wondered if there was a curfew; she'd seen armed soldiers at the airport. She felt she could travel all night, rocked to sleep by the rattling movement of the car through the darkness of her birthplace. She closed her eyes and inhaled, trying to connect with some familiarity, when the taxi lurched to a stop.

"Calle 14, Chalet Suizo," the driver said. He dumped her pack on the sidewalk and when he tried to overcharge her Paméla had her first argument.

Her first night in Guatemala City she dreamed of Palenque and the Temple of Inscriptions.

Mist rose from the earth, a fine breath whispering around her ankles, creeping up her body. She was held in the green air, suspended, in a place she hardly remembered. She climbed the worn stone steps of the temple and descended into a crypt, falling, falling, 1,200 years, the corbelled roof above her sloping downwards. A huge triangular stone swung back to reveal a tomb. Jade on her face, jade in her mouth, jade circling her neck, fingers and toes, ears spooled with jade. Suspended above her, floating in the breath-held air, a stone slab etched with the dancing figure of Pacal Votan ascending to the Heavens — thirteen layers: six ascending, one at the top, six descending back to Earth. Intersecting lines bit into the stone, Sun and Earth the crossing point. Four great cycles ending in 2012. 4 x 26,000 = 104,000 years, an end and a beginning.

"All our memories awaken, the history of the world is told."

*She rose from the tomb and followed the snake path
slithering up the stone steps to the top of the temple. She
was free and she dove from the pyramid, flying through the
green air; nothing but the sound of her wings.*

Sunlight woke her, flooding through the wooden
shutters, patterning her face. Paméla lay, savouring her
dream, holding it in her mouth, a jade fruit melting.
She'd forgotten Palenque. They'd been there after
Yucatán, the year she'd turned ten. Hannah and Fern
had held her hands as they'd descended into the tomb
below the Temple of Inscriptions, then they'd climbed
to the top again and Hannah had said, "Be careful, don't
go near the edge." Fern had told her that hippies ate
magic mushrooms and flew from the temple, believing
they were birds.

Paméla realized she was hungry. She'd fallen asleep
as soon as she'd gotten rid of the talkative check-in clerk
and had slept for twelve hours. She jumped out of bed
and dressed hurriedly. "No rush," she told herself. "I
have three months." But there was an urgency in her,
and after breakfast at the Chalet Suizo café she walked
out into bright sunlight and began her search. Almost
directly opposite her hotel she saw the huge gothic
structure of the police headquarters, a darkly comic
building with pretentious turrets and a sinister bulk.
Paméla turned down Avenida 6 and fought her way
through the dense, slow-moving crowd. The street
was lined on either side with stalls selling clothing,
toys, CDs, gum and cigarettes, fruit and candy. Music
blared so loud that it hurt. Paméla fell into the oozing
river of people and allowed herself to be carried along

as her senses filled with strange sights and smells. There was a rusted, musty, blood smell, something like money thickly layered with DNA from passing through many hands. Huge yellow irises had fought their way through the earth and stood tall outside the Iglesia de San Francisco, and *fuego del bosque* flamed with orange flowers overhead.

Tu sabor es Crush

Aleluya Cristo vive

Festival de camisas — quetzales 65

Paméla smelled gasoline or glue, something pungent, as a boy brushed past her, staggering between the stalls, holding a cloth to his face. She stared. No one paid attention to her. They bumped against her and pushed past her as though she were invisible. Of course, they take me for a local, she thought. She heard Spanish all around her and sometimes a soft guttural language, which was familiar to her, like music she couldn't identify. She supposed it must be Mayan, because the people who spoke it were Indians, mostly barefoot and dark-skinned, the women dressed in brightly woven cloth, the men wrinkled and round shouldered from carrying heavy bundles.

The stalls dropped away and the crowds thinned as she crossed Calle 8 into Parque Central. Through the spray of a triple-tiered fountain she saw the Palacio Nacional looming. It looked like an army barracks, a wide three-tiered greystone building with a central block jutting forward onto the concrete square and small towers at either end. Paméla turned away, walked briskly across the square and entered La Catedral Metropolitana. She was surprised to find it filled with people kneeling in prayer, others walking down the side aisles lighting candles to the saints. The air was cool and peaceful. She inhaled the sweetness of fresh flowers and melting wax. "I'm home," she told herself, "I'm home and somewhere in this city I will find my mother." But everything felt strange and she missed Hannah and Fern. On impulse she threw some coins into a box in front of the nearest saint and lit a candle. She stood a moment, eyes tightly shut and prayed for help in her search. She smiled when she thought of Fern's reaction. Fern was staunchly anti-Catholic, having grown up in a strict Catholic family and attended a convent school. Paméla knew little about Catholic saints or ritual and had simply suspended judgement, although she'd had some good arguments with Fern. She read the inscription under her saint and found that she'd been praying to Saint Jude Thaddeus, patron saint of the impossible.

By the end of the week Paméla was sick of Guatemalan food. It wasn't that she didn't like it or that it wasn't healthy — portions of rice with beans and salsa, fried platanos, steaming tortillas, all of it deliciously salty, but she craved something familiar and comforting. She sat in MacDonald's on Avenida 6, eating a greasy hamburger and drinking American coffee with cream from plastic containers, but afterwards she felt empty and cheated. If language and food are culture, she thought, I'm a miserable failure as a Guatemalan. Her head ached with the effort of speaking Spanish. Although she was fluent she wasn't used to total immersion. On the plus side, she now knew Zona Uno like the back of her hand and was beginning to negotiate the buses after several long journeys in the wrong direction and interminable waits in the blazing sun. Mostly she walked, map in hand, trying to forget her throbbing temples and the exhaust fumes from thick traffic. Walking was reliable. She explored what she came to realize was a huge, sprawling city, seeking orphanages, convents and adoption agencies, systematically going through the list provided her by the government office she'd consulted on her first day. Paméla was an efficient sleuth, but each time a door opened on a blank face and closed again with an apologetic smile her hopes were dashed. She could find no evidence of her existence in Guatemala, and she was constantly fighting back tears of frustration. She felt humiliated by her search, as though her mother refused to be found and was watching her, hiding from her around every corner, gloating over her failure. She entered her own strange zone in which she moved forward and backward in spirals, always returning to the Chalet Suizo at night, where she talked to the tall, dark-eyed owner and learned that his parents had started the hotel when they'd emigrated from Switzerland in the 1940s. When there was a power outage he brought her candles and lingered in the doorway. *"Gracias,"* she said, *"Gracias y buenas noches,"* and turned her back. She was learning to avoid eye contact.

She spent an entire morning at Guatel, waiting for a phone line to Canada, only to get Fern's voice on the answering machine. The sweet familiarity took her own voice away for a moment and when she spoke her words were clipped and snappy. "I'm not going through this again. I'll e-mail you, OK? I'm fine. Nothing to report yet. Wish you could see this crazy place. Why didn't you *tell* me! I love you both." She hung up, fighting an impulse to go straight to the airport and fly home.

She dreamed in Spanish now, the syntax hurtling into the day, fragmenting into phrases which echoed in her brain. She gave her watch to a woman on the street, begging with a baby in her arms and two more children hanging off her. She moved like a sleepwalker and saw clues everywhere, hanging in the trees, hidden in dusty bushes clinging to the cracked earth. She followed a woman down Avenida La Reforma, convinced that she was her mother. She'd almost caught up to her when she tripped on the root of a huge ceiba bulging through the sidewalk, and when she looked up the woman was talking to a man whose hand was grasped by a small child. The woman's face lit up as she swung the child into her arms.

At night, the dream again, grasping her by the scruff of her neck, shaking her awake.

Where is she? I know she's here, I can feel her! What does she look like? Is she like me?

∾

Fabiana awoke in their big bed in the high-ceilinged room. Her forehead was damp. She lifted her head and pulled her dark hair back with both hands, off her neck. It was heavy and she was hot. She tried to get up but slumped back into her own imprint. The languid afternoon. Her dream. One side of her face was streaked with tears. It had left her with a weight of sadness, undefined. She closed her eyes and glimpsed . . . but it was gone . . . only an absence, as though someone had just left that dark place she felt but couldn't quite see. Shadows, only shadows. She opened her eyes and turned her head to the window. It was barred to keep her safe. Yellowed grass struggled for life, small patches of green where the trees shaded it. Everything was familiar. She closed her eyes and drifted. She remembered nothing before she'd reached the city, her feet brown with dried blood. *"Pian wey nbi"*, my name is Fabiana, *"n'el nk'uu,"* I'm hungry. No one understood, *"No me entiendo, niña,"* until a Mayan man from the Mam-speaking region of Huehuetenango, leaning against a pillar in the cool air of the marbled Banco de Guatemala, stepped forward and translated, *"Su nombre es Fabiana. La muchacha tiene hambre."* A woman with thickly mascaraed lashes and red lips took her to the lunch room and fed her tortillas and milk. The child ate slowly, methodically, like a cow chewing on absence, then they opened the glass door and put her out onto the street. She slept curled around her own small body, listening to the soft murmurings of the Mayan street people, shaping her tongue to the strange sounds she heard, the hard metallic sounds of the Spanish speakers. The next day she slipped into the bank again and stood by the pillar. The red-lipped woman fed her and at the end of the day she took her by the hand and marched her over to Casa Central at Calle 13 and Avenida 2a. The child stood in front of the heavy wooden door, looking up at the woman as she lifted the brass-hand knocker, which had a ring on its third finger, and rapped on the door. They heard footsteps, a grille opened, Fabiana watched her red lips moving, heard whispered sounds from the other side. Then the big door opened and a small figure in flowing robes took her hand and tugged gently. The door slammed behind her.

She slept in a dormitory with many other orphans, none of whom spoke Mam. Fabiana learned slowly, reluctantly, repeating the Spanish words, thick in her mouth, as she stared into the courtyard, losing herself in the bougainvillea which spilled from the tiled roof like a cloud of bright butterflies.

"Fabiana!" Sister Rosa's voice was sharp. "*Mira, muchacha, presta atención!*"

For a long time she didn't understand what they said to her, but she learned to anticipate the nuns' wishes and eventually she was deemed fit for service. One bright morning she and Sister Rosa took the bus, rattling through the exhaust fumes of the city, swaying and stumbling in the crush of passengers. Fabiana gasped as they turned onto Avenida La Reforma; it was wider than a river. The roots of huge trees buckled the sidewalk as though there was a world under the concrete that she could not see. Enormous bronze creatures stood in the middle of the river — a snorting bull with curved horns, a lion with open mouth and tangled mane — and tall buildings like mountains.

"*Aquí, muchacha!*" Sister Rosa yanked her by the hand and shouldered her way off the bus. They walked briskly down a broad leafy street, away from La Reforma. This time the big wooden door was opened by a maid who tossed her head, gesturing them to follow her down a long corridor, into a bright room filled with vases of flowers. Señora Méndez sat in a bay window, painting her fingernails with a tiny red brush. She looked up with an amused smile, her lips parting to reveal perfect white teeth.

"What a tiny one. Your girls get younger and younger, Sister Rosa. I hope she can manage the work of kitchen maid." She resumed her manicure.

"She's a good girl, Señora, and quick to learn." Sister Rosa patted Fabiana's head.

"You will make the tortillas and wash the vegetables," Señora Méndez said, addressing Fabiana. "Go now. You must take a bath and put on a clean uniform before you start work in my kitchen."

Fabiana entered servitude as some enter Heaven. She served coffee to Señor Méndez in his study and stood by the side of his chair twisting her fingers. He smiled and gestured her to sit, but the child was shy. He asked about her village, but she couldn't remember a village and she didn't understand his questions. She was learning the new language fast, but it deserted her when she was nervous. He took down a book from the wall of books behind his desk and opened it, pointing to the black letters. Fabiana shook her head, so he began speaking, one word at a time, pointing to pieces of furniture, paintings, the fireplace, letters scattered on his desk, a crystal bowl, a letter opener, a paper weight, a vase, pointing and speaking until she had learned all his belongings. The coffee grew cold.

Fabiana remembered the first day Señor Méndez touched her. It was the day she learned to name the parts of her body — *boca, nariz, ojo, oreja, cabeza*. She was proud that she already knew some of these words. *Cuerpo, brazo, mano, pierna, estómago*; he was patient, pointing and speaking, smiling, praising her when she got the words right. "*Bravo*," he said, "*Bravo, muchacha*."

Señora Méndez had been angry with Fabiana that morning and had shouted at her. The child hadn't understood, because she'd spoken rapidly, her brow fierce and furrowed. She'd been afraid and had tripped and dropped her tray. The coffee cups had shattered in tiny pieces on the floor and Fabiana had wept in terror of losing her place in the grand house.

"*Espalda*," he said, placing his hand on her back, "*Cuello*," his hand gentle on the back of her neck, "*Nalgas*," running down her back to her behind, "*Muslo*," descending to her thigh. Then Señor Méndez took her hand and placed it in his lap. "*Pene*," he said, "*Pene, entiendo?*" Fabiana shook her head and pulled her hand away. He laughed. "Enough, *muchacha*. You can go." He dismissed her with a sweep of his big hand.

She lay awake that night, feeling the parts of her body, her lips moving, forming the strange words. She was afraid that she had somehow disappointed her teacher. The next day when she served his coffee as usual there was no smile, no greeting, only a nod. He didn't even look at her as she placed the coffee tray carefully on the mahogany sidetable, bobbing in a little curtsy as Señora Méndez had instructed her. For three days he withheld himself from her until the child could bear it no longer. "*Disculpe, Señor*," she lisped, "*Disculpe, disculpe, perdóneme*." He looked up finally from his newspaper, a cool, appraising stare over his spectacles into the child's face, wet with tears. He said not a word and she could not bear the silence. She needed more than anything to be forgiven, so she placed her small hand in his lap.

"Never tell," he said. "This is our special secret."

Fabiana grew up in the house of Señor and Señora Méndez. She spoke their language and ate their food. She had no memory of who she was, but she was not unhappy, because she had given her loyalty to Señor Méndez. She received a small wage for her work, enough to take the bus downtown on her day off and drink a cup of chocolate or visit the sad animals at the Parque Aurora Zoológico. She walked the sandy gravel paths and strayed barefoot onto the grass to stare into the wrinkled eye of the pacing elephant. Then everything changed.

Fabiana thought the bleeding was a punishment from God for what she did with Señor Méndez. She knew it was penance for her secret because it attacked her in the same place, hurting, so she told no one, neither Cook, nor the Señora, nor even the maid, Julia, whose room she shared. She thought Julia would surely smell her bloody rags, but Julia was in love with the gardener's boy and quite oblivious to Fabiana. She scrubbed the rags clean in the wash-house at night, swilling the bloody water down the drain and hanging them on a branch to dry. On her day off she went to Iglesia de la Merced and prayed to the Virgin. She lit a candle and begged the Holy Mother to intercede for her and ask God to end the punishment. When two months passed without bleeding she lit another candle and gave thanks to Madre María. But her body was not her own. Strange feelings invaded her; nausea and cravings she had never felt before. She was ravenous, devouring her food in the kitchen like an animal, sneaking downstairs in the night to gnaw on leftovers, hiding stale tortillas under her nightgown and padding silently upstairs to her bed to chew on them while Julia sighed in her sleep, dreaming of her boy.

"You are filling out, Fabiana," Señora Méndez teased. "We must find you another dress."

Cook gave her a sidelong glance. A week later the Señora walked in on Fabiana while she was washing herself in the bath. "Stand up," she ordered, her red nails scraping the air. "I want to look at you." Fabiana tried to cover her body, but Señora Méndez grabbed her by the wrists and spread her arms. "*Puta!*" she hissed, "Dirty little slut," and she slapped Fabiana's face. "Get your clothes on and get out of my house!"

She didn't have a chance to say goodbye to the Señor, to tell him that she had kept their secret, that she had been loyal. There was nowhere to go but back to Casa Central.

Fabiana sat up and swung her legs over the edge of the big bed. She stretched her arms and yawned, then her mouth curved into a smile. Ernesto would come soon and she would feel better. She missed him every minute. Her toes touched the floor as she slid from the bed and walked over to the window and stood there, watching for him.

∾

After the fall of Tenochtitlan King Carlos declared Cortés Governor, Captain-General and Chief Justice of New Spain. He set up his government in Coyoacan, a distance from Tenochtitlan, and set his men to clearing and rebuilding the city. The Franciscan Padrés wanted to smash every temple and use the stones to build churches on the same sites.

"Haven't we done enough damage?" Cortés asked. "Let us preserve what beauty is left in this landscape."

"The Catholic Church will triumph over heathenism," the Bishop said, "only when it is built atop the site of its atrocities."

The Church understood power and the accumulation thereof on strong foundations, feeding off generations of ancient faith. Cortés was a man of action, unaccustomed to the subtleties of silent power play. He was preoccupied; he failed to make a stand against the Church because he was faithful to it, to his Virgin who had brought him victory. So began a silent engagement which held him without his understanding in a war with the Franciscan monks and Spanish bureacrats. The Bishop gave orders. Priests were sent out with armed battalions to convert the Indians, to draw them out of their spiritual darkness now that they were subjects of the Spanish crown.

Cortés built a house for Malintzín in Coyoacan. Constructed on the site of a Culhua-Mexica palace, the walls of Casa Colorado were stained with cinnabar, the windows shuttered with fine timbers. Malintzín made a garden in the heart of the house where the sun cascaded into the inner courtyard. She took her pouch of earth from its hiding place and buried it in the garden, mixing it with the earth of Coyoacan to nourish her corn and beans.

"Why do you not grow flowers, Marina?" Cortés inquired.

"Flowers will grow themselves. Corn needs planting," she replied. I will never again be hungry, she thought. I will eat my homeland for the rest of my life.

The Casa Colorado was her first home since she'd been taken from her father's house and betrayed by her mother. Close by lay the rubble of a small pyramid. Malintzín watched her people picking through the stones, reshaping them into a chapel. When she tried to speak with them they turned away.

"I'm building it for you, *mi amor*. We'll celebrate our first Mass together in Capilla La Conchita. I've promised the masons a bonus if they have it finished for Navidad." The triumphant lover took Malintzín's hand, led her across the planks of the newly made floor, the wood still green and pungent, and made her kneel with him before the Virgin of Socorro. He fed her the words, the prayers of gratitude for his victory over the Culhua-Mexica, while she prayed silently to Tonantzin, her Mother Goddess, and to Cihuacoatl, uncertain still, her flayed soul shivering.

As the Franciscans smashed temples and built churches in the name of the One God, the True Cross, on all the power points of New Spain, Malintzín started her own construction, a dome in her belly.

"*Mi capitán.*" Her soft voice woke him. He rolled over and rounded her body into his palm, cupping her to him, drinking her like a shot of Spanish brandy. The sharp-boned Malintzín, bitter and hungry, stood on the shore of a fast-running river and watched herself swimming there under dark water, a creature without the need for breath. She watched the merchants' procession to the river, saw her own small body slung over a servant's shoulder, she watched her mother leave the place without a backward glance. She watched and plotted for the safety of herself and her bellyful.

"*Mi niño será español,*" she said, placing her hand over his, cupping her belly.

"A son!" he exclaimed, his hand softening. He didn't know how many there were, born in his wake to numerous women, but this was the child born of his conquest; this one he cared for. As Malintzín slept, curled around her new life, Cortés lay awake, his heart beating with something resembling fear; perhaps not fear exactly, but more a feeling of confinement. I cannot marry her. I'm already married and I need a legitimate son. The king . . . my governorship . . . He wiped his brow, beaded with sweat. She's an Indian. She's trapped me with her tongue.

∾

Paméla stood by the fountain in Parque Central watching a group of women walk slowly back and forth in front of the Palacio Nacional. Many of them carried placards with grainy blow-up photographs of young people. Crude lettering scrawled across the posters read:

¿Dondé tienen a mi hija,

Héctor Morales, desaparecido el 15 de mayo, 1989

There were many faces, many names. Slowly the women turned to face the Palacio and began to chant, some of them raising their fists in the air, "*Vivos se los llevaron, vivos los queremos!*" Alive they were taken, alive we want them back. A sad-faced man handed her a flyer with a picture of a small boy wearing a wide-brimmed hat.

> *Manuel Sotz,*
> *desaparecido el 24-6-1982 a la edad de 7 años.*
> *Ayudanos a Encontrarlos!*
> *Esclarezcamos el destino de nuestros niños y niñas.*
> *Asociación Dónde Están.*

There was an address in Zona 2.

Paméla started walking north. As she passed behind the Palacio she saw a group of little boys scrambling on the stone steps, making guns out of their hands, firing at each other. Their faces were fierce with intent as they ambushed each other. They fell on the sidewalk screaming with laughter as they were shot.

The first place she found seemed unlikely; a tiny *comedor*, the walls blackened by an open fire. A woman was making tortillas over the glowing coals. "No," she said, wiping her hands on her apron, "There is no office here. You have the wrong address."

She showed her the flyer, but the woman seemed uninterested. She looked past Paméla, her eyes squinting into the sun. Paméla realized then that the woman couldn't read and she told her the address.

"Zona Dos!" she exclaimed. "This is Zona Uno," and she waved her arm, "Two streets over, you will find Zona Dos."

The peeling blue door was grated with iron bars. There were four bells. Paméla pressed the top one and after a few seconds a voice crackled over the ancient intercom.

"*Quiero Asociación Dónde Están,*" Paméla said.

Instantly the buzzer went and the door swung open. One flight up a smiling woman in a bright yellow blouse stood at the door of her office. "Anna-María," she said warmly, extending her hand, inviting Paméla into a small room which contained little other than a desk, two chairs and piles of papers. "Please, have a seat. How can I help you?"

"I'm Canadian," she began wearily, "but I was born here in Guatemala and adopted in November 1982. I want to find my mother."

"I will try to help you," Anna-María said as she leaned across the desk to touch Paméla's hand. "Our work here is to reunite parents and children who have been separated. We need your date and place of birth and a blood test to match with your mother. Many children were separated from their families during the worst years of the war, in the '70s and '80s, but for you it's different. You were adopted." She pointed to a large bulletin board on the wall behind her. It was covered with photographs. "See these people? They're from Nebaj. They had to flee to the mountains when their village was destroyed twenty years ago. Two of their children were killed and the third child was lost. They looked many years for her and then one day they registered here with Dónde Están. We were able to match them, because their daughter — her name is Jennifer — contacted the office of Dónde Están in Chicago. Jennifer had been adopted by Americanos, but she wanted to find her mamá and papá. She remembered." Anna-María's eyes were shining.

Paméla looked at the photograph of the old Mayan couple holding their young American daughter. "Where does she live now?"

"Jennifer? She went back to the United States, but she visits her parents in Guatemala. Many children were lost in the war. They were taken to houses in the capital, *casas de engordas,* fattening houses where they were kept for adoption. There are people in Guatemala who will do anything to make money."

"My parents paid $20,000 to adopt me."

"Now it's $30,000, and there are approximately 3,000 children adopted every year, most of those children going to the United States. There is a great demand. You know that babies are stolen from the hospitals, and babies are smuggled in from Mexico and passed off as Guatemalan. The midwives forge their birth certificates. I know of one case where a girl gave birth in prison and they blackmailed her to give up her child in return for her freedom." Anna-María shook her head sadly and touched Paméla's hand. "At this agency we can only support people in their search. Unless a parent has registered with us there is little we can do. You see this girl?" She turned and pointed to a cheerful, American-looking girl in what appeared to be a high school photograph. "She lives in Texas and, like Jennifer, she came to us looking for her mamá. The mother had not registered with us, but we were able to find her from the hospital birth record. And do you know what she said? 'This is not my daughter. I never saw her. The doctor told me she was born dead.' Many women were raped during the destruction of their villages. And when a poor woman comes alone to the hospital they can take her baby. Selling children is big business in Guatemala. The children who are adopted are the lucky ones." Her face became solemn. "I am sorry to tell you this, but many children are sold as organ donors. There are rich families in the United States and in Europe who will pay for a healthy kidney, a liver, a heart." She turned to the wall of photographs. "But look! Here they are together," she said, pointing.

Paméla leaned forward and stared at the Texan girl in the arms of her mother. "So many lost years," she murmured. "It's a crime."

"In Guatemala there are many crimes. At least they're alive and they've found each other. This is all we can hope for. Come, you must fill out the form and we'll see what we can do to find your mamá."

Paméla sat down, pulled her birth certificate and adoption papers out of her wallet and started copying information onto the form. "My adoptive parents said I was in an orphanage run by nuns, but I've already been to so many convents and orphanages . . . "

"Have you been to Casa Central?"

"Casa Central?"

"A convent close to here. They used to take in children many years ago. It's on Calle de Niñado, a big building, it takes up the whole block. You can't miss it."

Half an hour later Paméla stood at the door of Casa Central. She reached out and lifted the brass-hand knocker with the ring on the marriage finger. The hand felt cool in hers. She let it drop, clanging against the heavy brown door. She heard footsteps, a bustling sound, then the metal cover on the grille slid back. "*Sí?*"

"My name is Paméla. I believe the nuns of this convent looked after me when I was a baby. May I come in?"

There was a long silence, then the metal cover snapped. A heart-beat later the door opened and a small hand reached out and grabbed her arm. The door closed behind her and she found herself in a dimly lit entry hall, with light flooding from an open courtyard at the end of the hallway.

"I'm Sister Rosa," the nun said, grasping Paméla's hand. "How did you find us? We're no longer registered as an orphanage."

"I've been to all the convents and orphanages in the capital."

"What are you looking for?"

"My birth mother. I was born in Guatemala and adopted by Canadians. I have papers from the hospital with the record of my birth."

"Show me, show me," Sister Rosa gestured impatiently. She was a tiny woman with bright bird-like eyes and a kindly, wrinkled face. Paméla pulled out her papers and the little nun peered, holding them inches from her face. "Ah, sí," she nodded, "the public hospital," she waved her arm heavenwards, "near to the church of Guadalupe."

"So this is the place?" Paméla asked eagerly.

"We will see," she said, handing the papers back. "Come, I'll take you to Sister María-Teresa. She's the one who can help you."

Sister Rosa led Paméla through the courtyard. She was dressed in a blue skirt with a darker blue cardigan, thick stockings and lace-up shoes. Her head was covered with a white scarf tied at the back, the sides falling onto her shoulders. "We have a school for career training," she said. "The children come here for nursing and secretarial studies, and some of them will be teachers."

As they passed through the bright courtyard Paméla glimpsed a wall of cascading bougainvillea. Trailing plants climbed the walls and the beds were filled with flowers and foliage.

"We have many students at Casa Central and we have a private clinic on the other side of the building, for those who do not wish to wait all day at the hospital." They walked down a long cool corridor branching off the colonnaded courtyard. Sister Rosa nodded to two young nuns, similarly dressed, walking briskly past. "Our Sisters go out into the city and into the villages to work with the poor and the sick." They stopped in front of a white door. Sister Rosa put her ear to the door and knocked gently. A voice answered from the other side.

It was a small room with a desk and several chairs and a tall filing cabinet standing in the corner. A handsome woman sat behind the desk, a crucifix hanging on the wall behind her. Sister Rosa spoke in a hushed voice, then the other nun nodded and Sister Rosa beckoned to Paméla.

"Sister María-Teresa will help you," she said and she patted Paméla's shoulder and left the room.

"Please sit. I understand you are looking for your mother."

"Yes, I . . . " She began to explain everything again, but María-Teresa silenced her with a single gesture of her hand.

"Your papers, please." Despite her curt manner the nun's eyes were kind and she had a full, generous mouth. She scanned the papers quickly and raised her eyebrows. "You are one of the lucky ones," she said.

"Lucky? Yes, I suppose — "

"Indeed," she said emphatically. She walked over to the filing cabinet, flipped through it and removed a faded folder. She leafed through the dog-eared pages, then replaced the file and returned to her desk. "It would be best if you did not look any further."

"Is she dead?" Paméla's voice was barely a whisper.

"She is alive."

"Can I see her?" Paméla was half-way off her chair. "Is she here in the capital?"

"She is in Guatemala City. That's all I can tell you."

"Where? I must know, please! I've come all this way." Paméla was standing now, leaning across the desk.

"Sit down, please," María-Teresa gestured to the chair and waited for Paméla to sit. "Your mother gave you a great gift when she gave you up for adoption. Don't you know about this country? Guatemala is a tragic place. Why come here looking for trouble? Isn't your life in Canada enough for you?"

"I *must* find her. This is wonderful, just to know that she's alive!"

María-Teresa held up her hand to silence Paméla, then she sighed and began, "I entered this convent twenty-five years ago. It was an orphanage then. We've had many children passing through our hands, Paméla. I don't know how aware you are about the political history of Guatemala, but — "

"I've been reading a lot, I — "

"So you know then that we've suffered a long war of genocide against our indigenous people. It began in

1954 with the fall of the Arbenz government, engineered by the CIA, all our land given over to the United Fruit Company and other foreign landowners, and when we protested we were silenced brutally."

"But surely it began with the Spanish in 1524 when Pedro de Alvarado murdered two thirds of the people?"

"Bravo, Paméla. You are a student of history. Yes, your history books are correct; resistance has been our way of life since the Spanish discovered us, but what they don't tell you, my dear, is how we live this conquest over and over, day after day, year after year. In my lifetime alone we have endured thirty-four years of armed confrontation. Imagine the number of women raped. Imagine the number of children orphaned. In '96 the Peace Accord was signed, which means what? That the war casualties are reduced for the time being, and Casa Central is no longer registered with the government as an orphanage."

"I'm not an orphan. My mother is here in the city. Why won't you tell me where she is?"

María-Teresa rose from her chair and walked over to the filing cabinet. She turned, leaning against the cabinet, as though protecting it. "You're not the only one to come looking for your birth mother. We're required by law to keep these files, but I have learned that it's better not to disturb the past."

"I'll tell you why I'm here," Paméla blurted out impulsively. "There's a dream . . . " She told María-Teresa about the destroyed village, the mountain of Papás, the bloody footprints. The nun nodded her head slowly as though she'd heard it all before.

"Yes, yes," she said when the story was over, "Four hundred and forty villages wiped off the face of the map, as though they'd never existed. My advice to you, Paméla, is to get on a plane and go back to Canada."

"Is that all? Aren't you going to help me?"

"There's nothing more I can do for you." María-Teresa fixed her with a steady gaze for what seemed like minutes, then she left the cabinet and walked towards the door, breaking the spell. "I'll see you out."

Paméla jumped up and moved quickly to the door. "No, I can find my own way," she said, pushing past María-Teresa.

"If you need help later you can come to me."

Paméla turned, her hand on the doorknob. "You're cruel!" she said, spitting out the word, then she slammed the door behind her and ran down the corridor. Hot tears stung her eyes as she rounded the corner into the courtyard and collided with a nun. She heard a gasp and felt herself resting in the softness of lemon-scented skin, sprawled on the ground, earth crumbling around her.

∼

Malintzín knelt with her head bowed over the green shoots of corn pushing through the earth, loosening it. She felt the child rooted in her belly, beginning to stir, and she knew she would not lose this one. Her new skin was growing as her conquered people rebuilt their homes and planted their land, bright dots of green patterning the hills around Coyoacan. She had a home with servants and more food than she could ever have imagined, yet she felt a sudden darkness come over her. She looked up, a wisp of hair trailing across her mud-streaked forehead. The sun stood brilliant in the sky, blinding her, then she heard the sound of hooves and a tall figure passed in front of her, his head eclipsing the sun.

"Where are you going?"

"To the city, to inspect the new hospital," Cortés said. It was the first in Mexico, the Hospital of Jesus; Cortés had supervised the building of it as a refuge for his wounded conquistadors.

"When will you return?" She pushed the trailing wisp behind her ear.

"Oh, there are many questions." He busied himself, tightening the girth on his stallion's saddle. "I must supervise the building of my palace, inspect the new cathedral, the churches . . . "

"I will come with you, Hernándo." With a quick gesture she turned and was about to enter the house when Cortés spoke, like a gunshot.

"No!" Then gently, reasonably, with the persuasive tone generally reserved for his men, "This is your home, Marina. You have served me well and now you must rest. I will manage." Gripping his reins in one hand he circled her neck with his left hand and kissed her lips gently.

"Hernán . . . when the child comes . . . "

"I will be with you. We'll baptize him together in Capilla La Conchita."

"And if it's a girl . . . ?"

"It will be a son," he said confidently. "You are the only woman in my life."

Malintzín caught her breath. "I will give you sons, many sons."

He caressed her thickening waist, his hand felt the pulse of her belly, then he mounted his horse and left her standing in the sunlight. She walked the short distance to Capilla la Conchita, entered the newly-built church and knelt in the sweet circle of the altar under the gaze of the Virgin. She knelt there a long time, savouring the warmth of the sun on her face, feeling the quickening of her child.

"Thank you Cihuacoatl, for giving me a new skin when I thought I'd lost my people, my life, my home. You cry for your lost children, but I am bearing a son and I will never be alone again."

When Cortés reached the city he went straight to the Hospital of Jesus, a stone's throw from the causeway where he had first encountered Moctezuma, staring down at him from his litter in the sky. He entered the hospital and marched to the end of the ward, stones ringing as his spurs struck them. A shiver ran down his spine, slithering through the cold stones, entering the earth like a fugitive; a part of Hernán Cortés entering the cool, dark earth of the New World, burrowing its way towards the north wall of the edifice.

"My poor old friend, you've served me well," he said, hunkering down by the pallet where Pablo Osorio lay, his waxen face sweating. This soldier had been with Cortés since the beginning, signing on with him in Santiago de Cuba. He'd fought fearlessly through all the battles until he'd been wounded in the final assault on Tenochtitlan. Gangrene had set in and, despite a double amputation, its progress could not be stopped. Cortés grasped the man's hand and brought it to his lips.

"*Mi capitán*," Osorio whispered, "Help me, please. I don't want to die here."

"God bless you, Pablo," Cortés said. "You must be brave." He smiled into the man's clouding eyes and held tight to his hand until he drifted into sleep. He knelt there a minute, one knee on the cold stone, stroking Pablo's face. Then he wiped his eyes roughly and walked out into the sunlight, across the plaza towards the cathedral, which had been built on the site of Huitzilopochtli's temple, and newly dedicated by the Bishop. Flickering candles circled the Virgin's feet and illuminated Cortés' face as he knelt to pray, eyes tightly closed, hands clasped.

"Madre María, I've lost my freedom. The battles are over and I'm beset on all sides . . . the Franciscan Fathers, Marina and her bellyful, the Spanish bureaucrats worming their way into my governorship . . . Oh, help me, Blessed Virgin, to find again the wildness in my heart that feeds my soul, the passion of the battlefield, side by side with my men. I live only for you, to spread your glory across this land, for you, Madre, not for the king. Help me, I implore you."

He opened his eyes and saw the Virgin's foot placed firmly on the head of a serpent circling the globe. No matter how devout his prayers, repeating his rosary morning, noon and evening, his heart felt increasingly constricted since he'd conquered the Culhua-Mexica and become governor. He longed for the days of battle when Malintzín was at his side, a wild girl, all bone and sinew, moving in his shadow as though she were a part of him. Whenever I turned she was there in my service, ready with her tongues. I gave my heart in the heat of battle. I forgot my station in life, my career, my wife in Cuba. Ah, but every man of standing has a mistress. Let Catalina come. I can keep Marina. I can have as many women as I want. I am governor!

He crossed himself and stood, turned away from the altar and marched out into the burning sun, his pale olive skin flushed. A tornado of feeling propelled him, deafened by the pounding of blood in his ears, until he found himself standing in the archway of the concubines' hall in Cuauhtemoc's sad palace, where the deposed Emperor lived on amid the refashioning of his lost Empire. Heads turned, one by one, eyes staring at Cortés. One of the women stood and bowed to the conquerer. She advanced slowly and stood before him, smiling, her head tilted slightly. The muscle in his jaw jumped as he turned and walked away, his boots striking the stones of the colonnade, ringing out above the soft laughter of the women.

Cortés was gone for many days. Malintzín lost count as her belly grew. She prayed to Ixchel, Goddess of her Mayan lords, and she felt like a slave girl again, a supplicant. "Weave me a spell, O Mother Ixchel, a spell to bring him home. Bind him to me with this child, I beg you, do not abandon me, do not cast me out!" Silence resounded through her heart and Malintzín heard the river and felt the swamp grasses brushing against her bare legs. Her stomach clenched as fear nested in her. It felt like hunger.

Zaachila had ground the corn three times to make a fine flour for the tortillas. She was mixing it with a little water, kneading the *masa* when Malintzín entered the dark kitchen. They had been given as slaves together to the Spanish, because Taabscoob had wanted to get rid of the unruly ones. Malintzín had helped Zaachila to abort her unwanted child with herbs and they had helped each other through the long journeys across the mountains. Now Malintzín shared her good fortune by employing Zaachila as her maid at the Casa Colorado.

"What are you doing, Zaachila? I'm hungry."

"I'm making *masa*. Soon the tortillas will be ready and I'll serve dinner." The girl spoke quickly, in her native Popoluca. She was loyal and eager to please her friend, who had quickly become her mistress as she had advanced in the new world with her gift of tongues.

Malintzín walked over to the table, stuck her finger into the dough and rubbed it between her fingers to test the texture as she'd seen her mother do and as her Tabascan mistress had also done.

"What is this? The corn is too coarse."

"But I've ground it three times, Doña Marina."

"I tell you it's not smooth enough!" she shouted and swept the bowl of *masa* off the table. Zaachila gasped as it crashed to the floor and broke into many pieces. "I'll send you back to your village, you useless girl!" she shouted and marched out of the kitchen.

When Cortés returned he brought with him Tecuichpo, the dead Emperor's daughter, and her three sisters, all newly christened with Spanish names. "As governer I am bound to provide for them, Marina."

"But in my house?"

"This is my official household until my palace is built, and I am their protector. I act in accordance with the Emperor's last wishes."

"He had not time for last wishes. He was murdered!"

A vein pulsed in his forehead, like a serpent under his skin. "What is it you want?"

"Marry me, Hernándo."

"You know I cannot."

"You said I am the only woman in your life."

"I am governor. I have responsibilities."

She was afraid he would leave her, storming out of her bedroom as he so often did now, but he grasped her shoulders and pulled her against him, pulsing against her belly. That night, as he lay snoring at her side, she trussed his body with her desire to be queen. "*Casarme*," she murmured in his sleeping ear, "*Casarme, casarme*," a marriage mantra. She knew he had a wife in another land, waiting for him three long years, but she didn't care. She walked with Señor Malinche who was a God and could do as he desired. He would give her a place beside him in the Heavens. It had been predicted.

∾

"I'm sorry, I'm sorry." She burst into tears and strong arms held her, cradling her where she lay, her head in a flowerbed in the convent courtyard. When she looked up finally, with snot on her nose, the nun laughed, revealing the most beautiful smile, and handed her a white handkerchief.

"The lilies are hurt more than we are," she said. "Look, this one has lost her head. I was planting when you came round the corner like a tornado." She had a quick, light way of speaking, as though her tongue might trip over itself. She laughed again and held out her slim hand, strangely formal after their embrace. "Guadalupe," she said, "and what is your name?"

"Paméla." She babbled her story while Guadalupe helped her up and brushed the crumbly earth from her hair. "But she wouldn't let me see the file. She wouldn't help at all and Sister Rosa was so kind. I can't believe it, to be this close to finding my mother!" Paméla kicked at the dirt, trying to push it back into the flower bed.

"Come and sit down." Guadalupe took Paméla's hand and led her over to a small stone bench. "I'll fetch some water."

Paméla noticed the startling clarity of her green eyes before she disappeared down the colonnade and left her staring across the courtyard at the bougainvillea. She brushed her hand across her face and smelled the lemony scent lingering there. She inhaled and closed her eyes, memory tingling through her body.

"Here."

She started as Lupe touched her shoulder and handed her a glass of water. "Thank you. I'm feeling a bit strange."

"You must rest. This has been a shock for you." Guadalupe put her arm around Paméla's shoulders and tipped the glass to her mouth. "I came to the convent in 1981. The nuns took me in."

"1981? You must have been a child."

Guadalupe nodded. "I was twelve years old. I had nowhere to go. My village had been attacked by the army. It was a difficult time for me, but I've found peace here." Her tone implied closure of the subject she had just opened and Paméla didn't know what to say.

"Are you the gardener?"

Guadalupe threw back her head and laughed. "Oh yes, my beloved lilies! But I'm very worldly. I travel and help people in the villages. I've just returned from Huehuetenango in the Highlands close to the border with Mexico. There's a village there called Huixoc and I go every month with Doctor Ramírez to work in the clinic. My friend, Chavela, is the village midwife. She lived in Canada like you. For twenty-two years she was a refugee with her family, but now she's come home."

"Isn't it dangerous for her?"

"Much less than before." Guadalupe leaned closer to Paméla and lowered her voice. "In this country we always live with danger. To be Guatemalan and politically active means to gamble with your life. There are less deaths and disappearances now, because, since the Peace Accord the eyes of the United Nations are on us, but it's only a matter of statistics." She smiled and pulled away. "I mustn't keep you inside the convent walls. There's the whole country for you to discover," she said gesturing in the air with her delicate hands, the nails clean and cropped.

"I didn't come here for tourism. I won't leave the capital till I find my mother."

Guadalupe raised her eyebrows. "Where will you go?"

"I don't know. I haven't figured that out yet, but I'd like to say goodbye to Sister Rosa."

"She's resting now. She always takes a nap in the afternoon. But you will come back again, won't you, Paméla?"

∽

Chavela took up her weaving, lifted the strap over her head, nestled it into her waist and leaned back. Her body was a loom, the weaving stretched between her and the tree at the corner of her house. Her threads shimmered in the afternoon sun: blue, gold, red and yellow, turquoise and white. She'd seen the ocean for the first time as they'd flown into Vancouver, the plane banking over deep blue water as though it would plunge in like a great bird and carry them to the bottom of the churning, white-capped water. She'd learned about the Pacific ocean, about the riches it held when she took her children to White Rock on Sundays to catch fish and crabs. They always ate well on Sunday night. She looked across the valley and saw the land dotted with corn and coffee, the plants patterning the earth as the bright threads patterned her weaving. She breathed the clean mountain air; it cleared her head. In Canada her head had ached, sometimes for days. She remembered those days, a refugee from the violence of her country. All the memories stirred when Guadalupe came, when they talked together in their language, in Mam. "What I have done to survive," she told her, "Twenty-two years in exile, first in Mexico at the refugee camp in Chiapas, across the border from my village, longing every minute for Mamá, for my sisters, my brothers. And my husand crying in the night for what they did to him. I was dragged by my hair into a new world, Lupe, where I had to learn a third language. In Vancouver I stared out the window at the mountains, longing for the mountains of Huixoc, as the teacher made us repeat the words in English — table, chair, door, floor, ceiling, wall. I learned Spanish in the house of a rich woman in the city of Huehuetenango when I was only twelve years old. I worked for her, washing her floors. But we are Mayans, Lupe. Our people are alive, our language is alive, and they will not kill us no matter how hard they try. Yes, it is safe for us to return now, but the war is not over. It will never end."

She looked through the open door of the house at her sleeping husband. Antonio slept in the bed where they raped her, after the army took him. Now, when they made love in that bed everything was new. He was up at dawn to work in their garden. They grew coffee, aguacate, mamaya, bananas, squash and beans. Their children were Canadians, their grandson was Canadian. The world had changed. Everything changes in time. They'd come home and everything was the same and different.

∽

A smile tugged the corners of Guadalupe's mouth as she swept the crumbled earth back into the border and finished planting her battered lilies. "Something about the girl . . . "

She prayed for her that night in the Chapel of the Medalla Milagrosa, attached to the convent. "Oh Lady of the Miraculous Medal, bless this child and help her to find peace."

Guadalupe imagined the relic of Santa Catalina's heart beating in Paris. Catherine Labouré had entered the convent of the Daughters of Charity in 1830 when she was twenty-four years old. She'd lost her mother when she was nine. She received several visitations from the Virgin Mary who appeared on a sphere circled by a snake. The Virgin revealed to Catherine a symbol with the letter M and two hearts, one pierced by a sword, the other circled with thorns, and instructed her to have a medallion made in this image. Guadalupe wore one of these medals on a thin gold chain. She believed in miracles and prayed to Our Lady to help the Canadian girl find her mother. She imagined the pale grey stone of the convent on rue de Bac, and the cobbled rue de Reuilly where Santa Catalina's heart was sequestered. But, like a screen, her visions crackled with interference . . . something in the background, unidentifiable . . . in her fingers a memory of soft silkiness.

That night she dreamed she was holding a baby, tiny fingers wrapped tight around her index finger. The child was light in her arms, lighter than Isabella had been. Guadalupe nuzzled her neck, inhaling the sweet scent, then someone ripped the baby out of her arms and she was stretched, her arms growing longer and longer like an endless scream. A wave of grief washed over her and she woke weeping in her narrow bed.

Guadalupe sat up gasping for breath. Unlike Santa Catalina Labouré, she did not share a convent dormitory, but had her own small room with a window looking onto a dilapidated park sprawling behind a line of purple jacaranda trees. She watched the sunlight filtering through her window, her throat thick with unshed tears, then something jolted in her body as she remembered. "It's her! *Caramba*, I know it's her!" she said aloud. She jumped out of bed and began pacing the bare wooden boards in her nightgown.

"Twenty years ago . . . adopted by Canadians . . . looking for my mother."

She splashed her face with water and brushed her hair back from her face, feeling the softness of her own skin. She nuzzled into the crook of her arm, eyes closed, body aching as she remembered the baby she had looked after when she was still a child herself, new at the convent.

After breakfast she knocked on Sister María-Teresa's door.

"Come." Her curt tone softened as Guadalupe entered and closed the door behind her. "Ah, Sister Lupe, how are you, my dear?" María-Teresa rose from her chair and took Guadalupe's hands. She looked into her eyes and her expression changed as she cupped Guadalupe's face. "You've been weeping, my child. What have you to tell me?" Her voice was low, almost seductive.

"There was a young woman here yesterday, looking for her mother."

"Ah yes, you saw her?"

"I want to know who she is."

María-Teresa shrugged. "One of the orphans from years ago."

"Twenty years ago. Do you remember her?"

"What is this about, Lupe?"

"You remember when I first came to the convent?"

"Of course. I was still a *novicia*. And you were a frightened little girl, on the verge of womanhood, your life suddenly taken from you."

Guadalupe nodded. "Then . . . after a while . . . Madre Superior told me I could look after the babies."

María-Teresa nodded. "She thought it would help you."

"There was one — we called her Flor de Maya — she was very special for me. I must know if this Paméla is the child."

María-Teresa went to the filing cabinet, rolled out the drawer and lifted out the tattered file folder. She held it in her hand a moment, looking into Guadalupe's eyes. "I trust you completely. All our years in this convent together. You know this information is confidential. The girl must not have it."

Guadalupe raised her eyebrows. "Why?"

"You will see why." María-Teresa handed her the folder and sat down, her hands folded on the desk.

As Guadalupe leafed through the papers, her eyes scanning the print, she found a tattered photograph, so faded it was almost a ghost image; herself, smiling, with Flor in her arms. It was the first time she'd smiled since the massacre of her village. A broad smile wreathed her face now. "It *is* her. It *is!*," she cried, then her face clouded. "Oh," she breathed, "Of course, yes, I remember. She disappeared."

"And then we heard. The girl must not know what happened. I doubt we'll see her again. She ran out of here in a temper."

Guadalupe opened her mouth, then caught herself. She closed the file and pushed it across the desk. "Thank you, Sister. As always, you've helped me." She took María-Teresa's hand and raised it to her lips.

"My child," María-Teresa said, the warmth in her voice pulling Guadalupe to her for a moment, holding her, then Guadalupe let go of her hand, pressed her own hands together in prayer, bowed and left the office.

❧

Cortés held the baby, three months old, tiny in his big hands. Malintzín had watched him fall in love with their son when he was but two hours old, a blind handful of new life, peering at his father through clouded eyes, mouth and fingers working, trying to focus.

"This child will be the resurrection of our city," he said, "Named for my father."

He screamed, his face a livid red, as the priest doused his head with cold baptismal water. "In the name of the Father, the Son and the Holy Ghost, I christen this child Martín."

Malintzín breathed her own silent prayer. *Merciful Lady Chalchiuhtlicue, Goddess of the Flowing Waters, wash him and deliver him, thy servant here present come into this world, sent by our father and mother, Ometecutli and Omeciuatl, who reside at the ninth heaven* . . . She remembered the ceremonial bathing of her newborn half-brother and her exclusion from her mother's life with his arrival. "Now I have my own son, I will never be alone again." In time she would perform her own ceremony for him, the ceremony of her people, giving him a spirit name. She would watch him, see what plants and creatures he was drawn to, choose an herb to heal him when he fell sick, an animal to protect him, his *nahual*, his double and protective spirit. Hers was the wildcat, the creature who teaches survival.

They walked the short distance from Capilla La Conchita to the Casa Colorado and stood in the courtyard, the sun in Cortés' eyes as he cradled his son. As Malintzín took the baby, their hands rested together on him for a moment, covering his body, then Cortés released him into her care and she carried him into the house. Her bedchamber was shaded with rich draperies cut from Spanish cloth. Cortés had followed her and as he stood in the doorway she turned and caught his eye. There was a moment of hesitation before she spoke. "I will call Zaachila to take him."

The birth of her son had burned her fire to embers, but she glowed brightly under Cortés now, igniting his memories of glory, and he was tender and solicitous with her, awed by the new life they had created together. After their gentle love-making she lay in the crook of his arm watching sun patterns dappling the edges of her draperies. His hand caressed her neck, sending ripples of pleasure down the brown sheath of her skin. I have him now, she exulted. He was never like this. I have a son and everything is different. But there was something weighing on her, something she had to say. Zaachila had heard a rumour in the market and had run home to tell her.

"Your wife will come." She said the words softly, almost a caress, but Cortés stiffened. He was silent and the afternoon lay heavily on them, a stifling blanket of dusty light as the silence lengthened. Finally he spoke.

"I am governor. I no longer have a choice. Our days of freedom are over, Marina."

She turned to him, her face inches from his, and traced the thin white line under his lip. She'd been curious about the scar when she first saw him, but by the time she'd learned Spanish it was so familiar a part of him that she'd accepted it without question, like a birthmark.

Two months later, on a sharp November morning in 1522, Cortés ushered Catalina Suarez into the Casa Colorado. Her dress was heavy with dust from the journey, but her beloved pearls shone around her neck. "How long I have waited for this day, Hernándo," she said, her pale cheeks flushed with pleasure. When she embraced him in the dark hallway of the western wing, he patted her shoulder gently.

"How pale and thin you've grown," he said, holding her at arms' length.

"I am starved for your touch, Hernándo," she replied, with an attempt at archery, but so filled with longing and wasted with solitary desire was she that her attempt at flirtation repelled Cortés. As he handed her through the heavy wooden archway of their bedchamber she felt strangely like a prisoner entering a death cell, and indeed Catalina Suarez met a mysterious death three months later in that very room. Her maid, Carmencita, screamed when she discovered her mistress lying in a wet bed, with a bruised neck, her pearls scattered across the floor.

"The governor is stricken with grief," she lamented, wringing her hands, raw from scrubbing the soiled sheets.

"Shocked by her sudden death, of course," said Cortés' ostler. "And so soon after her arrival. How did she look in death?" He leaned towards the girl, who pulled back, offended by the odour of horse manure that permeated his clothing.

"He would allow no one else into the bedchamber. He washed her body and laid her out himself."

"They say he had the coffin lid nailed down promptly."

"'Tis true. The governor didn't want anyone to lay eyes on her. He's a jealous man."

"They say your mistress was jealous too, of Doña Marina."

Carmencita pressed her lips together. "Tongues will always wag."

"Indeed. They speak of the dead Emperor's daughter and her three sisters. Some say my master has a house of concubines like Moctezuma. You must have heard some merry spats."

"Doña Catalina kept her dignity to the end," she said with a toss of her head.

"And who will you serve now that your mistress is gone? All alone here in a strange land. There's a few would like to lay eyes on you." He took her chin between his rough thumb and forefinger, holding her there, grinning at her. Carmencita's cheeks flushed and mottled and she dropped her eyes in confusion. "You need protection. And I'm looking for a wife."

She tossed her head, releasing her chin and looked at him squarely. Then her eyes travelled a quick appraisal of his person, from spindly shanks to muscled shoulder, coming to rest in his dark eyes. Like pools of horse piss, she thought, but beggars can't be choosers. She smiled and tilted her head coquettishly.

"You'll get used to the smell of horses," he said and pressed himself upon her.

Cortés lay in the darkness, haunted by the memory of Catalina's bulging eyes and the sudden warm flood of her incontinence. The arguments had started almost immediately after her arrival. His virility had failed him.

"You've spent yourself on your whore and saved nothing for me!" she'd hissed, "While I waited faithfully for you in that hell-hole, praying every minute for your safety!"

"Every man has a mistress, Catalina. It's the way of the world."

"And she has whelped, your bitch. Don't you think I want a child?"

"Be patient, Cata. I'm tired — "

"And there are others, I'm told, living in this very house. Are they carrying your bastards too? Your taste for Indian meat is insatiable, and you take them younger and younger! What's wrong with you, Hernándo? Are you losing your vigour after your great conquest?"

She taunted me. It wasn't my fault. She hated the New World and she knew I wouldn't return with her to Spain as she desired.

Cortés shunned the prospect of returning to Spain even more since his wife's death. There were rumours at Court and on the island of Cuba. No one would ever know what had passed between Cortés and his wife, but they whispered of murder. "Hernándo Cortés, a man of reputation," they said, "Surely not a murderer?" But they remembered Cholula and the whispers grew louder until the stain of the massacre and Catalina's demise began to blot his career. Master of the ocean, yet Cortés could not fathom it; the change in his fortune was a mystery to him.

"I would give my right arm to march south with you tomorrow, Pedro," he told Alvarado when the golden-haired captain came to bid him farewell on the eve of his departure for Guatemala.

"Come! Come with us," Alvarado urged. "Our quest for gold is not over, *mi capitán.*"

Cortés shook his head. "I must govern what I have."

"Let others govern. There's more territory to be won. This is only the beginning! There are lands in each direction waiting to be claimed, oceans and rivers, mountains and forests . . . "

Cortés pulled a bundle from under his arm and, like a magician, unveiled it in one swoop and thrust it into Alvarado's surprised hands. "Take her with you. I have no more need of her."

Alvarado lifted the Virgin of Socorro in the air, let out a yelp and kissed her feet. "I will return victorious," he said, "And we will make our next expedition together with the Virgin's blessing."

Alvarado's words echoed in Cortés' head long after his departure. He began to plan.

༄

Fern's foot twitched as her leg bobbed up and down. She twisted a strand of dark hair between finger and thumb, shifted the angle of her body, played with her earring. 'Keep still,' her mother had always said. 'It's just energy, Mom, I can't help it, I'm a fast burner.' Hannah had calmed her over the years, but tonight she was pent up. She glanced at Hannah, sitting across the room. She was reading, a bright pool of light falling on her coppery curls. She was so still, so beautiful, her legs curled under her, her breasts rising and falling almost imperceptibly. People used many euphemisms to describe Hannah — plump, voluptuous, comfortable — but Fern knew she was a Goddess. Hannah's mouth curved into a smile as she sensed Fern's steady gaze. She moved slowly, like a cat unfolding itself, stretching her arms, yawning. "It's so quiet."

"Without her, you mean?"

Hannah shrugged and smiled. "Play something."

Fern crossed the living room to the piano and plunked herself down with a sigh. She began to play *Fur Elise* from memory, but at the top of the three octave ascending arpeggio, just before the descending chromatic scale which brings the music back to the theme, she faltered and brought both hands slamming down on the keys in a jarring cacophony.

"Fern!" Hannah exclaimed, "What's the matter?"

Fern twisted her body round and stared at Hannah. "Something's missing," she said. She knew that Hannah was going to try and evade her; the phony concern of her furrowed brow, the puzzlement she hid behind.

"But you were playing so beautifully. I love that piece."

"Something between us. We haven't made love since she left."

"I've been completely absorbed by the backlog cases. You know how hard I've been working. And now, just as we have our final victory, you're on my case!"

"Ah, how quick you are to spring to your own defence," Fern said bitterly. "Have you forgotten how to behave outside the court room?"

Hannah had burst through the front door at six o'clock. 'We won! We won!' she'd shouted. 'Rashid has been granted refugee status. Now I have them all in, six clients. We had to rely almost completely on oral testimony, because he was so scared getting out of Iran he didn't have time to get his documents. Credibility was a crucial issue, and he was completely convincing. You could've heard a pin drop as he told his story, looking the judge straight in the eye. We had Justice Mahoney and he's a tough one. But I got him in, like all the others, under the old rules after that precedent setting case I told you about, remember?' Not stopping for an answer, she'd raced on, 'The Immigration and Refugee Protection Act implemented new selection criteria last year and that's what's been holding us up. You should've seen his face when Mahoney gave the judgement. "I've won the right to remain in Canada," he said, and he threw his arms around me. He's usually such a restrained man.' Fern had smiled and congratulated Hannah. She'd even opened a bottle of wine to celebrate the victory, but underneath it all she'd been tightly strung and now she snapped.

"There's always a case, isn't there?" Fern jumped up from the piano bench and began pacing. "Drama in the courtroom, media attention, lives under threat of torture and death, and you're the star. I thought it was no coincidence that you threw yourself into this double time the week she left."

"What are you talking about? It's my work. You never talk to me like this."

"Well I am now. I'm sick of it! I want you back!"

Hannah leaned forward in her chair, her slow body shocked by the assault. "I'm here, every night with you, at the table. We eat dinner together, we sleep together, we wake up together. Every day begins for me with your face, opening my eyes and seeing you there."

"I want more. I want my lover back." Fern's mouth was tight and thin. "I'm proud of the work you do, saving people's lives, it's a great achievement, Hannah, but surely you understand what I'm talking about?"

Her eyes were mean and narrowed. Hannah hardly recognized her. She felt as if something had entered her house while she was sleeping, something evil and shocking. She searched for words. "I feel . . . I feel like our . . . "

"Oh, don't look at me like that." Fern snapped. "You look like your mother with her befuddled mind."

"That's enough! Don't you speak to me like that." Hannah's chin began to tremble.

"I was talking to Helen after our faculty meeting," Fern continued, "And she said that when her son left home — "

"Paméla has not left home. She's on a trip, that's all, simply a trip." Hannah's cheeks were flushed.

"OK, OK. What's with the over-reaction?"

"Why are you talking to Helen about our private business?"

"Darling, we were talking about *her* private business."

"But you were referencing it to our relationship."

"What d'you think you are, a mind reader? Talk about making assumptions. I was simply going to say, if you could listen to me for more than two seconds — "

"Well that's snarky."

Fern took a deep breath. "I'm sorry. What I want to say is that it's a big transition when a child grows up and . . . steps out, even for a defined period of time. Paméla's on a quest and this journey will undoubtedly change her."

"You've never been as close to her as me. She's always called me Mom, always run to me when she gets hurt. All you can do is talk to her about academics."

Fern flinched as though she'd been stung. "I am an academic, remember?" she said defiantly. "You've always said that one of the aspects you love most about me is my analytical mind, a match for yours." Fern's eyes were shining now and Hannah, her face wreathed in concern, reached out her arms, but Fern stood rigid, six feet away.

"What's happening to us, Fern? Everything was fine till Pam left."

"I'm not going through this again when she really does leave home."

"What d'you mean?" Hannah hugged herself, shivering, stuck in her chair as though she were rooted there.

"All these years focussed on Paméla. She's been a buffer between us, and now . . . "

"Remember that time I was late to pick her up? What if someone had taken her? She's always been so trusting, ever since she was a tiny girl. Oh, the relief when I opened the front door and saw her red welly boots! One was on the stairs and the other was half-way down the corridor. She'd always kick them off and let them fly."

"Hannah, she's twenty-one years old. She's quite capable of finding her way home. She has a ticket."

"D'you think I worry too much?"

"There's only so much we can control, honey." Fern's voice was tired.

"We've tried to keep on top of things, processing as we go. I thought we were doing quite well."

"We've done our best, but there's never enough time, with our careers, the house, our daughter, my parents, your mom . . . " Fern took the few steps over to Hannah and knelt by her chair. She took hold of her hands, her face softening, recognizable again. "What about us?" she said.

"Let's take a trip of our own," Hannah said. "Can you get time off?"

"After my graduate seminar finishes on the 20th, yes."

"We could go to the Muskokas."

"Uncle Jack's cabin?"

"Yes!" Hannah's eyes sparkled.

"I'll call him tomorrow. Hannah, I'm not prepared to settle for a half life. We've always challenged the structures, the traditions, the mindless perpetuation of systemic oppression."

"Of course, that's how I was brought up. Who could be more left-wing than New York Jewish survivors. Why d'you think I became a lawyer?"

"That's your work, Hannah, not your personal life. I've always been a rebel too, you know that. I refuse to grow old and complacent and live some kind of charade of domestic comfort with you. It's just not who I am."

"So what is it? What are you trying to say?"

"Bottom line? I'd rather go through the pain of splitting now than the pain of . . . living like this for the rest of my life, with the distance between us getting wider. Why d'you think so many men die when they retire? First the kids leave home and the wife freaks out and starts doing volunteer work, then the husband retires, plays a round of golf and croaks, unless there are grandchildren living somewhere reasonably close. What a crazy world."

"Are you saying that you're my husband and you're afraid of dying?" Hannah asked quizzically.

Fern exploded with laughter. "A double theoretical cliché from Sociology 101," she spluttered finally.

"Oh darling, all this because our girl went on a trip?"

"OK, so I'm getting carried away. And incidentally, you're twisting things again. But yes, I've been feeling very lonely since Pam left and it's not her I'm missing most."

"I don't want to lose you." Hannah was solemn now.

"It's been years since we had a fight."

"OK, let's go up north and battle it out."

"Let's go to bed."

Hannah threw her head back in a gesture of surrender so sweet that Fern's mind went blank.

ᔕ

She stood in the caracol of Chichen Itzá, the Mayan tower of time, a calendar spiralling to the sky. She closed her eyes and marked the interlocking rounds: the sacred, the solar, Venus rising from the morning mist. "This is the Fifth World," a voice said. Then she was a baby, crawling up the circular walls of the tower, and Hannah and Fern stood outside calling to her, "Paméla, Paméla," holding out their arms. Fifty-two years ending in sacred and solar coincidence; 5,200 years times five, 26,000, the end of the Great Cycle. "We will enter the Fifth World on that day exactly. Extinguish the fires, break the vessels, abandon the cities, the pyramids, the hearth. Everything must change in time." She began to cry, her baby voice spiralling into the sky . . .

Paméla woke in confusion. She didn't understand the prophetic nature of her dream, but she remembered Fern and Hannah reaching out, calling to her, and she went to the nearest internet café after breakfast and wrote to them.

I may be onto something. Registered with an agency called Dónde Están and found a convent which has a file on me, but no real news yet. Bravo for winning the immigration case, Hannah! Still thinking about Malinche and the conquest. Wish I'd written the paper before I left, but who knows, maybe I'll learn more while I'm here. I'm fine. I'll keep in touch.
Love, love, your Latina Babe.

Paméla wasn't sure what she was going to do next until she put her hand in her pocket and found the nun's handkerchief. Ten minutes later she was at the convent door. The metal cover slid back and the green eye at the grille was Guadalupe's. Paméla held up the handkerchief and smiled. The door opened and Guadalupe came out onto the street. She seemed flustered as she stared at Paméla and stroked her face.

"Extraordinary! I was going out to pray for you and here you are. You must come to the chapel with me."

She took the handkerchief and tucked it into the sleeve of her blue cardigan and started walking down the block to the entrance of the Medalla Milagrosa. They entered the chapel and knelt in a pew near the front. Guadalupe crossed herself and started praying, her lips moving silently. Paméla wished she would talk to her instead of praying for her. She looked up into the vaulted roof where light streamed in, illuminating the robin's egg blue of the ceiling, splashing down on the swirling ochre-tiled floor. She heard the whispered prayers of the nuns and the dripping of water into the deep basins of three fonts. Red and turquoise lozenges splattered the grey stone pillars supporting the structure of the chapel. She saw the Virgin floating above the altar, surrounded by flashing blue lights. In the halo around her head were written the words, *Oh María Sin Pecado* . . . Paméla turned quickly as Guadalupe touched her shoulder.

"You must have this," she said, holding out a tiny medallion on a thin gold chain. "It is the Medalla Milagrosa. It will help you. Turn around."

Paméla turned and let Guadalupe fasten the medallion around her neck. It was warm on her flesh. She turned back with a surprised smile. "Thank you. Can we go outside? I'd like to walk with you."

Guadalupe hesitated a moment, then she rose from the pew. "Of course. Come with me."

They walked around the block to a street lined with purple jacaranda and crossed the street into a dusty, dilapidated park with leaves piled in corners along the edges of a large building.

"This building is part of the University of San Carlos," Guadalupe said. "It's for students of dentistry and medicine."

A young soldier patrolled the forgotten pathways, a gun slung over his shoulder. Paméla had grown used to the army presence. She'd seen soldiers everywhere since her arrival — at the airport, in the bank, outside the National Palace, at the cathedral.

"We can sit here if you like." Guadalupe swept the leaves off a stone bench which looked as though it had been there as long as the tired palms and rustling jacarandas. Shadows danced through the leaves, tattooing their faces with lacy patterns of light. The stones in the pathway were cracked and pitted.

"Why don't they take care of this park?"

"It used to be very beautiful. See that statue?" Across the yellowed grass stood a classical figure of a woman holding a scroll. She wore a long gown, scalloped at the hip, hair piled on top of her head, but her right hand was missing. "I remember when it was new. My room is up there," Guadalupe said, turning to point at the convent building.

Paméla saw a small window on the second floor in the middle of the huge building. "So this is what you see every day."

Guadalupe surveyed the park, opened her arms in a dramatic gesture and laughed. There was an awkward silence, then Paméla said, "Can I ask you something? You said your village was attacked. What exactly did you mean?"

Guadalupe took a breath and hesitated a moment.
"The army came. They burned everything," she said in
a low voice. "Everyone was killed."

"How did you escape?"

"I hid under the table. Then . . . I don't know how . . . I
ran away. I didn't even stop to save my brothers and my
sister, Isabella. I lost all my family."

"What did you do?" Paméla's voice was a whisper.

"I kept on running, then I walked when I couldn't run
any more and I slept in a field. It was a long time before
I reached the city of Huehuetenango."

Paméla wanted to touch Guadalupe, to comfort her
somehow, but she was afraid. It was too much like her
dream. They sat in silence. Nothing moved except the
shadows playing on their faces."I'm Mayan . . . at least
partly. I wonder if the same thing might have happened
to my mother."

"Why? Why do you say that?"

"There's a dream I have . . . about the total destruction
of a village. It's like a nightmare. I — "

"Shhh." Guadalupe gave a subtle toss of her head in
the direction of the soldier who was patrolling within
earshot. "*Orejas* everywhere," she whispered. She took
Paméla's arm and they started walking on the cracked
pathway, Guadalupe with her head down, listening as
Paméla told her dream.

"That's why I came to Guatemala," Paméla said, "I
know this isn't my dream. It's driving me crazy."

"Ah." Guadalupe smiled. "Perhaps your mother is a
survivor like me. If so, it's best to let her be and go home
to your parents."

Paméla stopped suddenly. "You know something, don't you."

"I want you to have peace in your life."

"I'll have no peace till I find my mother. Please help me, Lupe. You told me you came to Casa Central in 1981, and I was born in '82. I was nine months old when I was adopted. I guess there were a lot of children around and you were just a kid yourself, but . . . do you remember me?"

Guadalupe's eyes shone with tears as she looked at Paméla. "Of course I remember you, of course. I dreamed of you last night, about them taking you away from me." She took Paméla in her arms, grasped her long hair in her fist, and held her.

"Are you . . . are you . . . ?"

"No, I'm not your mother. I looked after you at the orphanage. I was an orphan then too, before I joined the Sisters. You helped me come to life again after the loss of my family, then they took you away."

"I can't believe it!" Paméla gasped. "You must be the girl who took me to the adoption agency. They said you cried when . . . "

"Yes." Guadalupe hugged her tightly. "I've prayed to the Virgin for your return, but I didn't recognize you until my dream. It was something . . . something about the feel of you, your smell . . . "

Paméla rubbed her face against Guadalupe's, like a cat. "You smell of lemons," she said, "sweet, tangy lemons."

"When I lost you I decided to take orders. Until then I was only taking refuge and I wanted children of my own,

but I was afraid of losing them too. I've lost so much."
She stopped suddenly, as though she might cry.

"Guadalupe? Is that your real name?"

"It's the name I was given when I entered the convent,
for Our Lady of the Flowers. She gave Juan Diego the
miracle of red roses in winter emblazoned on his coat.
You can see it at the shrine of Guadalupe in Mexico
City. They say the roses are still fresh after nearly 500
years."

"I might go to Mexico. I have three months. Would
you like to come with me?"

Guadalupe laughed and shook her head. "I travel
only in Guatemala, for my work. Next week I'll go with
Doctor Ramírez to Huixoc. I can help the people there by
translating for them into Spanish so that Doctor Ramírez
can treat them, because my mother tongue is Mam. I
have learned also to speak Cakchiquel, because I used
to work in the villages near Chimaltenango."

"What is your real name?"

"I was . . . Calixta. And we called you Flor de Maya.
It's a beautiful tree with big orange flowers. Sometimes
they call it *fuego del bosque*."

"D'you know my mother's name?"

"Sister María-Teresa is right. It's better for you to
forget about your mother. This search can only bring
you pain."

"You do know something."

"Please, don't ask me. You must trust me and accept
that she's lost to you forever. I'll pray for you."

"I don't want your prayers! I want to find my mother."
Paméla stamped her foot angrily. "Why all this mystery?
I know she's alive and she's in the capital, and I'm going

to keep searching until I find her. If you won't help me, I'll . . . I'll break into the convent and take my file."

"Impossible."

"It's mine. It's my right." She swung suddenly, from anger to supplication. "Get it for me, *please*." She went down on her knees, pleading clownishly. Guadalupe shook her head and Paméla rolled over on her back, arms and legs pumping and kicking the air. Guadalupe broke into laughter and pulled her up from the ground, brushing the dust off her back. Then Paméla's eye caught hers and they stared at each other, a foot apart, Guadalupe's mouth open in surprise as she saw the expression in the girl's eyes. "I remember you," Paméla said softly.

"I must go now." Guadalupe looked down at the trampled grass.

"Can I see you tomorrow?"

"I must prepare for my journey. We have a strict schedule at Casa Central."

"Just for half an hour. Here in the park?"

Guadalupe hesitated. "In the afternoon, at four o'clock."

∽

July 1524: Casa Colorado

"Mamá!"

"Martí, Martí! *Xochitl xolotl.*"

Malintzín turned and swept him up in her arms as he ran at her, trying to bury his face in her skirt. His childish, throaty laughter entered her heart.

"*Xochitl xolotl? Que significa, Mamá?*"

"My Flower Prince of Darkness," she said, kissing his neck.

Martín could barely speak a full sentence in a single language yet, although his vocabulary was large. Often his talk was an indecipherable babble in a mixture of Spanish, Nahuatl and Popoluca with a phrase or two of Chontol Maya thrown in. Malintzín talked to him constantly in all her tongues, crooning and cooing to him, light of her life. "I will never be alone again," she said, "now that I have you, *xochitl xolotl*." Cortés' eyes stared back at her, dark with love.

Over the child's head she saw him approaching with his long stride, crossing the courtyard. Martín saw too and scrambled out of her arms. He ran, stumbling, into Cortés' arms. "Papá!" he shouted and pulled on Cortés' beard as he was lifted onto his shoulder.

"*Mi pequeño caballero.*"

"*Xochitl xolotl!*" the child insisted.

"What's that? You must speak Spanish with him, Marina. You'll confound the child with all your tongues."

"Ah, he's only a baby, Hernán. There's time for him to learn everything." Malintzín wrapped her arms around Cortés and laid her cheek against the softness of his beard. Martín was nestled between them squirming to get down and when Cortés released him he ran across the courtyard to pat the horse's legs.

"Be careful, Martí," Malintzín called.

"Don't worry. I've ridden him hard. There's no kick left in him."

"But, Hernán . . . "

He silenced her with his hand over her mouth, pulling her against him with his other arm.

"I have news for you, *mi amor*, very good news."

Her mouth softened and she flicked her tongue against his palm. She thought he was going to say it finally, the words she'd prayed for, "Marry me." On the night of Catalina's death he'd come to her. He'd said nothing, but the next day she'd heard the rumours and thought he'd done it for her, to gain his freedom so that he could marry her. She'd been waiting patiently, eighteen moons since, praying to Tonantzin, her marriage mantra, "*Casarme, casarme.*"

"We are leaving this house."

"Leaving the Casa Colorado?"

"You will come with me to Honduras." His eyes sparkled. "I'm preparing an expedition to leave in three months. I need you at my side as interpreter."

"Martín must come."

He shook his head. "It will be a dangerous journey, Marina, into some of the harshest territory we've yet encountered."

"But we can't leave him."

One of his officers, Cristóbal de Olid, had been sent into Honduras the previous year to seek a passage to the South Seas, but Olid had betrayed Cortés by proceeding under his own banner. He'd learned the trick from his master and the situation had provided Cortés with the excuse he needed. He would pursue the mutinous Olid with a retinue of thousands and make an example of him.

Cortés turned and walked across the courtyard. As he turned to face Malintzín his eyes made a study of the earth. "I have a kinsman, Don Juan Altamirano, a man of great honour and means. He is cousin to me, and he has a household in Mexico-Tenochtitlan."

"What is this to me?"

"He has agreed to take Martín under his care."

Malintzín gasped and ran to scoop Martín up from under the stallion's belly. She held him tight, pulled back on one shoulder. "Never! You'll never take my son!"

The little boy began to cry.

"We can't risk the child's life by taking him with us, Marina, and I don't want to risk my own life by going into Honduras without you. Who knows what hostile tribes we'll encounter?"

She stared at him, uncomprehending.

"It's only for the period of our journey," he shrugged. "Your decision."

"It would break my heart to leave him."

"The jungles are said to be almost impenetrable. Water will be scarce and brackish and we will lose many men to fever and disease. I can only pray that you will make the right decision, Marina, and begin weaning our son now, in preparation for our departure at the beginning of October."

On the 12th of October, 1524, Malintzín left the Casa Colorado forever. Her son had gone ahead with his father to the house of Juan Altamirano. And she travelled with Zaachila to join Cortés once more on the long journey east across the mountains to the Gulf. At every step she ached with the absence of her son, and milk drizzled from her nipples, staining her blouse. Cortés was solicitous, keeping her close to him, his eyes upon her as she translated greetings in every town and village along the way. They were billetted below Mount Orizaba when Cortés came to her in the shadow of the mountain.

"Marina, *mi lengua,* how would I make my way in this new world without you?"

"Help me, Hernándo," she grasped his arm. "My heart is aching."

"I too am thinking of our son and of his future," he said, pulling her close. "I have spoken with Don Juan Jaramillo and he has agreed to give Martín his name."

"Jaramillo? That long-faced hound! What has he to do with my son? You are his father!"

"Ah, Marina, you do not understand. You are from another world. In Spain we have certain customs that must be observed."

She pulled away sharply, wrapping her shawl around her in the cold night air. "This is not Spain. You live in my land now and we have our own customs."

"Don't oppose me, Marina. I want only what's best for you and Martín."

"And what is that?" she demanded.

"I will settle you . . . my family . . . on lands assigned to you by governor's decree in your native province of Coatzacoalcos. A wedding gift to you and Jaramillo."

Malintzín gasped as her hands flew to her mouth. Cortés grasped her shoulders, but she wrenched free and turned her back, shamed by her sudden tears.

"I thought you would be happy to go home, eventually, to your own land," he continued. "He's a good man, Marina, a fine soldier. He will provide for you and the child."

Her body shook, with grief or fury, he couldn't tell. He reached out and his hand hovered in the heat of her shoulder as he spoke. "Nothing will change, Marina. This is merely a convenience, for the good of everyone. You must remember that I love you . . . all that has passed between us . . . our son . . . "

He was completely taken by surprise when she whirled around and slapped his bearded face. "You know nothing about love!" she spat, "You . . . you Spaniard!"

The marriage secured for Jaramillo his Mexican estates in the city and to the north of Tenochtitlan, in accordance with the new law requiring Spanish bachelors to marry or forfeit their land holdings. The celebration of his sudden security rendered him drunk during the marriage ceremony while Malintzín stood rigid in the early morning light that crept over Mount Orizaba. As her marriage mantra collapsed around her in four fragmented languages, cries and wordless whispers echoing down the years, the grief in Malintzín's heart held her focussed on the child who was part of her body, pulling and pulling, soaking her blouse. That night as Jaramillo snored at her side she heard Cihuacoatl wailing. She rose and followed the keening, her footsteps sure and rapid in the darkness until, as the crying became louder and louder, she realized it was her own voice she heard.

On December 15th the expedition reached the Isthmus of Tehuantepec, the ancestral homelands of Malintzín's family, no longer independent territory now, but fallen under governance of the Spanish crown. They encamped at Coatzacoalcos and Cortés sent out runners to summon all the local leaders. Among those who came were Malintzín's mother and half-brother, christened Marta and Lázaro since the Franciscans had passed through in a fever of conversion. Lázaro had been a baby when Malintzín was taken by the men from Xicalango, so she didn't recognize the twelve-year-old who stood at his mother's side. But she knew Marta, even before the woman gasped to see her daughter, identical to her younger self, and fell to her knees begging forgiveness for her betrayal. Malintzín reached out her hand and raised her mother. As they embraced she smelled her skin and felt the old surge of childhood love, as though everything that had happened was a dream and now she was waking with a clear heart. Malintzín forgave it all and bestowed lavish gifts upon her family before she resumed her journey.

On the last day of February 1525, by the rushing Candelaria flowing in from Guatemala, Cuauhtemoc was executed, along with the other Culhua-Mexica nobles taken on the expedition as hostages. Malintzín translated his final bitter words to Cortés and the young Emperor was hanged from a ceiba, the sacred tree of life, and left to rot far from his birthplace. This cruelty shocked even the Spaniards and it struck fear into Malintzín's soul, fear for her own life and the resting place of her soul. For the first time she gave thanks for her wedding gift, the granting of her ancestral lands where she could go one day to die. And she gave thanks for the reconciliation with her blood family.

Juan Jaramillo fell a hair's breadth short of handsome. He was indifferent to his captain's cast-off mistress and her bastard son, but he was not unkind; rather he was distant. They surveyed each other across a vast distance and barely spoke, despite her fluency in Castilian Spanish. But something was changed with the separation from Martín and the forgiveness of her mother; and her marriage finally, albeit to the wrong man, contained her like a vessel, altering the tenor of everything around her. She accepted it and entered into a state she had never felt before, something which, with all her tongues, she had no word for. It was a slowing of the river within her, something she had never guessed at. Malintzín lay under the moon in the fetid air of the jungle and closed her eyes, listening to the breath of a thousand creatures rising from the earth. She dreamed of her *capitán*, Señor Malinche, joined with her forever in Martín's blood. She hated him for his betrayal, but her body remained true, with its exquisite memory and an ability to enshrine even this cruelest of lovers. She held him in her heart, framing his soul, like an image at an altar; she held him in governance. Malintzín had changed hands again, but this time she had borne a child. They had mixed their blood and changed her world. She would bear another. As Jaramillo rolled off her and fell into a deep sleep she crept through the darkness of the fevered night, silent as a cat.

ॐ

Cuauhtemoc's angry words rang like a curse through Cortés' dreams. When he reached out in the night for Malintzín she was not there. He took instead a swig of brandy and in the dawnlight he drank again to clear his ringing head. More and more he drank to clear the way and soften the memories of his past mistakes. The terrain became increasingly inhospitable as they moved south towards Honduras, travelling through Guatemala where Alvarado raged his bloody pathway south to the city of Antigua, the Virgin of Socorro forgotten in his trunk at the back of the convoy.

Many men were lost in the quicksand of the swampy bushland which gave way to dense jungles where trailblazers wandered in circles, lost to the world, starving to death. Many died from fever, thirst and disease; many were hung for mutiny as they tried to escape. The expedition was a disaster from the outset, but Cortés was desperate. He repeated the only pattern he knew, of exploration and conquest, but, without the Virgin to succour him he fell ill with fever. As he lay sweating in the jungle night in a delirium of prayer, rows of skulls sped past him. Or was it he who ran through the darkness, the dead grinning at him from the *tzompantli* at the foot of Huitzilopochtli's pyramid? A ghastly face, half bone, half rotted flesh, rushed at him and he jumped aside as it dissolved into the darkness. He felt a cool hand on his brow. "Marina," he whimpered, and he remembered how she'd tended him on the road to Tenochtitlan and wept for the lack of her. "Madre María", he prayed, "Guide me safely out of this hell. Bring Marina to me. Let me see my son again."

Skilled fingers moved over his body, delving beneath his sweat-soaked doublet. He felt the pressure of someone sitting astride him. He peered into the darkness but he was blind with fever. He smelled her, he tried to raise his arms to grasp her darkness, but she held him down and moved against him, pulling, pulling all the fever from his body.

"I am dying," he whimpered. "Oh Madre María, I am dying, take me."

In the morning light his face was waxen, his limbs weak and limp, but the fever had broken and Cortés recovered slowly.

"We will continue," he said after a few days. "Give the orders to decamp, Jaramillo."

"The men are afraid, *mi capitán. No meterse en honduras* is what they say. Don't go in over your depth. This territory is like a deep river."

"They are cowards. We must move forward. That's how we conquered this land." Cortés was not one to heed warning, so his dwindling retinue lumbered forward into the mouth of the jungle where their lives were inhaled by the long night.

◕

Fabiana stood in the shower, water streaming down, plastering her hair flat against her skin. She opened her eyes and let the warm water stream into them. She felt dirty all the time now as though some darkness were rising in her, a rip tide surging against the pumping of her heart. She took several showers a day, and sometimes in the night as Ernesto lay sleeping at her side she would rise quietly and tiptoe from their room to shower secretly. She would powder and perfume her body. She would shave her legs and rub fragrant cream into the prickling skin and finally, calmed by the ritual, she would go back to bed and nestle into Ernesto's big body, solid as a wall.

She stepped out of the shower and wrapped herself in one of the fluffy pink towels he'd brought her from the United States. Ernesto travelled sometimes with President Portillo and he always brought expensive gifts; jewellery, perfume, silk undergarments. The towel felt luxuriously thick around her small body. She looked into the steamy mirror, wiped a small patch with her hand and saw her face looming. She looked like a ghost. Tears stung her eyes and she ran weeping from the bathroom.

∾

Guadalupe knelt in the front pew, her eyes closed, her lips moving. She recited the words mechanically, hardly aware of what she was saying. Then she opened her eyes wide and gave thanks for Flor's return. But the joy of reunion had drained from her body, leaving it like a bundle of live wires, and part of her wished the girl had never come. She heard a soft thudding and realized that she was pounding her chest; "*Mea culpa, mea culpa, mea gran culpa,*" she chanted. "Mother Mary, what is this test you've given me? What am I to do? Help me, give me strength to remain silent, to send her away so that she may have peace of mind." She bowed her head and wept for the loss of her equilibrium, for the joy of finding Flor, for the girl's pain in her desire to find her mother. But everything had to be contained. There was no room in the convent for these feelings. Deep within she heard the soft guttural sounds of her Mayan language, kept alive by monthly visits to Huixoc where she talked with Chavela. She'd been invited to attend a Mayan ceremony with her, with the priests and priestesses of the village. She'd refused, but she had imagined what it might be like. She remembered kneeling with her father at the altar in the corner of their house, the aroma of copal all around them. She smelled it now, as though it came from her own body. She saw hundreds of candles clinging to a rock, tiny flames surrounding her, burning on her body, and she felt everything in her solid state of immobility. Wax covered her like flesh, soft and fragrant, coming to life on her bones. The air was red and yellow, pink and white. She spun inside her stillness, faster and faster until she reached the centre and there was Ixchel, the Old Goddess of Medicine.

"This child will heal you, Calixta," she said. "Surrender."

She would talk with Chavela next time she went to the village. She couldn't bear this conflict alone.

∾

I've met a wonderful woman, a nun. She looked after me when I was a baby, before the adoption. I think she'll help me, but she's afraid. There's so much secrecy here. I'm wooing her! Love, love, love, Paméla.

She arrived early at the park and paced the dusty pathways impatiently. She'd spent the morning at the internet café, then she'd bought a bunch of postcards and sat in Café Rey Sol, drinking coffee and writing cryptic messages.

Dear Fern & Hannah, The street vendors look like Mayan sculptures escaped from the museums of the world, stone turned to flesh. Their breath rises in spirals with the howling of dogs, prayers flying from split tongues;

*the world rests on the back of a crocodile. Thank you for
pushing me to come; it was the best thing. Malinche still
simmering. Love, love, love.*

She'd waited patiently in two long lines at the post office,
first to buy stamps and again to have the stamps cancelled
and her cards deposited in the mail sack. She'd wandered
the hallways of the post office staring up at its crumbled
elegance. Everything in the city seemed a monument to
the past, a living museum struggling to keep up with
business-as-usual in a condemned structure. Outside
the city she knew there were tourist resorts catering
to people like herself, on land appropriated by foreign
developers, land where she might once have lived had
she not been adopted.

It was almost four o'clock. Paméla circled the one-
handed woman in the centre of the park, and leaned
her aching forehead against the warm stone of her
leg. When she saw her she almost ran, but Guadalupe
waved from across the street and flashed her brilliant
smile and they walked quickly towards each other. They
both spoke at the same time, then a quick embrace and
they linked arms and walked, heads down. There were
many stories to tell.

"You slept in the nursery with the other children,
but you cried in the night and often I'd take you into
bed with me to quieten you. I was afraid of rolling over
on you, so I hardly slept. We played a game with our
fingers, making them dance, and you laughed. I was
thirteen years old. I pretended that you were my baby
and that we would be together always."

"Did you meet my mother?"

Guadalupe nodded.

"What was her name?"

"Fabiana."

"Fabiana?" Paméla breathed the name as though it were a secret code to another world. "How beautiful."

"She was very young, like me. She wanted to see you, but the Sisters wouldn't allow it because of government regulations. Mother Superior found her a position as a maid in the house of some rich people."

"Where? D'you think she's still there?"

Guadalupe shook her head. "She ran away, onto the street. We never saw her again."

"So what's in that file?"

Guadalupe shrugged. "Documents. A photograph of you and me before I handed you over to the Canadian women."

"Who took it?"

"Sister Rosa. She had a small camera then. She used to photograph the flowers in the courtyard."

"There must be more, isn't there? Please, Lupe, please tell me," Paméla begged.

"I can tell you only that she loved you and she wanted to take you. It's too cruel that you should not know that."

"It's cruel not to tell me where Fabiana is now."

"I cannot bring this trouble on our convent. You have no idea what could happen. This is my home, Paméla." She gestured towards the huge building, a city block, her own small room embedded in it.

"I'll never tell, I promise. You can trust me." She gripped the nun's hands in hers. Guadalupe's head was shaking back and forth. She wouldn't look her in the eye. Paméla pulled the *medalla milagrosa* out of her shirt and held it up. "In the name of the Virgin I promise I'll never betray your trust."

A light flared in Guadalupe's eyes. "You're Catholic?"

"No. But I understand about love. What else is there?"

When she spoke her voice was low and toneless as though she were reciting something without thinking. "Your mother lives in a secret apartment inside the Palacio Nacional. She is the compañera of General Ernesto de Cuevas. He has had a long career in the army. They call him Generalísimo Carbonero — the charcoal maker — because he has burned many villages and many of our people. We all know about him and we wanted to save you from this."

"That can't be true. There must be a mistake. Are you sure it was my file?"

"The general's sister works with us at Casa Central. She's a teacher in the school. She disowned her brother many years ago, but she heard through her family that he'd taken Fabiana as his mistress and she reported it to Mother Superior, because the government requires that records on the parents of our orphans be kept up to date."

Paméla pulled away. "I'm not an orphan. I have a mother and now I know where to find her."

"You can't see her, Paméla. It's impossible. They won't let you into the Palacio."

"I've seen tourists going in there. It's a museum."

"Only part of the Palacio; the staterooms and the murals. You'd never find your mother in there."

"I'll ask for the general."

"No! You cannot see him. It's dangerous. He gave the orders for so many massacres."

"But the war is over."

Guadalupe tossed her head in exasperation. "I told you, nothing has really changed despite the so-called Peace Accord. Now Fabiana's generalísimo is a respectable member of the Estado Mayor, La Defensa, a group of high ranking officers in charge of national security. But even though he's only a watchdog to protect President Portillo and his family, he can still bite your head off."

"You judge her, don't you?"

"I'm sorry if it seems that way to you. It is not my intention."

There was an awkward silence as Guadalupe withdrew into herself. What have I done? Oh, Mother, what have I done? I've broken my trust. I've betrayed Sister María-Teresa.

"Well . . . thanks for helping me, Lupe. Let's keep in touch."

"No!" Lupe grasped Paméla's arm. "You mustn't go like this. You don't understand the risk you're taking, Paméla. If you had grown up in Guatemala you would know how dangerous this is."

"Stop talking down to me. I'm not stupid."

"Of course you're not, but it's hard to see what is invisible." She lowered her voice to an intense whisper. "There are so many layers of corruption and violence. I only want to help you, Paméla, to protect you."

"You have helped me, and I'll always be grateful."
She hugged Lupe impulsively and drew back quickly.
"Can I telephone you at the convent?"

"It's better for us to meet in the chapel. I'm always
there at five in the afternoon."

"When do you leave for the village?"

"Next week." She reached out her hand.

Paméla took her hand and looked into her eyes.
"Please don't worry about me," she said, then she
leaned forward and kissed Guadalupe's cheek. "You're
beautiful," she said.

Guadalupe stared at Paméla a moment, then she
touched her face. Her hand dropped to her side and she
held it away from her body like a dancer as she turned
and walked down the path towards the convent.

That evening Paméla stood in front of the National
Palace and stared up at the impenetrable façade.
Tomorrow I'll be inside, she thought. She was in such
a turmoil of feeling that she couldn't think clearly,
couldn't even begin to imagine what might happen.
She turned abruptly and walked down Avenida 6,
watching the vendors pack up their stalls. Where do
they go at night? she wondered. Two boys piled their
wares into huge plastic sacks, loaded them on a trolley
and trundled down a dark sidestreet. Everyone was
scattering, separating like mercury, down sidestreets,
into doorways, bedding down under the colonnade
that lined Parque Central in front of the Palacio. She
went back to Chalet Suizo, lit a candle and lay in bed
thinking about what she would say to Fabiana the next
day. She couldn't believe how fast everything was going

suddenly. She was wide awake and didn't sleep until long after the candle had spluttered out.

∾

Discovering Olid and his mutineers long dead by the time he arrived at the Gulf of Honduras, Cortés commandeered a small fleet of caravels and set sail for home around the Yucatán peninsula. The voyage was as cursed as the overland journey. One of the caravels was lost in a tempest and everyone drowned. When the other members of the fleet finally straggled ashore at Veracruz in May of 1526 Malintzín carried a baby in her arms, a girl born at sea and christened María by her father, Juan Jaramillo.

It was the height of summer by the time they stood on the outskirts of Tenochtitlan. Cortés wiped the sweat from his brow and remembered his first vision of the city, a jewel-studded lake teeming with life. He remembered the battles, the deaths, *La Noche Triste,* the long siege and the final surrender. He remembered the houses filled with death, mountains of corpses smoking and spitting as the fires raged. Before him now lay a shining city of newly-built churches and palaces. "I've given my life for this land. I have built this city for God and my king!" he shouted, turning to his exhausted men.

Instead of the welcome he'd dreamed of, he found the capital taken over by Spanish bureaucrats wielding quill pens and parchments. He was greeted by Gonzalo de Salazar and Rodrigo de Chirinos, treasury officials who'd taken over the government of the new territory in his absence.

"Don Hernándo! We thought you dead and were about to assign your lands elsewhere," exclaimed Salazar, stroking his beard.

"You might wish you had not returned, Don Hernándo. There is a Commission of Inquiry into your governance, your unorthodox methods of conquest, the suspicious death of your wife . . . " Chirinos ended on a suggestive inflection.

"Your lands have in any case been confiscated and Don Luis Ponce de León has been sent from Spain to sit as Judge in the Inquiry," said Salazar, flicking a parchment under Cortés' nose. It was a scroll of charges which included the theft of Moctezuma's treasure, the defence and protection of Indians from slave labour, the strangulation of his wife and the poisoning of several rivals to his governorship. The two men sat back, hands folded on their bellies, and smiled as Cortés read the charges against him. His sallow skin flushed and a muscle worked his jaw as he read.

∾

Malintzín woke to the cry of her daughter. At first she didn't know where she was. After almost two years of travelling, waking up in jungles and swamps, Mayan palaces or huts thatched with swatches of corn leaves, she was unaccustomed yet to the stability of her husband's house close by the central plaza of Mexico-Tenochtitlan. She took her bearings as she emerged from the dreamworld, tugged into the day by María, and picked her up, looking intently at her tiny features. The child wept inconsolably, as though she had suffered some great loss. Malintzín put the baby to her breast, watched her rosebud mouth suck urgently, felt the milk coursing through, quietening the child. "Give me a sign, Tonantzin, oh Mother Goddess, tell me she's Hernán's child."

She stroked her tiny arms and touched each finger, splayed in the ecstasy of feeding. She cupped her downy head and gazed at her fluttering eyelids with their milky blue skin, almost translucent, like a bird's egg. A longing for Martín stabbed Malintzín's heart and tears sprang in her eyes as she remembered him like this, new in the world, lying in Hernán's arms so trusting, his milky eyes trying to find his father. She imagined him running into the room.

"Mamá, Mamá, my sister is like me, half Spanish," his merry dark eyes laughing at her. "When will Papá come? Can I go to Spain, Mamá, what is it like there?" Crouching on the bed, legs folded under his perfect body, staring at her with his father's eyes, waiting for her answer.

Malintzín lived a double life since her marriage to Jaramillo. She came now from the shadows of the past, rife with memory.

"Hear me, oh Tonantzin. I lie in Jaramillo's bed, my daughter in the crib beside me, and dream of Hernándo and our son, and when I wake my heart is filled with light. But as I enter the day I am turned to stone. Oh, Mother Goddess, only you can stand in judgement of me. My heart gives me no choice. I wasn't divided then, when I spoke the words of the Cholulan wife. I had to live, to be loyal to him. I've split my tongue three ways and now my body is divided. I stand in the shadows, longing for Hernán and watch myself living, bearing another child, even enjoying my husband's body moving against me in the night. This is my betrayal. This shadow girl is me. It is she who looks into my child's face, searching for a sign. Oh Tonantzin, tell me I have not betrayed him."

A flood of light blinded her as the door swung open.

"Señora, I have brought you chocolate." Zaachila carried a steaming cup and placed it on the dressing table amidst a clutter of necklaces and Spanish hair combs. "You must drink, Señora. It will give you strength."

"Ah, Zaachila," she sighed, "What would I do without you? You served me well on that long journey to hell and delivered me in a stormy birth at sea. Now we can rest."

"The Señor wishes to see you. Can he come?"

She nodded and removed the sleeping baby from her breast. "But don't leave me, Zaachila. I'm not ready for his appetites."

Zaachila stifled a laugh and bobbed in a curtsy as she'd been taught, then her skirts twirled as she left the bedchamber to fetch Jaramillo.

Malintzín leaned over to put the sleeping baby in her crib. She climbed out of bed and buttoned her bodice and had just time to wrap a shawl around her shoulders before Jaramillo entered the room. He strode forward and kissed his wife's cheek, then he looked down at the sleeping child, reached hesitantly into the cradle and fondled her soft head. "A miracle," he said. "We will baptize her María in the name of the Holy Virgin."

"María Malintzín."

"Malintzín is not a Catholic name."

"It was my name . . . before."

"Of course . . . a small matter," he shrugged.

"Not to me," she said sharply. "It's her right . . . her mother's blood." She turned her head away and closed her eyes.

"You're tired, Marina. I'll leave you to rest."

"No," she grasped his arm and looked into his eyes. "Take me to Altamirano's house, Juan, to see our son."

Zaachila's eyes grew round as she hovered in the doorway.

"Cortés says the boy must not be disturbed."

"Disturbed? What do you mean? I'm his mother. You've given him your name, my husband, now he must come to live with us." She held onto his arm with a vice-like grip.

"Martín is well cared for in Altamirano's house. He learns to speak in Castilian and grows up like a Spanish boy."

Her nails dug into the sleeve of his doublet. "But, Juan, what about — "

"You have another child now, Marina, our daughter, no?"

"I demand to see Martín!" She tried to pull away, but he held her arm.

"She is our daughter, isn't she?"

"Of course. What do you think?"

"I don't know what to think of Señor Malinche's mistress."

"Let me go! I must see my Martín. It's been almost two years."

He released her suddenly so that she almost fell, stumbling into the dressing table, setting the beads and combs aquiver, causing the dull mirror to tremble.

"Go," he said defiantly, "You will be refused entry at Altamirano's house. These are not my directives. They are orders from Cortés himself, for the good of your son. What kind of mother are you, leaving your new baby? Could it be that you don't care for this one?"

Malintzín lashed out quick as a cat and slapped his face. For a moment she thought he would retaliate, but he stood there, his face turned crimson, a thick vein pulsing in his forehead, then he swept past her, knocking Zaachila against the doorframe as he left the bedchamber. The baby began to cry, her face red and wrinkled, her little fists quivering. Malintzín ran to the crib and lifted her. They paced the room together, the baby's head wobbling with each intake of breath, while Malintzín smoothed circles on her tiny back. She saw the chocolate congealed in the cup as she passed her dressing table, and she saw herself reflected in the dull mirror, a dark shadow from the past, holding another baby. "What have I done? What will happen to my son with his mixed blood?" A chill ran down her spine, setting each vertebra resonating until her entire body was alive with premonition. She turned from the mirror. She would not look, she could not, so great was the darkness in the wake of the serpent path.

∿

Paméla handed her pack to the guard and passed through the metal detector. "You must check your bag here," the woman said and handed her a ticket.

Paméla climbed a curved flight of stone steps. On the walls flanking the staircase and along the marbled hallways on the upper floor were murals showing metal-clad Spaniards and naked Indian women, priests converting clusters of Indians. Above an ornate, wrought-iron archway was the battle scene of Kumarca'aj, showing Pedro de Alvarado slaying Tecúm Umán, the feathered Chief of the Quiché Maya. He lay on the ground like a wounded bird as Alvarado leaned down and pierced the proud Chief with his sword.

A couple of gardeners whistled as they plucked dead foliage from the many plants that cascaded from the balconies into a central courtyard bordered by colonnades. Lanterns hung from a lapis-inlaid roof over stone walkways, and shimmering water filled long mosaic pools with fountains trickling from the mouths of massive stone fish. Each time Paméla turned a corner there was a clock and they all told a different time. She felt like Alice entering wonderland; all the rules were different here and she must rely on her instincts.

She stood on the second level, looking down into the courtyard. A freshly cut rose rested in a huge sculptured hand, the petals white, still beaded with dew. She walked to the back of the colonnade. There was no one around so she stepped over a chain, slung between two posts, into a darkened area and walked silently in her rubber-soled sandals until she saw a light coming from an open doorway beyond a broad staircase. She peered into an office where a man sat at his desk poring over a pile of papers. He didn't even look up. She felt like an intruder as she turned and walked towards the staircase. At the top of the second flight was a hallway with two closed doors, and on the wall a silent face indicated five o'clock. She listened, heard nothing, turned the handle of the first door. It was locked. She tried the next one and it opened into another dark hallway with more doors opening to either side. As she stood wondering what to do next she heard footsteps on the stairs outside. She'd left the door open. As she turned a figure appeared, silhouetted; a small man with his hand on a hip holster. For a crazy moment she thought he was going to pull a gun and shoot her, so she raised her hands. The guard walked towards her, staring as though he had seen a ghost.

"Señora?" He was a young boy with a fine down of hair on his chin and upper lip.

"Señorita," Paméla said, her voice trembling.

The boy looked closely at her face, then his body stiffened. "*No hay admisión,*" he said and repeated the words with emphasis.

"I came through security at the front desk," Paméla said. "Please help me. I'm looking for Señora Fabiana. She lives here in the Palacio."

"You must come with me." He took her arm roughly and started down the stairs.

"I want to speak with General Ernesto de Cuevas," Paméla demanded.

"The general doesn't give interviews."

"So you know him!"

"Shhh, you mustn't cause a disturbance," he whispered, hunching his shoulders and raising his finger to his lips.

"I must speak with him. It's very important."

"No, no." He shook his finger in her face and hurried her down the stairs, holding her arm firmly. "This area is out of bounds for tourists. You must stay on that side," he indicated the chain. "Go. Don't let anyone see you."

Paméla's protests were to no avail, so she stood her ground waiting for the guard to leave, but he stood firmly at his post by the chain, and eventually she left defeated.

On her way out she bought a postcard of the Palacio Nacional and pinned it to the wall of her room at Chalet Suizo. She lay awake puzzling the strange world she'd entered, its shifting borders blurring the distinction between fantasy and reality. She was frustrated and angered by the web of secrecy she encountered at every turn. El Convento, El Palacio: huge grey buildings filled with secret passageways and closed doors; stone monuments to a culture cloaked in terror. Yes, the general exists, so Fabiana must exist too. But everything I want is forbidden, hidden inside a tangle of rules and regulations, whispers and fears.

In the morning she returned to the Palacio. She smiled at the guard as she passed through the metal detector, checked her pack like a veteran and walked purposefully towards the office in the front entrance. "*Buenos días*," she said to the man behind the glass booth. "I'm a Canadian journalist," she flashed her passport with the three month visa clearly visible, "And I've been granted an interview with General Ernesto de Cuevas."

The man spoke into a small microphone on the other side of the glass. "The general does not give interviews."

"Oh, but I arranged this with the Guatemalan embassy in Canada. They said — "

The man shook his head as she spoke. "The general is away," he cut in, "on official business with President Portillo."

"When will he return?"

"The general does not give interviews." His face was like a slab of stone.

"Could I speak with his wife?"

"Please. You're wasting your time."

Paméla broke into a brilliant smile. "I know you can help me," she said in as confidential a tone as she could manage through glass. "The person I would really like to speak with is a woman who lives in a private apartment in the Palacio — "

"No one lives here. These are government offices."

"Her name is Fabiana."

He shook his head, "No one lives here," and turned away.

Paméla was left staring at the back of his head, tears of frustration welling. She wandered around the courtyard and stood by the fountain. The white petals of yesterday's dewy rose had turned brown and curled at the edges. The sight of it somehow defeated her. She had imagined Fabiana strolling through the gardens in the early morning, cutting a fresh white rose each day, placing it in the sculptured hand as a symbol of Guatemala's Peace Accord.

That evening she sat in Parque Central, alone amidst the music and chatter of the evening vendors. With fairylights, fireworks, the splashing of fountains, the city seemed like a long fiesta amid the ruin of her dreams. She wished that Talya was there to love her and make her feel like she existed. She didn't know where the day had gone. After leaving the Palacio she'd circled the building, staring up at the barred windows. She'd felt like lying on the Palacio steps, kicking and screaming for her mother, but she'd wandered aimlessly all day and found herself eventually drawn back to Centro Histórico at dusk when little birds swarmed the trees and the night life of the city began. She felt so painfully alone in the crowded square, watching the Palacio, knowing that her mother was inside and yet totally inaccessible to her, that eventually she could bear it no longer and made her way back to the hotel, pushing angrily through the slow crowds on Avenida 6.

She lay awake for what felt like hours, but she must have fallen asleep eventually, because she woke sweating from a dream in which Fabiana and the guard whispered in a corner, refusing to look at her. She shouted at them, but no sound came out of her mouth. They walked away as though she didn't exist and when she tried to follow she found herself rooted in the park like a great tree with tiny birds swarming in her hair. Somewhere in the background, although she couldn't see her, was Guadalupe, an aura of light shining from her body.

She sat up in bed, swatting at the mosquitoes that whined around her head. She flipped the switch of the bedside lamp, but there was no electricity, and all the candles were burned to stubs. She fumbled for her flashlight. Three a.m. She found a cool spot on the damp pillow and tried to relax, but her head throbbed and she was soon tossing and turning in the damp sheets. She began to count, a childhood ritual, counting the steps, down, down into the earth, counting her breaths, in and out, counting the levels of her existence until she became a tiny speck suspended in the darkness of eternity. All around her was a high-pitched humming which vibrated her body, snaked down her spine and left through the soles of her feet. A clamour of voices mouthed unintelligible sounds which she understood in a place beyond thought, a place where the air shimmered with the jungle sounds of a many-layered universe. Then suddenly she was travelling back at a tremendous speed. Her body grew larger and became sentient as she slammed into it and felt the sick thud of absence. Fabiana's absence, Hannah and Fern, Talya, Lupe . . .

At dawn she fell into a deep sleep. Like an enormous boulder, she sank to the bottom of a great body of water and lay there immersed. The water was filled with light, and she was held in liquid turquoise, shimmering with bright limestone. She was pulled under and coated with dripping white stone, soft and safe like a cocoon. Upriver, by the big rocks, she could see a whirlpool eddying. A girl and a boy lay there, twinned, coated with ancient limestone. They'd jumped from the rocks and never surfaced. *Agua azul . . . agua azul . . .* a crocodile beneath her, guarding the steps to hell; nine layers under the water, four steps down, then the rock and four steps up. Above her the Heavens; six ascending in the east to the seventh layer, six descending to the west; and in each corner of the world a sacred ceiba, a wild cotton tree. A giant green ceiba stood in the centre, rooted in the underworld, its branches reaching to the Heavens. She was inside the tree, her legs entangled with its roots, but she was also outside — *q'ab q'anup* — a branch of the ceiba. She could see everything; white in the north, yellow in the south, red to the east, black to the west, and all around her the blue of the universe. She was complete.

Paméla woke at 9:30, covered in mosquito bites. Getting out of bed was like pulling herself through liquid clay. She looked in the cloudy bathroom mirror and hardly recognized her swollen face and puffy eyes. She splashed water on her face and slowly her head cleared, until she knew what she must do. First she would go to the convent and talk to Guadalupe.

A clear blue eye appeared at the grille. "*Si.*"

"I want to see Sister Guadalupe."

"She's not here."

"Where is she?"

"I cannot say."

"But I'm a friend of hers. I must see her."

The nun pushed a slip of paper through the grille. "You may write her a note."

"I don't have a pen."

The paper withdrew and she heard the snap of the metal grille closing, footsteps receding. Paméla headed for the park, where she sat on the stone bench and looked up at Guadalupe's window. She thought she saw a shadow moving there and kept watch for some time before she realized it was the play of light through the jacarandas.

At five o'clock exactly she stood waiting at the chapel, but there was no sign of Guadalupe. She sat in a pew at the back and prayed for her to come. A touch on her shoulder. She raised her face.

"Did you find her?"

Paméla shook her head. "I'm going away. I wanted to say goodbye."

Guadalupe paled. "When?"

"Tomorrow, if there's a bus."

"A bus?"

"Yes, I'm going travelling like you. You're going to the country, aren't you?"

She laughed and her colour returned. "Yes, to Huehuetenango, to a village not far from there. I thought you were leaving Guatemala." Her light tripping tone. Their eyes met.

"No, just leaving the capital, for a while." She paused.

"The park?"

Guadalupe nodded.

"I'll wait for you there."

"I'll come with you."

"But your prayers . . . "

"There'll be plenty of time for prayers."

∾

Of all people Zaachila knew Malintzín's heart; she who had shared with her the years of slavery and the coming of the Spaniards, then the joy of Martín's birth and babyhood at Casa Colorado, who had witnessed her humiliation as Cortés filled the house with his mistresses, who had washed the sour milk from her clothing and walked with her on the long and hopeless journey to Honduras, who had seen her married off to an indifferent man, swollen with a second child, sustained only by her desire to hold Martín in her arms again, her son, her firstborn.

"I will go to Don Altamirano's house. His cook is from my village. I will bring news."

"Oh Zaachila!" Malintzín grasped Zaachila's hands and a wild hope lit up her eyes. "You must be careful. Tell Martín I love him. Do you think he remembers me? Nineteen moons is a long time, almost half his life."

"I must make the tortillas for *la comida*, then I will go."

"If anyone sees you say you're going to the *mercado*."

Zaachila nodded and ran to the kitchen to mix the *masa*. She comforted herself with the steady slap of the tortillas between her hands. All her desire was to help her mistress now, because she understood grief and loss, she recognized it, although she wondered if it was for Martín that her mistress grieved or for Señor Malinche. On the journey to Honduras when they had passed through the Gulf town of Coatzacoalcos, as Malintzín reunited with her mother, Zaachila had learned of the death of her parents and her brothers from the Spanish disease. When she heard about their skin erupting in volcanoes, about their dying agonies from the all-consuming fever which had swept across the land, reaching even to her village of Acayucan, she had wished for death herself.

"I'm an orphan now, I am all alone," she had wept. But Malintzín had helped her once again.

"The Gods have chosen you, Zaachila," she had said. "You must stop wishing for death. It was your destiny to become a slave and leave your family. This is what saved you, and now you're free."

But Zaachila didn't want to be free. She had given her loyalty to Doña Marina and vowed to serve her and her Spanish lords.

Martín was four years old. He did not recognize the woman in the green skirt, a bright shawl draped across her brown shoulders.

"Martí, *xochitl xolotl*," she whispered, stooping to take the boy's hand, and a memory stirred in him. As she held him close he felt the warmth of her skin, then his face burrowed into her neck and he smelled her, like earth and corn and rich red hibiscus.

"Mamá!" he cried, "Mamá, Mamá!" and he pummelled her back with his fists, angry that she'd left him and that he had forgotten her. The bright little boy from Coyoacan who had patted the horse's legs fearlessly was clouded already with knowledge. In his uncle's house he heard whispered words, "*La Malinche . . . bastardo . . . traidora . . .* " He didn't understand the words, but he felt the scorn behind them. He had begun to lose his childhood in the big, flagstoned kitchen where he crouched under the wooden table and listened to the servants whispering and laughing, ugly sounds that made him feel dirty, made him want to run and run until the wind picked him up in its big arms and carried him away.

And as she spoke to him in the soft sounds of Nahuatl memory flooded in and he began to laugh, joy bubbling up to fill his loneliness. "Take me home, Mamá," he said, throwing his arms around her neck. But she could not, it was forbidden by the governor. If she had been able to speak to Cortés she would have begged him, she would have abased herself, done anything for the sake of this child who was enshrined in her heart with his father. But Cortés was like a phantom since their return. She heard news of him, rumours snatched from her husband's lips and savoured in the night, but months went by and she was unable to make her petition, so she visited her son secretly, Zaachila paving the way, arranging with the cook in advance to have Martín at hand in the kitchen. The proximity of Altamirano's house was a mercy. It lay only four streets away. Sometimes she left her baby girl sleeping under the watchful eye of Zaachila and walked the streets, hoping for a glimpse of Martín. And sometimes she saw him, his hand firmly clasped in the hand of a Spanish servant woman, and her heart leapt with the desire to run forward and claim him. But most often it was some other small boy, dark-eyed and sallow-skinned, but never with quite the same demeanour that characterized Martín, that particular self-containment of the child abandoned by his parents, the demeanour which Malintzín herself carried, matured into the grace of independence.

∾

Paméla sat above the trees looking down into the jungle. She had climbed the breathless stone steps to a changed perspective, and a young man from Québec had snapped her with his digital camera in the arms of this monstrous pyramid; a traveller, well met in the Heavens, touching briefly. She could not see where she sat exactly — atop one of the four giant pyramids of Tikal facing onto the plaza of a once-thriving community where Cortés had stopped briefly on his journey into Honduras — but only that she was surrounded by a dense jungle stretching into swampy scrubland. She felt as though she could

~ 169 ~

fly, diving off the pyramid, covering the world with her wingspan.

The nights were hot and slow. She heard the jungle breathing like a sleeping animal as she lay half asleep, naked under her thin sheet, her consciousness spread out, barely held, touching everything. In the morning she drank coffee with Denís, the Québecois. Their paths had crossed and now she was leaving, heading south on a crowded bus, bumping over the damage they call roads in Guatemala. In between stretches of rubble there were sections washed out by monsoon flash floods, smooth and dangerous, rich with mud. She looked out through smudged glass at a soaring landscape as the bus curved so close to the edge that she couldn't see the road under them. The corners were blind, the horn incessant, the bus filled with bodies pressing, the people's faces passive and inscrutable as they stared at the patterned land, sweeping and plunging in a patchwork of green, yellow, reddish brown. The fields were planted with corn and coffee, their delicate leaves breaking through the earth and rising through a thin mist blanketing the hills. She wondered what Guadalupe was doing. They had arranged to meet at Iximché when Guadalupe was finished her work in the village. Paméla was on her way, moving slowly, trying to contain the exultation that leapt in her like a fish in sunlight. Since she'd given away her watch a new sense of time had grown in her, a line curling in on itself, past and future clasping the moment.

Working in the house of God, there shalt thou draw
blood, there shalt thou make penance. It shall be thy
duty to offer parchment and copal, to give alms to the
needy who starve, to clothe those who go naked and in
rags. Their flesh is as thine.

— Bernardino de Sahagún,
Historia de las Cosas de la Nueva España

Guadalupe held the sleeping baby and translated
from Mam into Spanish as Doctor Ramírez examined
the woman's ear, questioning her. "How long since it
started, have you had this pain before, where exactly
does it hurt?" The child was warm against her breast,
like her brothers had been, her baby sister, like Flor de
Maya. The last day, before they had come with their cans
of gasoline and their flaming torches, she'd been playing
with her brothers. Mynor and Felipe were rough boys
and she had told little Isabella to keep away. They ran
at each other, grabbing legs, ankles, shoulders, rolling
in the dust. At twelve she'd been a skinny girl with a
body like a boy and she'd loved wrestling. Isabella ran
at her and pummelled her belly with little fists. "I want
to play, I want to play!"

Calixta picked her up. "You can't play with us, baby.
You'll get hurt. Come on, I'll take you to Mamá." The
child screamed and kicked, but Calixta took no notice
and carried her into the house.

"There you are. Where've you been, Calixta? I need
your help with the tortillas. Here's the *masa*, now get
to work. And show Isabella how to do it. She likes to
help."

She remembered feeling so angry that she'd kicked her sister under the table and Isabella had screamed. But they had made the tortillas. She could still hear the steady slap of her own hands mixed with Isabella's erratic slap and flop as her tortillas fell apart. "No, no, this way, baby. Watch me." She'd had a big pile of tortillas almost finished when they had heard the first scream. After that it was like an echo chamber, screams and gunshots circling them until Calixta was deaf with it. She'd crouched under the table, Isabella clasped to her body, her hand over the child's mouth. A heavy boot had kicked them apart, then Isabella was screaming and Calixta was running, running, running for her life through thick black smoke, choking and coughing, running like snaked lightning. She'd been so scared that she'd forgotten Felipe and Mynor until she was a mile from the village. She had turned back, but all she could see were spirals of black smoke rising into the clear sky, gathering in clouds as though a storm were coming. She had never smelled anything like that before. It was the smell of human flesh burning, hot and sweet.

She handed the baby back to his mother and brought the next patient in; a woman with three children hanging onto her skirt. Coming to the village was Guadalupe's penance. Her wounds re-opened and each time she suffered again the devastation of her neglect. But this time was different, because her heart was not fully engaged in penance. She had told Chavela about Flor's return and about the joy she felt at seeing her. Now she counted the days till they would meet at Iximché.

ɘ

Chavela's shuttle passed back and forth, feeding the threads. Through the earth she felt the movement of her people; the soft vibration of bare feet travelling the pathway to the shrine, walking down to the river to drink, climbing the hills, furrowing the earth, sharp thud of the planting stick, plop of the kernel dropped into darkness. She felt the slow growth of life in the earth, life in the bellies of the village women, death in the bodies of the village elders. Slowly, inexorably she wove the story of the sky, sitting on the earth, Mother-Father, Earth-Sky. Soon the priests and priestesses would gather again and she would be one with them, wearing the colours of life on her body, a story unfolding across her shoulders, covering her. Hands of the living, bones of the dead whispering beneath the ground. Chavela's father spoke to her as she worked, the man she'd never known, buried in the garden of her brother's house. He had died during her long exile, but he spoke to her now, calling her. Chavela rolled up her rainbow and placed it under the tree. She glanced across the valley as though she were waiting for someone. Then she walked slowly down the dirt road, mud splashing her ankles, to Manuela's house to see if her baby was ready to be born.

∾

Kumarca'aj, Utatlan, near Santa Cruz del Quiché. *Silence, all around me a dark silence; shapes of the dead stretching the earth. So much blood shed here the grass will never be bright again.*

Kumarca'aj was a national monument. Paméla had read the history of the place in the small museum at the site: how the Quiché Maya were defeated by Pedro de Alvarado, how Tecúm Umán flew like a quetzal, his green wings swooping as he beheaded Alvarado's horse, how the heroic leader came to earth and was killed, his breast gaping where Alvarado's sword entered. She sat in the dark grass and wrote.

Silence has entered the stones that contain this place. Giant ceibas drink the silence through the darkened earth, the wind snatches the silence and disappears, leaving the place breathless. I sit here and imagine the Quiché Maya standing startled, their mouths circles of surprise, as Alvarado gives the order, "Secure the prisoners! We march south!" Blood running down the pyramid steps, from the wounded priests, cut down in the middle of a sunny day. An endless line of people standing in the sun with bleeding ears, Alvarado's men ripping gold and turquoise from their ragged ears. The Maya were accustomed to blood sacrifice; they pierced their own ears with obsidian, their bodies with cactus thorns, passing thin willows through tongue, lips, penis. The pain they suffer is nothing compared to the terrible misunderstanding of the strangers who think they must tear what they want from their bodies. This earth is scarred forever. I'm moving south, to Iximché, sacred city of the Cakchiquel Maya. I move in Alvarado's footsteps. I wonder if Guadalupe will be there. I wonder if she really exists. Nothing can be taken for granted in this place.

∾

Chavela prepared chocolate for Manuela. She boiled
water, honey and chocolate over the fire inside a circle of
stones. They were high above the valley and the nights
were cold. She had heated a rock in the fire and wrapped
it in thirteen big leaves from the tree with red and white
branches near Tomás' house. She would wrap it again in
a red woven cloth and massage Manuela's stomach to
stop the bleeding and take down the swelling. Manuela
lay in bed, her baby tucked into the crook of her arm.
Chavela had caught the baby when it came, her hands
drawing it out of Manuela, and Guadalupe had cut the
cord. The other children were playing outside in the
muddy road, screaming and shouting. Chavela heard
them as the chocolate began to boil. Every afternoon the
rains came, heavy like a sheet of white hair from the sky,
then it was over and the sun made rainbows across the
valley. She poured the dark liquid into a cup, cracked
two eggs into it and took it to Manuela, so small in the
corner of her bed. In the darkness of the house you could
miss her, Chavela thought, like the soldier had almost
missed her, under the covers of her bed with her baby
son. If he hadn't looked back one more time. Afterwards
he shouted to the others.

"My children are Canadian now," she told Guadalupe
as they left Manuela's house and walked back down the
road. "But they will come to visit soon. My youngest son
has never been in Guatemala. He was born in Vancouver,
and Julia in Mexico."

"Why did you have to leave, Chavela? Was your
husband fighting with the guerrilla?"

"No, he was working for our village, to get drinking water for the people of Huixoc, and a school for the children. They took him away for thirty days and tortured him. They said he was a communist, but he only wanted to help our people."

"And did they torture you?"

"I took my son and went to my mother's house in La Democracia. She wanted me to cross the border into Mexico. It is very close. But I didn't know if I would see my husband again, so I had to wait. I looked for him every day, and when he came finally we escaped and I didn't see my family for twenty years. This was the torture. But for you life has been more cruel, Lupe, losing everyone, your whole village."

"Paméla is here now, the child who brought me back to life. Since she came everything has changed. I don't know what to do, Chavela."

"What do you want?"

"To know who I am, and what I should do."

Chavela took Guadalupe's hands in hers. "Tomorrow there will be a ceremony with the elders. You can come with me if you want."

PART THREE

Dearest Hannah and Fern, Do I really have two mothers?
Or are you actually one wonderful double-faceted woman?
I love you both so much and miss you terribly. I'm sitting
on the steps of the cathedral in Chichicastenango. In front
of me is the market place. Everyone here is Mayan, apart
from the gringos. Yesterday I saw a procession around the
square, everyone in ceremonial dress, carrying effigies of
saints. Lots of incense and strange music. I'm on my way
to Iximché to meet Guadalupe, the nun I told you about.
Iximché is the spiritual centre of the Cakchiquel Maya. I've
had a great trip, met some interesting travellers and have a
whack of photos. This land is like a skirt spread out over a
huge expanse of mystery. Sometimes I feel I am getting lost
in Guatemala, staring at the terraced mountains rolling
down into the valleys, leaving my body.

There is a saying here, that the women speak their skirts.
They all weave, sitting on their heels outside their homes,
backstrap looms stretching between their body and a tree,
and the patterns and colours they weave tell you which
village they're from and what Mayan dialect they speak. I

can see the contours of the land in their clothing, as though
they wear the earth itself and speak the soft sounds of it. I
feel optimistic about resuming my search in the capital. No
ideas as yet, but I feel that something wonderful is going to
happen. Love, love, love, Pam. (Ignore my opening remark.
It's probably a projection. I'm beginning to feel like two
people).

∾

The earthen floor was strewn with pine branches. Chavela knelt beside Guadalupe in the small room filled with the aroma of pine and copal. The Mayan priests and priest-esses had come from all around, some of them rising at dawn to travel many miles for this ceremony. They came silently out of the forest, crossing the dirt road, feet gentle on the earth, greeting each other softly, creating a stir in the air around them, like wind in the trees. Behind the house the Rio Selegua flowed. It was on the banks of this river that the tortured had been left to die and in those days the river ran with blood and limbless corpses floating. Chavela had been there every day to look for her husband. When they had released him from the army barracks, a few miles down the road towards the city of Huehuetenango, he had crawled to the road and found help. A man drove him to La Democracia, to his mother-in-law's house. When Chavela saw him she could not believe this was her husband, one saved out of so many thousands. Why? A dog lapped at the edge of the Selegua, its pink tongue lolling from its mouth. The water was clean now. Where had all the blood gone?

In the newly built house, cement bulging from between the bricks, Juan Xiloj lit the candles, one for each direction, and Lucinda Pacheco recited the invocations. Everyone was dressed in their woven garments, in reds and pinks with electric blue, white and yellow jags. The priestesses wore ropes of beads and their heads were covered in coils of brightly coloured cloth. The priests wore brimmed hats, excepting Juan who had a red cloth tied around his brow and in his bolsa, the woven bag looped over his shoulder, he carried tobacco, a small bottle of alcohol, candles, matches, copal, for offerings to the Great Spirit. He lit a cigarette, pulled on it, exhaled and prayed to the Mother-Father, Earth-Sky, his prayer in the smoke that had travelled his body, swirled in his lungs and hung heavy now in the air. He passed the glowing cigarette around the circle. Each one must pray. They were the daykeepers, the midwives, the matchmakers. They understood the significance of the days in the sacred Mayan calendar that interlocks with the agricultural calendar.

Guadalupe's plain skirt pooled around her where she knelt, listening as one of the elders told his story of how he had suffered and been ill until he had found his path.

"Life can be harmonious," he said, "When we follow our calendar; health, marriage, children. The day on which we are born will tell us our path in life. We follow it exactly or we suffer and create disharmony around us."

It seemed as though he spoke only to her and she wrapped her cardigan tightly around her body in her wish for invisibility. She felt like an intruder amongst her own people, as though everyone's eyes were on her, and when she thought of the convent she was consumed with guilt. But memory stirred in her as Lucinda told the story of the *Popol Vuh*, the *Mayan Book of the Dawn of Life*. Guadalupe heard her father's voice as Lucinda told of the creation of the first people from corn, of Hunahpu and Xbalanque, the celestial twins, of the unity of life, the zero, the prophecies. She told of the sacrifice she made in order to be a priestess, her husband and children who must take second place. Guadalupe felt herself astride two moving islands, wanting to be in one place but unable to make the leap. I will be split in two, she thought. The world is moving under me. Oh help me Mother, Madre María, Mother Ixchel . . . Who am I?

Chavela also was listening. She was to be initiated as a priestess now that she had come home to do her work, bringing life into the world, receiving the new souls in her hands, settling them in the arms of their mothers. In Canada she had worn jeans and T-shirts, like the young men who crowded the outer edges of the room, but today she wore a bright *huipil* embroidered with many colours on the red cloth. She prayed to her grandmother to send her wisdom. She prayed for Guadalupe.

The prayers continued all day. The prayers do not end. Everything in life becomes a prayer.

∾

1528: She thought he was a spectre, standing in her imagination under the arched entry to the hallway. She walked slowly towards him and touched her fingers to his face.

"I've been ill, Marina." His arm reached around her waist, his hand in the small of her back. "I've lost my governance. They've put me on trial and I must defend myself. I will go to Spain and appeal to the king in person. It's the only course."

There was a commotion in the courtyard; dogs barking, a child screaming. Zaachila appeared in the doorway, holding María, who screamed louder when she saw her mother.

"Doña Marina . . . Señor Malinche, Oh . . . " The girl blushed and Malintzín reached for her child.

"María, María, quiet my darling, come to Mamá."

"María?"

"Her father's choice. He's a good Catholic," she said, formal now, as though a door in her had closed.

"I'll speak with Jaramillo."

"The master is away from the house, Señor," Zaachila said, bobbing in a curtsey, "He will return for *la comida*."

"Ah." He turned to Malintzín, who was fussing with the child and would not look him in the eye. "Will you entertain me in your parlour, Doña Marina, like a Mexican woman of nobility? As I remember, your father was a *cacique*."

She looked up sharply, meeting his eyes. "Zaachila! Bring refreshments to the parlour. Captain Cortés will drink pulque."

She led him inside, to the cool shuttered room, tiled with great slabs of blood-coloured stone. She sat in a narrow upright chair, María on her lap, all her attention focussed on the child. María leaned against her mother's heart, felt its beating. She sucked her thumb and watched

Cortés, as he watched Malintzín, like a hunter waiting for his prey to stumble. She saw herself crouched in the shadows, twisting a knife into the wound of his long absence.

"So you're a happily married woman, settled in your husband's household, the past behind you." It was almost a question. María whimpered and stretched, wriggling on Malintzín's knee. "And now you have a legitimate child."

María arched her back suddenly and threw her head against Malintzín's breast. It jolted her. "You are cruel!" she spat. "I will never forgive you, Hernán, for taking my son."

Zaachila entered with a bottle and two glasses. She placed them on a table, bobbed and left the room quickly. Cortés poured two glasses and offered one to Malintzín. She shook her head, but he downed the fiery pulque in one gulp.

"And do you think my daughter would be better off in your kinsman's house? She too has mixed blood."

"You must ask her father."

"Perhaps I have."

Their eyes locked and for a moment Malintzín felt herself sucked under by the current of his darkness, then María squirmed in her arms and she surfaced, the moment broken. Cortés downed the second glass and slid to his knees before her. Malintzín clung to her daughter like a shield and the child sat solemnly, staring directly into Cortes' eyes now that he was at her level.

"Marina, *mi amor*. We must take what is ours. Our lives are ebbing."

"You took my son," she said.

María struggled free and ran across the room, her bare feet pattering on the flagstones. Malintzín started after her, but Cortés caught her arm. "Let her go."

She fought him, but with her husband absent from the house and Zaachila out of earshot there was no one to protect her from herself. Her heart swallowed the years of deprivation in one gulp. She would never be hungry again but he was still her survival. Her body remembered everything in an instant and carried her like a bolting horse, she clinging to its mane, fighting for control. Cortés was lord of the world again, released from his months of humiliation, riding the land with Malintzín at his side, For a timeless instant which fed the years, they were like one creature breathing the darkness of itself, igniting its own body to create the light. He watched her mouth twist, felt her rippling like a river over stones and boulders, falling over rapids, splashing in the bright sun, then he slumped against her and returned to himself, renewed by her loyalty. She had lit a candle in his soul and their troubled love was a prayer to the new world.

Malintzín found herself pinned in the corner of her own parlor, her skin imprinted with the heavy material of Cortés' doublet. She was panting like a dog which has been running and running, looking for its master.

"Now," he said. "Now I will accept your hospitality," and he poured himself another measure of pulque as she rearranged herself.

"*El capitán* will dine with us," Malintzín said when Zaachila entered the parlour with a basket of fresh tortillas and a dish of goat cheese. Seeing her knowing eyes, she said sharply, "Go now, there is work to be done in the kitchen."

She took his hand and led him through the empty house, filling it with his presence, the essence of him which she would feed off, as she had fed off the earth of her homeland.

At dinner they sat across from each other at the long table, Jaramillo at the head, Cortés and Malintzín on either side of him. Zaachila served brimming plates of pork and tamales with chiles and atole, and a basket of steaming tortillas. Jaramillo poured more wine into Cortés' cup. "You will leave for Spain, *mi capitán*?"

"Yes, I leave for Villa Rica de la Veracruz and set sail from there."

"But surely you will return to our land, Don Hernándo?" Malintzín asked.

"When I have gained an audience with the king, a full pardon and the reinstatement of my lands."

Her shoulders fell in relief and she resumed eating.

"There is another matter I must settle," he said casually, his eyes making a study of the damask cloth, "I will take my son with me and settle him in — "

"No!" Her fork clattered to the floor as she stood.

"Marina — " Jamarillo cautioned.

"You cannot take Martín!"

"He must learn about his heritage, Marina."

"He's too young, only six years. You can't do this!"

"I will place him in the care of my relatives until he's old enough to go to Court. There he will serve as a page to the Royal Household."

"So this is why you came!" she spat.

"I came to inform you of my plans. I give you at least that courtesy, Doña Marina."

"Juan," she ran to her husband and took his arm, "Don't let him take our child. Martín looks to you as his father. You have given him your name."

Jaramillo stroked his beard thoughtfully. He wanted a son of his own. This could be their chance. Another son and she would soon get over the loss of Martín. Malintzín stood behind him, hands on his shoulders, staring at Cortés. Mine, her eyes said, Mine. This is the man who shares my bed every night, who protects me. He will speak for me.

But before Jaramillo could speak, Cortés said, "Martín has Indian blood. There is no future for him in this country. He must come with me to Spain and there the Indian will be trained out of him. He will learn about his true Spanish heritage, adopt our customs and our ways within the Holy Catholic Church. I will have him legitimized as my true son and heir and he will become a Knight of the Order of Santiago. Then he can return to the land of his birth, if he so wishes."

Jaramillo nodded sagely as Malintzín sank to her knees. She knew she was beaten and there was nothing in her to fight with, because she loved Cortés as she had loved her mother, even when she'd taken the purseful of coins by the river. Cortés could offer their son everything and what could she offer? Blood, the power of blood; we have mixed our blood, you and I, Hernán, and we are joined forever, but what will happen to my son with his mixed blood? The serpent quivered and her eyes clouded like the dark mirror of her bedchamber. She couldn't see through the darkness, but she smelled death, the smell of dry bones.

Jaramillo left the dining room and Cortés rose from the table and stretched out his hand to Malintzín. As he raised her from the floor their eyes met and she saw a softening in his eyes.

"You have my heart," he whispered.

The worst had happened and now she knew what she must do.

Malintzín kept to her bedchamber the next day.

"Watch over him, Tonantzin, and keep him safe. It is a chance for our son to leave this land and escape his destiny."

When she had returned to her homeland during the journey to Honduras she'd slipped away to see the priestess who had foretold her own future as an infant, and she had given her the day and hour of Martín's birth and asked her to foretell his future.

"He is born under the sign of sacrifice and endurance. His life will be lived astride the ocean, in perpetual exile, wandering, rootless . . . "

When Malintzín had protested the old woman had raised her hand to silence her.

"This is his destiny, my child, to right the wrongs of others, to create balance in the world. Give him freedom. His *nahual* is the bird in flight and only when he lands will he be caught and sacrificed, as the fish which swims in the sea and gives its body to be eaten."

"Oh Mother, what can I do to help him?"

"There is a bitter herb he must take for endurance. It is called *ruda*, and it grows in the sun. You will know it by its leaves and by its taste . . . see? This will protect him and keep him true."

The priestess had spoken harshly, but her face softened as she took a pinch of rue and put it on Malintzín's tongue. The taste had been bitter and intoxicating. She had tried not to believe the cruel words, but once said they held power over her imagination. "Astride the ocean-.-.-." Now it made sense, "In perpetual exile . . . "

"Oh please, no, it cannot be." She filled a pouch with *ruda*, picked from her own garden behind the house, and sent Zaachila to speak with the cook one last time so that she could bid her son farewell.

"You will go with Papá on a voyage, Martí, to Spain."

"Why?"

"Because you are Spanish. You will go on a big boat across the ocean."

"Are you coming, Mamá?"

She shook her head, struggling to find her voice. "Mamá will stay here. You're a big boy now, Martí, ready to go out into the world. You will ride to Villa Rica with Papá on his stallion." She took Martín in her arms and explained to him about the bitter herb. She made a game of it, placing a pinch on his tongue and nodding her head at him, open-mouthed, until he swallowed it. "*Xochitl xolotl*," she murmured, "Prince of my heart, flowering always," and she attached the pouch to Martín's belt and told him to keep it safe and to remember her when he tasted the *ruda*.

"You have my heart, you have my heart . . . " His words echoed in her dream-laden body, through the night as she woke, and as she attended to her daily tasks. Each morning she went out and waited near Altamirano's house, waiting to see them leave, until she heard that they had gone and she had missed them. She remembered how they'd landed at Villa Rica de la Vera Cruz and Cortés had knelt in the sand and prayed. She remembered how he had betrayed her time after time and how she had forgiven him, because he was a man and not a God after all. She had her own deities and she trusted in them.

"Tonantzin watches over me, Chicomecoatl feeds me with ripened *maíz*, Cihuacoatl has given me a new skin to make my way home. I have my place on this earth, the place of my birth where my spirit dwells."

Yes, she would go. She would follow them and stand on the cliff and look out to sea, watching for their return.

∾

The pyramids of Iximché were surrounded by pines. Golden drops of sap oozed from the trunks, shining in the sun. Paméla inhaled the pungent smell and watched a woodpecker tapping high in the branches, a flash of red as its head hammered back and forth. She rolled a ball of sap between finger and thumb, wrapped it in a leaf and started walking back to the entrance. Before she reached the gate she heard a voice behind her — "Paméla!" She turned around and saw Guadalupe standing in the middle of the path. Paméla was the first to move. She ran forward, the wrapped leaf in the palm of her hand, and gave it to Guadalupe.

"Ah," she said, smelling the sap, then she laughed and they embraced.

AMANDA HALE

"I thought you weren't coming. It's so good to see you. I've had the most wonderful time, Lupe, I've been everywhere. Have you been to Tikal? It's incredible!"

Guadalupe shook her head, smiling. She had seen Tikal on the map. It seemed impossibly far, up by the northern border with Mexico and Belize. She took Paméla's hand and they walked along the pathway under huge trees, red and gold spots of light glancing through the branches, spangling their skin. Guadalupe's heart was lighter than she could remember. She cautioned herself to contain this feeling; she didn't understand it and feared it might be the presager of something terrible. She listened to Paméla's adventures as they passed the tiered pyramids of Iximché. There was so much to say that Guadalupe was silenced by the weight of it, as though if she started she might surprise herself by saying things she hadn't understood until they were spoken. But Paméla questioned her and finally she began to speak. She told her about the village, about the women with their sick children, about the long days and evenings at the clinic, the crowds of people waiting patiently, the ones they'd had to turn away because Doctor Ramírez was exhausted.

"I wish I could help," Paméla said. "I'd like to do something useful."

"You could . . . come with me . . . next time."

"But I must find Fabiana. I haven't given up, Lupe. Something's going to happen when we get back to the capital, I know it."

"I will take you to a special place, where we make our ceremonies." There, she'd said it and her heart was pounding. "You can pray for your mother." She

~ 190 ~

led Paméla down a narrow pathway at the back of the archaeological site which opened into a clearing surrounded by trees. In the centre was a charred circle full of glowing copal embers and, behind it, a mound of stones covered with wax. Guadalupe knelt before the mound and lit two candles, white for purification, yellow for the seed of faith in her heart, the faith of her childhood, reawakened. She sliced a green orange into four sections and offered them, cleansing the stones with the tart juice, splashing her face. A man climbed the rock pile and placed two bunches of flaming candles there, then he took a mouthful of alcohol from a small bottle and spat onto the ground. Paméla watched as a small group of people, dressed in indigenous clothing, paced around the charred circle, spitting into the sizzling copal embers. Tendrils of dark hair escaped from Guadalupe's head covering and her lips moved as, behind closed eyes, she saw her father at the altar in their house, his head bowing rhythmically as he prayed.

"Remember, Calixta, to honor the earth, the stones, the fire, the birds of the air, the rivers and oceans. They remind us of who we are."

She remembered the rough texture of his hand on her arm, the light in his tired eyes. She peeled a scrap of bark from a ceiba trunk, bit her lip and kissed the parchment, then she laid a nugget of copal on the bloody bark and lit it. As she inhaled the aroma of the hard resin, a memory awoke in her of her father speaking through the smoke of the burning copal.

"This is the blood of the trees, see, Calixta, it is red and sweet, given to us for our ceremonies. When it burns it becomes the breath of the Mother-Father."

She brushed her lip where a fly had settled, a flash of shimmering green as it flew, catching her eye.

"Jade carries spirit in the other world, carries the soul to another place. Jade on the eyes blinding the dead, jade in the ears silencing the world, jade in the mouth consuming the breath, spiriting the soul to another world. See the blood of the ancestors circulating inside the funerary jade; everything is over, over and over."

"I offer my blood," she murmured, "*Cha'x a'jan*, you come to drink, soul of the dead on your wings."

∾

Their canoe glided across the lake, soundless save the drip of water off the paddles as they lifted, slicing again into the smooth surface. Fern was a veteran paddler and Hannah had learned from her over many seasons at Uncle Jack's cottage. She was in the back, steering, and had a perfect view of Fern's body, the movement of muscles under her skin as she dipped and lifted, the scapulae lifting with the power of invisible wings, pulling her oar through the water rhythmically. It was at the lake that Fern's body triumphed. They had been there three days and she'd finally relaxed and stopped carrying her entire graduate class. Of course they were her survival; the students, the ideas, the words and books. Hannah had forever imprinted on her retina the image of a tough little girl in cut-off shorts and a pink t-shirt, clutching a book under her arm, squinting into the sun. Fern had been 'shaped like a board' as she put it, the skinniest, smartest kid in her class. When the other kids teased her about her good grades there'd been nothing else to fall back on, so she kept on studying, but by the time she was in her mid-teens it was fashionable to look like a stick insect. The Twiggy look was back, and she was popular suddenly. When she started university everyone wanted to date her, and she'd made up for lost time, rebelling against her Catholic upbringing. Something had to change. Then of course she'd gotten the infection. Strange how the dots connect, Hannah thought, one thing leading to another. There had been lots of time for reflection at the lake. She stared at Fern's neck, the fragility of it, like the stem of a flower that could snap if it were not cherished. They dipped and pulled in perfect rhythm, like one body, joined with the canoe, the water, the earth, the sky. She felt the whole world and Paméla too, as though she were still a baby in her lap, even the weight of her, her lightness and warmth. Hannah's face creased into a smile so persistent that her jaw began to ache. Love hurts, she thought, love and pain are indistinguishable in their extremes. She clasped that moment, knowing that she would need the memory of it to sustain her when they returned to the city.

∾

"Glorifica mi alma al Señor y mi espíritu se llena de gozo, al contemplar la bondad de Dios mi Salvador. Porque ha puesto la mirada en la humilde sierva suya y ved aquí el motivo porque me tendrá por dichosa y feliz todas las generaciones. Pues ha hecho en mi favor cosas grandes y maravillosas . . . " Guadalupe's lips moved silently as she knelt to remove dead blooms from the rose bush at the corner of the courtyard. Petals fell as she snapped heads off. She gathered them in her hands and made a little pile.

"Good morning, Sister." María-Teresa held out her hand and brought Guadalupe up off her knees. "Is this your report?" she asked, pointing to the folder on the bench.

"Yes, I was on my way to your office, Sister."

"We can sit here. The clinic is running well?"

"Yes. Doctor Ramírez was pleased. We saw many follow-up patients with significant improvements." Her light, tripping voice was like water over stones. There was a bubbling beneath the stream that María-Teresa had not heard before.

"You seem . . . refreshed by your journey."

"I am pleased. But there are still too many patients, Sister. We had to work very long hours to fit them all in. Perhaps if we could go to the village more often?"

"What are you pleased about?"

"Our work, the growth of the lilies, the new roses coming . . . " Guadalupe laughed out loud; she couldn't help herself.

"If I didn't know you better, my dear, I would say you were forming an attachment. Doctor Ramírez is a married man."

Guadalupe burst into laughter and immediately sobered, her hand over her mouth. "Oh no, Sister, Doctor Ramírez is a model of decorum. There is no question."

María-Teresa remembered when Guadalupe had entered the convent, a traumatized child on the verge of womanhood. María-Teresa was twenty-one years old then, four years at Casa Central, a seasoned *novicia*. She remembered the moment that had decided her vocation. As a child she had suffered terrible fits of anger that came out of the darkness and left her devastated at the pain she had inflicted. Her mother was a gentle woman who deferred to her husband in everything. There were three more children after María-Teresa, two more girls with the brown skin of their maternal grandmother, then finally a son. Her father was a devout Catholic, but in her mother's face there was only acquiescence, though María-Teresa searched every day for passion. She had strong feelings herself and couldn't believe that anyone might exist without the same intensity. When she began to break things her mother prayed to the Virgin, but when she bloodied her sister's nose her father said, "You've gone too far!" and put her out of the house. She climbed a broad-limbed ceiba in the neighbour's garden and crouched in the fork of two branches. As darkness fell she heard her father calling. She held her breath till he'd gone, but the tension in her limbs made her muscles quiver and she got pins and needles and had to shake her arms and legs to release the blood flow. In the middle of the night the Virgin appeared at the foot of the tree, a strange light all around her as though the pale grass were on fire and the air were being consumed. María-Teresa closed her eyes and opened them again; she was still there. Her lips moved silently and the child heard her, as though the Virgin were inside her head thinking her thoughts.

"You must enter my house, María-Teresa. Give your life in service to my Son and I will save you, child. You are a danger. You must be saved from yourself."

In the morning she entered her father's house and knocked on the door of his study. "Papá, I've received a vision. Madre María wants me for her daughter." His smile told her that her vision was true. Her father's eyes shone, and in the kitchen her mother wept.

María-Teresa loved Guadalupe; she was her atonement. She had nursed her through the initial months when she had stared vacantly and refused to eat. Her care had pulled the girl back slowly, then Mother Superior had given her charge over the babies and she had come to life fully with her quick words and gestures, her bright eyes. When María-Teresa witnessed the transformation she knew they were both saved and she gave thanks to the Virgin.

She sat in her office, the file from the clinic on the desk in front of her. She placed her hand on it and looked at her own slim fingers outlined against the buff folder. A narrow gold band shone on her third finger. She needs my help again. Thirty-five years old, her body crying out for a child. I will guide her through this crisis. I too have suffered such desires and you, Blessed Virgin, have spared me. I will send Sister Rosa to work with Doctor Ramírez next time. It will be Guadalupe's penance, for her own good.

∾

When she looked up he was staring at her and Paméla recognized him immediately. Her hand tightened on Guadalupe's arm as he walked towards them, his arms swinging loose, his body swaying from side to side. *"Buenas días."* He removed his hat with a slight bow. "Your first time in Parque La Aurora?"

"Sí," Paméla replied.

The young man replaced his hat and tilted his head. "I think I've seen you before, no? You were trespassing." He laughed and offered his hand, "My name is Miguel."

"Paméla," she said, placing her hand briefly in his, "And Sister Guadalupe."

He nodded politely, barely able to take his eyes off Paméla. "You wanted to enter the Palacio!" he laughed, "*Qué caramba!* You scared me."

"I still want to," Paméla said.

Miguel shook his head, still laughing. "This is my day off. Will you walk with me?"

Birds chattered from the massive tree canopy above them, so raucous that they seemed almost human. Paméla and Guadalupe rose together, arm in arm.

"We come here," Miguel indicated a cluster of young men nearby, "to meet our compañeras. We're from the same village, Santo Domingo Xenacoj. We come to find work in the capital. Our sisters and cousins work for rich people, as nannies and maids."

When he found out that Paméla was from Canada Miguel threw his hat in the air and caught it with a flourish. He asked if she would be his pen pal and if he might take her to see the animals in the zoological section of the park.

"I don't like to see things in cages."

"But you want to see inside the Palacio, the biggest cage in Guatemala!"

"Will you help me?"

Miguel shrugged in a gesture of apology. "*No es possible,*" he said sadly. They walked in silence for a while, then Miguel asked, "You like to dance? Come with me to La Sanpedrana tonight. They play *música típica* and everyone will be there; my sister, her compañero, my cousins, my brothers."

"Do your brothers work at the Palacio too?"

"My brother Pedro works in the kitchen. He's a cook."

"I like to dance," Paméla said, smiling at Miguel for the first time.

She waited for Miguel the next day on the steps of Catedral Metropolitana, in full view of the Palacio. It had taken all her charm to persuade him to help her and she blessed Hannah and Fern for raising her bilingual; she could never have wheedled her way so far into the heart of the capital without fluent Spanish. They had danced at La Sanpedrana to a tedious selection of outdated North American music: Cindi Lauper singing *Girls Just Wanna Have Fun*; Cher's *Gypsies, Tramps and Thieves*; Michael Jackson's *Beat It*. Miguel had twirled her around the dance floor, his hands hot and clammy on her shoulders. It had been a relief when the *música tipica* came on with its steady repetitive rhythm and the comforting sound of marimbas.

Miguel's face lit up when he saw Paméla and he made a masterful show of embracing her. "Paméla, my Canadian girl. You're the best dancer," he said. He kept his arm firmly around her waist as they crossed Parque Central and walked around to the back of the Palacio, where he led her down a flight of concrete steps to a narrow basement door. "I shouldn't be doing this," he whispered, "But I'm crazy in love with you." He produced a key from his pocket and opened the door, closing it quickly behind them. Immediately he pressed himself against her and tried to kiss her. Paméla held her breath and tried not to move. When she gasped for air he released her, grinning ear to ear, and put his finger to his lips. He took her hand and they tiptoed down a long corridor. It was hot and airless in the basement of the Palacio; she wiped her sweating hand against her skirt and followed Miguel, trying to take note of all the twists and turns. "Behind that door," he pointed across the corridor, "is an underground path that leads to Casa Crema where the president used to live. More than fifty years ago President Carlos Castillo Armas was assassinated in that tunnel. You want to see?"

"Not now," she whispered impatiently. "Where's the kitchen?"

Miguel dragged her down the corridor to a door which revealed a long flight of metal steps. They climbed up, their feet clattering on the metal, and she figured they were on the ground floor of the Palacio as they emerged into another long corridor punctuated with doors at regular intervals. Miguel opened a door on the left and immediately she heard male voices and the clatter of plates. He motioned her to stay where she was and disappeared. Minutes passed before Miguel reappeared with Pedro.

"*Caramba*! You look just like her," Pedro said; the same comment he'd made at La Sanpedrana the night before. Miguel kissed her full on the mouth before she could avoid it, then he ran down the corridor, leaping in the air. "*Venga*," Pedro said, starting off in the other direction.

After a long, labyrinthine journey through the innards of the fortress, they reached an open courtyard, bordered by a colonnade. "We're in the centre of the Palacio. Turn right at the end and there's a door. The romance suite is there," Pedro grinned.

"*Gracias*," she said, clasping his hands, afraid suddenly.

Pedro blushed. "Don't tell them nothing," he said. "I'm risking a lot for you."

Paméla was alone in the final approach. As she turned, she found herself under a stone archway that opened into a colonnade of grey stone pillars where sun penetrated into a courtyard containing a rectangle of yellowed grass. To her left, at the end of the colonnade, was a heavy wooden door. She walked up to it and knocked. There was no answer and she knocked again, her heart beating high in her throat. I'll wait, she thought, I've come all this way. She sat on the warm stone at the corner of the rectangle, feeling as though she were in a bad movie and might fall any moment onto the cutting room floor.

Fabiana lay in rumpled sheets watching the play of light on her belly. She had lain like this for hours at a time, her mind vacant while her body entwined with a part of Ernesto's life. She remembered how he'd come to her and pulled her by the shoulders, up from the sidewalk where she'd been crouched in a doorway. She had smelled the alcohol on his breath as he dragged her along the street, lurching from side to side. She'd been afraid he was from the police and that he would put her in jail, but he had taken her to a hotel and fallen on top of her, fumbling. She was still sore from the birth and had cried out when he tried to enter her.

"Please don't cry," he'd said, "please, please, no more crying." In his drunkeness he'd started babbling about the smell of burning in his hair and on his clothes, crazy talk. He'd ripped off his clothing and sat naked on the bed, arms clasped around his knees while he stared into the distance and spoke of swollen bodies floating in the river, bubbling flesh lumped into unrecognizable shapes. He had talked until dawn, his eyes staring into the darkness, and Fabiana had listened without understanding. Then, as light crept slowly through the blinds, he had lain down and she had held him in her thin arms, cradling his head, heavy on her collarbone. When he woke there was a new light in his eyes as he gazed down at her. "*Mi niña,*" he'd said, "You've saved me."

She jumped up when she heard the knocking. It must be Ernesto, she thought. But why doesn't he use his key? She dressed hurriedly, smoothing the sheets and pulling up the covers, then she opened the blinds to look, but Ernesto was not there. Someone was sitting, her back curved, head bent. Fabiana moved silently towards the door.

Paméla didn't hear the door open. She heard a sharp clicking of heels and turned, her face in shadow, and saw an image of herself standing in the archway. At first she thought it was her own shadow, standing behind her, cast into the future. Then it spoke.

"Who are you? What do you want?"

"Paméla . . . " Her mouth was dry and sticky, her tongue threatening to choke her. "Flor de Maya . . . "

"What are you talking about?"

"I am your daughter," she said, moving out of the shadows. Paméla reached out her arms, but the woman gasped and took a step back, her stiff arms outstretched, palms flattened against Paméla's approach.

"No, no," she said. "You must not come here."

"Please, don't send me away," Paméla begged, and she began telling her nightmare, as she had told María-Teresa, as she had told Guadalupe, hardly aware of who she was telling as she ran the movie yet again. As the words tumbled, splashing in the blood of the village, tracking the jungle floor, the woman's hands rose in the air, covering her ears. She fell to her knees and hunched in on herself like a wounded bird and Paméla, silent now, embraced her mother. She felt a frozen stillness in her before the shuddering broke. She held on tightly until she heard footsteps and the squeak of leather; a handsome man striding into the courtyard, encased in the tight uniform of a general.

"*Qué pasa aquí?*" he asked, taking hold of Fabiana's arm, pulling her to her feet. She looked up at him, her face strangely blank.

"*Mi niña,*" she said, "*Mi niña, Ernesto. Mira.*"

He looked at Paméla, and his frown dissolved into a slow smile. "*Qué bonita!*" he whistled. "How did she get in?"

"I brought her," Fabiana said quickly. "Come, we must go in. I need to talk with her."

Ernesto hesitated a moment, then opened the door. The room they entered had a high ceiling with moulded cornices and a large stone fireplace. The chairs were monumental, covered with red velvet studded onto curlicued wood. The general threw himself into one of these chairs and leaned back, the shining leather of his boots squeaking as he crossed his legs.

"Come, we will go to my bedroom," Fabiana said, touching Paméla's shoulder hesitantly. Ernesto nodded, his face a mask.

Paméla moved like a sleepwalker into the spacious bedroom with its large canopied bed. She looked around her at the lead-paned casement windows giving onto the courtyard, the heavy, floor-to-ceiling drapes, the carved wooden headboard rising above the brocade bedspread, the huge candelabra in the centre of a marble mantel, obscured by nights of dripping wax. Then her eyes came to rest on Fabiana's face and it was like looking in the mirror.

"How did you find me?"

"I went to Casa Central."

"Ah, the Sisters. They took you from me. They said they would send you away to a better life, but it broke my heart."

They heard the creaking of the general's boots, the thud of the door as he left the apartment. His shadow fell across Fabiana's face as he passed the window, obscuring the sunlight for a moment.

Paméla turned and caught their reflection in a long gilt mirror hanging on the wall. "Look at us!" she said. They stared at each other in the smoky glass, twinned in all but time, only fourteen years apart. "We're like sisters." She watched herself take her mother's mirrored hand, the slow entwining of their fingers, everything slowing, her heart thundering in her chest at the feel of Fabiana's skin. "If you knew how long I've dreamed of this," she heard herself say, the words stretching and distorting as they left her mouth. They moved together silently and climbed onto the bed where they lay curled into each other, one translucent, the other opaque with the years. Fabiana brought her small hand up to Paméla's face and cupped her cheek, exploring with her eyes and her fingers, stroking her hair rhythmically.

"It was my life you dreamed," she said finally.

Paméla tried to speak, but she could not. Fabiana's words echoed deep in her skull, deafening her. "So it happened," she said finally, her tongue thick behind swollen lips. "Everything?"

"Everything. You're the only one who knows."

Paméla could hardly distinguish one object from another in the room. She felt miles away, a pinpoint in the universe, and yet so large that she could not maneuver her body. Fabiana's red shoes lay, one in the corner with the metal-tipped heel pointing upwards, the other on its side near the door, pulsing against the heavily-grained wood. Her head felt light as though it were spinning her body away to another place. "*Madre*," she whispered, and with a great effort she began to trace the outline of Fabiana's face with her finger, their hearts beating together in the long silence, seeking the old rhythm of each other. "What happened?"

"I ran away from Casa Central. Ernesto found me on the street. I was so hungry."

The room was beginning to focus around her, objects coming clearly into view, her mother's world. "Ernesto?"

"He is my life," Fabiana whispered, her eyes riveted on Paméla as though she could not believe in her existence.

"The general? Is he my father?"

"No."

"Who was he?"

"He was Spanish, a Ladino." Fabiana bowed her head. "I'm sorry, it was a long time ago, I can't tell you any more."

Paméla shook her head back and forth, clearing it, trying to bring herself into the moment. As she shook she gathered energy. "I'm *your* daughter . . . yours, yours, Mamá. I can't believe it. Here we are together finally. Are you real? Oh tell me you're real."

"Yes, yes! I've thought about you every day, and for a long time I've felt you, I knew you were coming. But I didn't believe it."

Paméla watched dust particles dance in the sunlight, little explosions from Fabiana's mouth as she spoke, each word flying through the air, settling in the folds of the heavy curtains.

"You were so eager to come into the world. I couldn't stop you. They had to cut me."

The room was filled with whispers, all the words piling on top of each other, collapsing in sighs and sweet sounds, the honey of Fabiana's voice trickling down Paméla's throat, silencing her.

"I only held you once, but I've never forgotten the feeling of your life in my arms. You were a miracle," she said, a faraway look in her eyes.

"Will you come with me," Paméla asked very slowly.

"I can't leave."

"Why? Do you have children with — ?"

"Ernesto has children with his wife. But I belong to him. That will never change," she said vehemently. Then she buried her face in her hands and sobbed. "Oh, why did you come!"

Paméla held her shoulders and rocked with her. "Mamá, Mamá, I had to find you. The dream . . . your life . . . things I need to know. What was the name of your village?"

Fabiana shook her head. "All I remembered was my name and my language, Mam."

"Your village was in Huehuetenango?"

"How do you know?"

"I know the names of the villages that were destroyed, 440 villages, Mamá, destroyed by the army under Rios Montt's scorched earth policy. They learned it from the CIA, because the American army did the same thing in Vietnam in the 1960s. There was the Panzos massacre in 1978, San Francisco-Nenton in '82, Chuabaj Grande, Corinto, Chajul-Quiché — "

"Shh, you mustn't speak of these things." Fabiana's eyes were wide with fear. "*No es seguro a hablar de esto,*" she whispered.

Paméla stroked her mother's hair, dark and silky like her own. "Let's go outside and sit on the grass. I want to feel the sun."

"No! There's danger everywhere, even in the Palacio. On the street there are *orejas*, everywhere spies and murderers. Dolores hid in the *tamascal*, the steambath in our village. They found her, my sister. They cut her throat. They cut open the bellies of the women who were big. I saw a baby lying in a pool of blood, its mouth opening and closing like a fish." Fabiana's face was like stone, all the life gone from her voice. "*Disculpe, disculpe, perdóneme,* I can't remember the name of my village. I'm sorry."

"It's all right, Mamá, it's all right. Now that I've found you I don't ever want to lose you again."

The door slammed in the outer room and Fabiana shuddered. She jumped up and ran for her shoes. She reached the bedroom door and was wobbling on one heel, pulling on the other shoe, just as Ernesto knocked. "*Mi corazón,*" she said, throwing the door open wide, "Where have you been?"

"Outside, only outside," he said gently, his big hand stroking her hair. He nodded to Paméla who was still sitting in the middle of the bed, a shocked expression on her face. She felt as one might feel being interrupted with a lover.

"You are a guest. You are welcome, but now you must go. You see, your mother is tired."

Paméla rose from the bed, her face flushed with anger. She smoothed the covers with great attention to detail, then she walked towards them and offered her hand to Ernesto. "My name is Paméla," she said.

"*Mucho gusto.*" He gripped her hand. He smelled of cigarette smoke.

"I'll come tomorrow in the afternoon, to the office at the front of the Palacio. Tell the guard to bring me here."

Ernesto turned to Fabiana, his eyebrows raised. She nodded. "Very well," he said, "Three o'clock."

Paméla tried to kiss Fabiana's cheek but caught her earlobe instead as she turned her face to Ernesto. "Will you see me out, Mamá? I don't remember the way."

"Please, I will call a guard to escort you." Ernesto was already dialing on a cell phone he'd taken from his breast pocket like a pack of cigarettes. He spoke rapidly into the mouthpiece then clicked the phone off. "A guard will meet you in the courtyard immediately."

She was dismissed. She felt his eyes on her as she walked across the outer room and let herself out.

Fabiana laid her head in the crook of Ernesto's arm, her dark hair spread across his chest. She felt herself curled by the hearth, heard hands slapping, shaping the tortillas, *thunk, thunk* as they landed in the steaming *comal*. Circles of light danced across the floor, flickering like fish in moving water. She felt Ernesto's hand laying lightly on her belly and a tear trickled into her ear.

"*Mi amor*," she murmured.

"More than twenty years and still it's for you that I live, no one else," he said as he rose from the bed and leaned down to kiss her.

The years were densely woven in her body, tied and wrapped and intricately worked so that she could no longer feel where the threads began or ended. All the loose ends were secured and she inside again, swinging in a hammock; red, yellow, turquoise, blue and gold. She watched Ernesto as he dressed, buttoning his shirt, pulling up the fly of his tight pants, smoothing his ruffled hair with the palm of his hand. He was a handsome man, proud of his good looks. He sat on the edge of the bed and pulled on his boots. The effort brought out beads of sweat on his brow. When he turned to kiss her mouth her eyes were a question.

"The boy has a football match," he said. "I must be there, it's important."

"Will you come tonight?"

He hesitated a moment. "I'll try."

In truth he was her captive. She was the only one who gave him freedom. Ernesto's wife expected him to be everything he was not and, although she rarely questioned his absence, she wanted him to be there at the appropriate times to play the proud generalísimo: at dinner parties and family fiestas, at the girls' concerts and graduations, for their son's sporting events. Alicia was titillated by his reputation and she liked him to be rough with her, to take her to the edge of her bourgeois existence. She had been born into a wealthy Ladino family and would never know what it was like to be an Indio, but Alicia loved to flirt with possibility. She was a frustrated actress and the generalísimo was her leading man. It was Fabiana who knew the real Ernesto, naked, free of all reference. He shed his skin when he entered their secret apartment. It was a bunker, sealed against intruders . . . until now.

"Will you bring tortillas?"

"You can make them, no?"

She wound her arms around his neck. "Bring me some fresh from the tortillería, Ernesto. And *pan dulce* for our breakfast." She wanted the energy of someone else's hands, slapping the tortillas from palm to palm, flipping them into the *comal*, feeding her with their life.

"There's a reception tonight. I must attend."

"I'll wait for you."

"*Mi amor.*" He kissed her tenderly, cupping her face in his big hands. It was always a wrench to leave her.

He left the bedroom briskly and was through the living room in four strides and out the door, marching down the colonnade. How did the girl get in here? There must have been a security breach. He didn't believe that Fabiana had brought her. She was covering for someone. He sensed her fear and was determined to protect her. He owed it to her, because she had saved him.

Now that he was gone her mind exploded with memory. It wouldn't stop. She paced the room, but she couldn't stop the shuttered images slicing through her brain. She ran out into the courtyard half expecting Paméla to be there, but the colonnade was deserted, the pale grass brittle in the shadows. Had she dreamed her? She crouched by a pillar and leaned her cheek against the warm stone

∾

1528: The flotilla was stocked like a sailing circus. The prodigal did not intend to arrive home empty-handed. Cortés ordered the holds of his galleons to be filled with caged creatures; jaguars and ocelots, chattering monkeys, hummingbirds and quetzals. The decks teemed with tumbling acrobats and conjurors, dwarfs and albinos, time travellers crossing into another world. Cortés' hearty laugh rang out during the long voyage as he triumphed at the gaming tables, scooping up his winnings and tossing back shots of brandy. His luck at cards had not deserted him, nor his bravado in the face of a dubious homecoming after twenty-four years. Surrounded by his men and flanked by his loyal friends, Gonzalo de Sandoval and Andrés de Tápia, he resolved to act the Spanish *hidalgo* and father legitimate sons in order to win back his governance of New Spain. He paraded the deck, striding along the slippery planks in long stockings and ribboned shoes, carrying Martín on his shoulders. He was an exultant hunchback with his velvet cape flung against the biting wind, covering the boy's body and his own.

"What is it like in Spain, Papá?" Martín chirped, a bird on the head of his father's hump.

"It is a great land filled with birds and animals, and more horses than you've ever seen, Martín. There are olive trees and vineyards bursting with fruit, multitudes of people with big families, and churches, many churches. Spain is governed by a powerful king whose Court moves from Barcelona to Madrid, Valladolid to Toledo, wherever he goes, across plains and deserts, with all his retinue."

"What is a desert, Papá?"

"A desert, Martín, is a dry place with sand and red earth, bright and warm in the day, cold and harsh at night, and sometimes beautiful flowers spring out of the earth like miracles."

"Will Mamá be there before us?"

In the privacy of his cabin Cortés slumped with head in hands and prayed to the Virgin to release him. "Give me back my heart, Blessed Virgin. Marina has bewitched me. Free me from my desire for her savage body." He smelled her skin, soft and musky, travelled her body, exploring valleys and rivers, mountains and volcanoes, smooth plains and thick undergrowth. He was haunted by the sad little face of his son looking out to sea, watching for his mother. He marvelled at the child's memory. He too must learn to live with a burdened heart. Cortés abandoned his prayers and took another swig of brandy.

Sandoval died of ship's fever soon after their arrival at the port of Palos de la Frontera. No sooner was he buried than news came of another death; old Martín Cortés, gone before he could see his grandson. Cortés had written to his father about the boy and had anticipated their meeting — a gathering of blood, their line continuing — but now it was curtailed. He travelled with Andrés de Tápia and young Martín to his birthplace, the town of Medellín, where he embraced his grieving mother and knelt at his father's tomb in the church of Santiago. Weighted with loss, Cortés wanted only to return to Mexico and govern his lands. He put Martín into the charge of Tápia, who promised to deliver the child to Cortés' relatives, while Cortés himself hurried to reassemble his scattered circus and catch up with the king's retinue, thence to defend himself and petition for recognition of his achievements in New Spain. Although his eyes were dull with grief and his forty-two-year-old body was losing vitality, desire still lived in him as it had in the full-blooded youth who had scaled Doña Carmen's wall in Salamanca, his head filled with chivalric tales.

"I give you another chance," said Carlos magnanimously, reaching for an oyster stuffed with anchovies. Cortés watched the king's cheeks puff, hanging on his words, laboriously translated by a poker-faced courtier. Carlos was German, born in Ghent, and he spoke Flemish and German, but little Spanish. His long Hapsburg jaw moved up and down as he chewed the fishy mess and swallowed finally, smacking his lips.

"The estates confiscated by us in your absence in the wilderness are returned to you, in perpetuity, for you and your line. I declare you Marqués del Valle de Oaxaca. You may return to New Spain as a *hidalgo,* a gentleman of means with estates and palaces filled with Indian servants. You have served us well, Don Hernándo, and now you may rest on your laurels."

The muscle in Cortés' jaw trembled as the king's proclamation was translated, then it froze as he clamped his teeth together. I'm being pensioned off, he thought as his past glories called down the years, mocking him. He wanted governance, nothing else would do. The cruel streak in him hardened as he began to plot. He would not surrender.

Martín lay shivering in his new bed under a new sky. He'd felt cold ever since he'd arrived in his uncle's house, even though it was early summer and the sweet smell of orange blossom drifted through the windows. He missed the close heat of Mexico-Tenochtitlan, the smell of the kitchen and the cobbled courtyard where he had played. It was all he'd ever known of the world, that he could remember, and the sweet spicy smell of his Mamá's skin as she'd held him close. When Señor Tápia had left the house he'd felt the last thread breaking and he had disgraced himself by crying. "Where is Mamá? I want my Mamá!" His aunt had crossed herself, her thin lips pressed close together, then she'd picked him up in her arms and carried him to bed. As she had tucked him

in she had explained to him about his new home, that he
would not see his Mamá again, but Martín didn't believe
her. When she'd gone he climbed out of bed and stood
at the window. Everything was quiet. He looked up
into the sky and saw the moon, full and round, shining
down on the earth. He had seen the moon many times
before they'd crossed the ocean. It was the same moon,
he felt sure. He had watched it growing rounder as the
days passed, just as it grew rounder at home and then
disappeared bit by bit until the sky was dark. He padded
over to the bed, his bare feet silent on the cold tiles, and
felt in his clothing for the leather pouch. He pinched the
dry leaves; *ruda*, a familiar smell. He crumbled a leaf on
his tongue and held it there, savouring the taste. He felt
his Mamá close by and he was comforted.

∾

Guadalupe's thoughts were far away beyond the
convent walls as she washed her clothes at the *pila*, her
hands deep in the basin. She jumped when she felt a tap
on her shoulder.

"Come, Sister Lupe. We're wanted in Sister María-
Teresa's office." Sister Rosa tugged at her sleeve.

"What is it?" She was annoyed by the intrusion on
her reverie.

"It's not for us to question, Sister. We are summoned.
Quickly, quickly, you can finish that later."

Guadalupe had often marvelled at Sister Rosa's
acceptance of authority. She prayed for such humility
and obedience.

María-Teresa greeted them with a smile. She clasped
Guadalupe's hands and looked deep into her eyes.

"Sister?"

"Sit down. I have something to tell you both." The Huixoc clinic folder lay on her desk. She ran her hand across it, paused a moment, then looked up and began to speak, her eyes shifting back and forth from Guadalupe to Rosa. "I've been speaking with Doctor Ramírez. He is appreciative of your efforts at the clinic, Guadalupe, but he has requested the assistance of a more mature Sister for his clinical work. You will accompany him on the next tour of duty, Sister Rosa."

"But why?" Guadalupe exclaimed. "I know all the patients! I know everyone in the village! Can't I go too?"

María-Teresa inclined her head sympathetically and leaned across her desk. "My dear, this is a delicate situation. Doctor Ramírez feels that with an older nun to assist him perhaps more of the men in the village will come forward for treatment."

"But he never spoke to me of this."

Sister Rosa clicked her tongue in disapproval.

"This change comes through no personal fault, Sister. You must rise above your disappointment and think of the good of the whole village."

"But Sister Rosa doesn't speak their language."

"You mustn't worry about these details, Guadalupe. One of the Spanish-speaking villagers can translate."

"But there's more to translation than — "

"I've thought very carefully about this matter."

"Of course." Guadalupe bowed her head over twisting fingers, her face flushed with anger.

"Sister Rosa?"

"Yes, yes, Sister, I am happy to serve."

"I knew I could rely on you. Sister Lupe will go over the file with you and brief you on each of the patients. You can go now, Sister. I'm sure you have plenty to do in preparation. The next clinic is, I believe — "

"In two weeks," Guadalupe said curtly. "You will travel with Doctor Ramírez in his car, if it is working. If not you must take the morning bus, Sister Rosa, at eight o'clock."

As soon as Rosa had left the room María-Teresa rose and walked over to Guadalupe. She stood behind her chair and rested her hands gently on Guadalupe's shoulders, her fingers clenching as she kneaded, reaching up into the muscles of her neck. "Relax, my dear. I understand the tension you're under. It will pass and you'll look back and smile to remember these difficulties."

"What difficulties?" Guadalupe whirled around. "I have no difficulties in the village, Sister. I don't understand."

"I've tried to be as discreet as possible, Guadalupe, to save your dignity. You must trust me. You are in my charge and I pray every day for your soul." María-Teresa's face was solemn, but her eyes glittered and suddenly Guadalupe understood and she covered her mouth to stifle her laughter. "Pray for strength, my child."

"Yes, Sister, I will go to the chapel. Thank you, Sister, thank you." She took María-Teresa's hands and kissed them.

∾

Paméla arrived promptly at the Palacio and a stony-faced guard escorted her to the colonnade leading to

Fabiana's apartment. When she rounded the corner she saw her there, alone in the courtyard, leaning against a pillar, smoking. Paméla watched her for a few moments before she spoke. "Mamá." Fabiana whirled around, fear and then surprise streaking across her face. She threw her cigarette to the ground, crushed it with the toe of her high-heeled shoe, and ran to Paméla. As they embraced Paméla felt the slight dampness of Fabiana's freshly washed hair. She wore a subtle trace of lipstick and she smelled of cigarette smoke and roses.

"Ah, my child. I hardly dared to believe it was true." She took Paméla's face in her hands, cradling it like a precious object, then she pinched her cheeks and laughed. "I thought perhaps you were a dream."

"It's a dream come true. Are you all right, Mamá. You look tired."

"I couldn't sleep last night," she said, still gazing into Paméla's eyes. "You've turned my life upside down." She turned abruptly, grasping her hand. "Come inside. I'll make coffee."

Paméla followed her into the apartment, through the shuttered living room, into a small kitchen in the back. "Do you still wish I hadn't come?"

Fabiana shrugged, a gesture of helplessness. She tried to smile but her face contorted. "I don't know." Her hands moved, trying to grasp the air. "I've longed for this, for you to come to me, but now I don't know. It's the memories . . . too painful."

"I'm sorry."

Fabiana turned away and busied herself with the coffee, spooning finely ground beans into a pot, adding water, lighting a blue flame.

"Mamá, what happened after you left your village?"

"Ah, my child, don't ask me these questions. It's too difficult for me."

"I'm sorry, but I have a right to know. Promise you'll tell me, when you're ready."

Fabiana turned to face her. She took her hands and looked deeply into Paméla's eyes. "You must be patient with me."

"I have lots of time." She looked around the tiny kitchen, at the cracked blue tiles, the two-ringed burner, the deep sink. She took a few steps, casting around for something. "*Puerta* . . . door," she said, pointing, "*Muro* . . . wall, *cocina* . . . kitchen . . . "

Fabiana's face flushed with anger. "What are you saying to me?"

"It's English, Mamá. This is what we speak in Canada." She touched Fabiana's hair, feeling the softness, wanting to smell its freshness and rub her face against it. "*Pelo* . . . hair, *piel* . . . skin." She caressed her mother's cheek, unable to keep her hands off her, but Fabiana pushed her away, scratching her wrist with her long nails.

"Enough!" she said sharply, "I've already learned Spanish." She stared into Paméla's eyes as though she were looking for something there, then she shook her head and turned away. Paméla licked the blood from her wrist where the veins stood blue against her brown skin. She remembered a kitten that Fern had brought home from the SPCA and how it had lashed out at her with its sharp claws. She'd cried and Hannah had hugged her better and put a band-aid on the scratch. It was strange to think of her two mothers now that she'd found her real mother. She stood silently while Fabiana brewed the coffee and poured it into two cups arranged on a small plastic tray with spoons and a bowl of sugar. "Leche?" Paméla shook her head. "Negro."

They entered the cavernous living room with its monumental furniture and the whirring of the ceiling fan high above them, powerful enough to lift the hem of Fabiana's skirt as she passed under it. It was a man's domain, filled with dark wood and leather. Fabiana had made no mark on it. She sat like a child with nothing to say, crossing and uncrossing her legs. Paméla was strangely moved by the sight of her mother's bare legs and her old-fashioned stiletto heels with pointed toes. She wanted to hold her, to stroke her body and smell her skin, but there was a distance between them and Paméla didn't know how to bridge it.

"Do you remember Guadalupe at Casa Central?"

Fabiana shook her head.

"Calixta?"

"Ah, Calixta! Yes, I remember her. She was a girl, like me."

"She looked after me when I was a baby."

"She spoke Mam, but the nuns made us speak Spanish."

"Is that why you were angry with me in the kitchen?"

Fabiana shook her head. "*Perdoneme, mi niña.* What about Calixta?"

"She told me where to find you. We've become friends. Could *we* be friends, Mamá? Would you come out with me tomorrow? We could go to Parque Aurora."

"We've already been there, together."

"What d'you mean?"

"When you were inside me," she whispered.

Paméla slid from her chair and knelt at Fabiana's feet. She laid her head in Fabiana's lap, her head pressed against her belly, her face resting between her thighs, so she didn't hear the footsteps. Ernesto opened the door and took a step back in surprise. "*Ah, la hija,*" he said, recovering himself. "*Cómo estás?*" He grasped Paméla's hand and pulled her to her feet, appraising her with a subtle smile, then he leaned down to kiss Fabiana. "*Mi corazón.*"

"I wasn't expecting you, Ernesto."

"My business is finished for the day." He threw himself into a leather chair and crossed a booted leg over his knee.

"Would you like coffee?" she asked and, without waiting for a reply, she hurried to the kitchen.

"This is very good for our country, to have American tourists."

"I'm Canadian," Paméla said, bristling.

"Everyone is welcome," he said with a nonchalant gesture, then in slow deliberate Spanish, "But always there comes time for the vacation to end."

"This is not a vacation, Ernesto. I came to find my mother."

The general leaned forward and dropped his voice. "I must speak honestly with you. Fabiana is in delicate health. It's unsettling for her to see you after all these years. She was awake in the night, crying. If you love your mother, Señorita, you will return to your own country now, you understand?"

"This is my own country. And I've only just found her. I'm not leaving now!"

"Shhh. This apartment is our refuge. We don't want disturbance here."

They heard the clink of a cup and saucer in the kitchen, then footsteps.

"Please, my ticket's good till August 1st. There's time for her to get used to me, for us to . . . " Paméla stopped as Fabiana entered the room.

She stooped to give Ernesto his coffee and he held her there with his arm and whispered rapidly in her ear. *"No viene aquí otra vez . . . terminado . . . desembarazarse de ella."*

Paméla caught the gist of it — "Mustn't come here again . . . finished . . . get rid of her."

"But Ernesto . . . " Fabiana began.

He sprang to his feet and strode across the room like a caged tiger. "Good-bye, good-bye," he said in exaggerated English. "I will wait outside while you say goodbye to your mother, then I will escort you to the Palacio gate." In two seconds he was gone, leaving the women in confusion. They could see him through the slats of the shutters, pacing back and forth outside, smoking a cigarette, his body strangely disjointed by the horizontal lines of the shutters.

"Mamá? What are we to do? He says I can't come here again."

Fabiana seemed unable to speak.

"I must see you. Meet me tomorrow," she whispered urgently. She shook Fabiana's shoulders gently. "Mamá?"

Fabiana snapped upright suddenly, as though waking from a dream. "Peñalba," she said.

"Peñalba? What's that?"

"A restaurant, on Avenida 6, half way down, on the left."

"Ten o'clock?"

She nodded. "In two days."

"But that's too long."

Fabiana held up two fingers. "Two days."

"Alright. I'll buy you breakfast." Paméla leaned forward and kissed her mother, holding her face a moment, their eyes locked, then she walked across the room and let herself out.

Ernesto was waiting. He put his arm around Paméla's shoulders and started walking her down the colonnade. She turned her head and looked pointedly at his hand, but he didn't seem to notice. "We both want the best for your Mamá, yes? It's difficult for her, you understand. She didn't want to tell you herself."

She tried to say something, to protest, but she couldn't think. His touch had drained the energy from her body. He talked on and on until they reached the guard station.

"Claudio! You will escort the Señorita. A great pleasure," he said, removing his arm finally and grasping her hand. "Goodbye, goodbye, *que le vaya bien.*"

∾

Juan de Jaramillo absented himself from the house with increasing frequency. His fortune was rising. He'd been proclaimed lieutenant of the city and granted a tract of wooded land beside the wall of Chapultepec. He'd set to and built a grand residence there, but when it came time to move their household Malintzín refused to go.

"I want to return to my homeland, Juan. You've secured your lands with this marriage, now let me go."

"And you have secured your position in this city, Marina."

"I don't deny it," she said wearily. "But this is not my place. I want to go home."

"What about María?"

"She will stay here with you, her father."

"You are an unnatural woman."

"I have done my best, husband, but I am worn with longing for the earth of my homeland."

"And what of your child? You think she won't long for her mother?"

"María will be better cared for in your household."

"By Zaachila?"

"Zaachila will come with me. I will find a woman to take care of María."

"Perhaps I will find a woman . . . another wife," he said defiantly.

"As you please. I grant you your freedom and make no claim on you."

One more journey east, past Cholula — risen again under the eyes of three great volcanoes — and across Mount Orizaba. The two women huddled together for warmth in the bone-chilling night; they hugged each other and jumped up and down in the morning to start the circulation in their frozen feet; then descended into the fetid swampland of the Gulf where Malintzín felt embraced by the air, as though a swaddling blanket had been wrapped around her. It was a journey with a sense of finality, following her heart's desire, each step bringing her closer to him.

"When he returns he will land on the Gulf coast," she said. "I will wait for him."

She stood at the edge of the cliff, on the lands assigned her by Cortés, her body a beacon above the pounding waves that wore the rocks smooth. Malintzín was home, rooted again in the dark earth of the town of Paynala where her father had once ruled. She stood above the ocean, a closed circle, filled with a knowledge she could not have suspected when she'd stood on this same cliff, a child in her father's shadow. She waited and waited until the reality of Cortés' words reached her, echoing over the interminable days.

"The Indian will be trained out of him . . . my true son and heir . . . a Knight of the Order of Santiago . . . our customs and our ways within the Holy Catholic Church . . . "

Martín would not be coming back. Cortés would not come. She'd lost count of the moons. She could wait forever, but they would not come. Jaramillo's child stirred in her, unmistakably.

"I'm going to the river," she told Zaachila, "Stay in the house with my family. There are tortillas to be made. We are many people."

They were living with Malintzín's mother in the household of her half-brother, Lázaro, the young *cacique.*

When she reached the river she stood on the bank listening to the rushing water. The river was swollen with summer rain and Malintzín was affected by its turbulence. This was not the gurgling stream she remembered from childhood. The river had grown with her, swelling with the power of her heart, and it pulled her now as she plunged her toes, knees, thighs, her green skirt lifting. She walked into the water, her toes squelching the mud, until she was inside the dark water swimming for the cave on the far bank, finally escaping the men from Xicalango. Her heart filled as her limbs knifed through the water. Who will guide me through my journey on earth, O Lord Quetzalcoatl, now that you are gone?

"You will rule over many people, but never over your own heart."

Malintzín was swept downriver, held by the current as she swam in its arms.

"Death and destruction in your wake . . . "

But her people were recovering, moving towards their destiny, mestizo nationalism growing from their mixed blood with a force as strong as the *maíz*. Blood pounded in her ears as she entered the cave. She began to remember everything as she swam towards the light of a sinkhole high in the roof of the cave. She remembered the golden ring on her father's wrist, the smell of her mother's hair, music of the river running over stones, earth on her tongue, the God moving inside her, teeth tearing horsemeat on the retreat from Tenochtitlan, baby kicking inside her belly, copal burning, Martí's tiny fingers circling her finger, his wrist but a crease. Malintzín's heart constricted as she broke the surface and gulped for breath, her eyes filling with the sky until she saw nothing, only heard the snapping of a ceiba branch as she pulled herself out of the cave and fell backwards into the mouth of the feathered serpent, travelling the bright tunnel of his body into the radiant earth, one, silent.

Zaachila found Malintzín's green skirt on the far bank of the river, hidden in the weeds like a discarded skin. She clutched the damp fabric to her breast and wept. She was far from home, a home that no longer existed. She was bereft.

∽

Guadalupe knelt in the chapel of the Medalla Milagrosa. A brilliant light played behind her closed eyes and she smelled the aroma of lilies as she felt again the soft thud of their collision, lilies flying from her hands, the earth receiving them, joined without yet having seen each other. She opened her eyes, but no one was there, no one except her Sisters and a few people who'd come in off the street to pray. The battered lilies had taken root and grown in the corner of the courtyard. She hoped Paméla was safe. There had been no word since she had gone to La Sanpedrana with Miguel.

∽

Paméla found herself talking once again through a pane of glass.

"Does your mother have a passport?" The man spoke into a microphone.

"No, I told you, she's never been outside Guatemala. I want you to issue her a passport as a refugee with me as her sponsor." The general's attempt to come between her and Fabiana had brought out her fighting spirit. She knew he was lying, that Fabiana wanted her to stay, and she knew that her mother was the sole survivor of a terrible massacre and that she needed help.

"Señorita, this is the Canadian Consulate. We don't issue passports for Guatemalan nationals. And officially there are no more refugees since the peace was declared in '96. You must apply from Canada to sponsor her." Enrique Ruiz smiled apologetically when he saw her face drop. "These are the rules. Also, you're in the wrong place. Immigration is downstairs and I'm sorry, it'll be a long wait."

Paméla's face flushed. She took a deep breath. "OK, first of all, where can she get a passport?"

Señor Ruiz was hungry. He rubbed his little round belly. He'd lingered in bed with his wife and missed breakfast. It had definitely been worth it, he thought, remembering her eager kisses, the warmth of her breasts pressing against him, but now his stomach rumbled painfully. "Here is the address." He scribbled on a notepad. "Also she needs a medical examination." He pulled off the page with a flourish and pushed it under the glass.

"If there's no more refugee program how can I sponsor her?"

"As a relative. She's your mother, isn't she? They'll tell you all about it at Immigration, two floors down," he gestured with his thumb. "In my opinion she won't stay. Everyone comes back. It's the tortillas."

Paméla stared at him, dumbfounded.

"We Guatemalans love our tortillas and frijoles. Nowhere in the world do they have tortillas and frijoles like in Guatemala. I've been in the United States, and their tortillas, huh, like cardboard. You can't eat them. And the frijoles, agh, those gringos don't know how to cook beans. It's a small thing, yes, but it's important."

"Is there a way to sponsor her without going back to Canada."

He stared at her with heavy-lidded eyes and sighed. It was almost time for his lunch break. He scribbled something and handed her the note. "Give this to the receptionist at Immigration and she'll take you to my friend, Alejandro. Maybe you won't have to wait all day. *Buena suerte.* Good luck, Señorita."

When Paméla emerged from the Immigration building two hours later the afternoon heat held the city in a close embrace. She heard the clamour of traffic and honking horns in the distance from the Obelisco, a monument to Guatemala's independence marking the intersection of Avenida La Reforma and Calle 13. Her spirits were soaring after the interview with Alejandro. She walked briskly down the broad, leafy street through Zona 10. *Dearest Hannah, this is my plan. You get the sponsorship thing started in Canada, and I'll help Fabiana with her passport.* Bougainvillea spilled down high walls topped with glass fragments embedded in concrete. *We'll put a rush on it. We have six weeks, that should be long enough, but I may need you to send some money.* Fuego del bosque trumpeted forth its orange flowers. *I've already started the application for her visa. She'll come with me for a visit, then, if she decides to stay the sponsorship will already be under way and . . .* Tall palms sliced the sunlight with their shadows. She passed a high wrought-iron gate, beside it a brass plaque with a German name . . . *and I can return to Guatemala with her, file the sponsorship papers and she can officially emigrate with me as her legal sponsor. Brilliant, eh!* Paméla saw two Mayan girls in maids' uniforms, shaking a carpet. Dust rose in the hazy air and from somewhere far away she heard a dog barking. *You'll love her. She's beautiful, just like an older version of me. I feel like I've finally grown up.*

Paméla hurried downtown to send her e-mail. She was impatient to get everything organized. It never occurred to her that Fabiana might say no. Guadalupe's face floated into her mind and she thought of going to Casa Central to tell her the news, but no, she thought, no, I'll wait until after our meeting at Peñalba tomorrow. She relished her anonymity in this strange, secretive city and now she had her own secret to savour for the day. She boarded a bus on impulse and found herself once again on Avenida La Reforma, close to the Popol Vuh Museum, a place she'd been meaning to visit since she'd arrived in the city, so she got off at Marroquin University and walked through the lush grounds to the museum. Once inside, she wandered the cool corridors, her mind whirling. Time is a structure, each moment a cluster of all the moments, past and future, a tower of time balanced in my brain. Everything is piling up in the tower and one day it will fall and the hours will splinter into minutes, seconds, ticking away, and the eternal moment, which has nothing to do with time, will be lost. Something pulled at her, an object glimpsed from the corner of her eye. It was a small figure with bent back and bejewelled head-dress, *Ix Chak Chel, La Diosa Vieja*. Paméla was intrigued by the figure. She leaned on something — a cane or a planting stick — while her body curved like a snake and her face lifted to the sky. Paméla bought a replica of Ixchel in the museum shop, for herself, for Fabiana, for Guadalupe. She bought it for all of them, but she wasn't yet sure who would receive it. She thought sometimes of her research paper, of the long hours she had spent hunched over her books in the library. Toronto felt like another world despite her frequent communications with Hannah and Fern, and with her friends, but the story of Cortés and Malinche stayed with her as though it were planted and was growing inside her. She saw them in the night, appearing with darkened flesh and white eyes in the negative of her dreams. She saw their child alone in a strange country, yearning for his parents.

∾

Toledo: 1532
Martín could not remember when it had begun. Perhaps when he had first come to Court three years ago to enter the service of the Empress Isabel. The day after his seventh birthday his uncle had put him onto the coach bound for Toledo. After his uncle's modest country home the Palace seemed like a dream of golden fabrics and chandeliers, with ladies in voluminous dresses on the arms of gentlemen dressed in skirted doublets with high ruffled necks. He'd been given into the care of Don José, Master of Pages, and took his place in a narrow cot in the long windowless dormitory where all the pages slept.

One day his father had come to tell him he was returning to Mexico.

"The king has commanded me to take up residence in New Spain and govern my lands there."

"Can I come with you, Papá?"

"No, Martín. You must remain at Court and serve the Empress with all your heart and soul as befits a page of the royal household."

"But Papá —

"Shhh," Cortés had placed his finger on Martín's lips. "Be patient, my son, one day you will be a man and then you will choose for yourself." He'd leaned over and whispered into the boy's ear, "To fight the enemy you must learn to be like them. We must protect ourselves against the Spanish. Remember that, Martín. They would be lords over us."

"But I am half Spanish, Papá."

"You are a very special boy, Martín," he'd said, looking into the boy's almond-shaped eyes, noting the golden hue of his skin. "In your veins flows the blood of the old world mixed with the blood of the new world, our true home. You will learn what this means as you grow. You must always be proud of your mixed blood."

Cortés had fallen silent as Martín questioned him about the voyage, about his step-mother, Juana de Zuñiga, who had recently married Cortés and was sailing with him to take up residence in New Spain, and about his mother.

"Will you see my Mamá? Tell her I am well and that I think of her." Martín remembered the beating of his father's heart through the thick material of his doublet.

Before Cortés left he had received acceptance of his firstborn as a Knight of the Order of Santiago. The seven year old page pledged to wage war on the Infidel and to adhere to the Order's rigid code of schooling. Cortés himself had been refused, but his son was young and stood on the shoulders of his dissolute father.

Martín remembered how the whispers had started; like a breeze, a slight movement of leaves swirling in the palace courtyard, dust around his feet. He remembered crouching under the kitchen table in his uncle's house in Mexico, the cook whispering to Zaachila, words he hadn't understood — "*Bastardo de los Malinches, sangre soucio . . .* " — and their laughter. Now the same ugly sounds, the laughter that made him want to run away, back to his aunt and uncle in Estremadura.

Don José had taken Martín under his care from the beginning. The boy had shown unusual promise, but when he had begun to daydream and drop things in the presence of the Empress, the Master had spoken sharply to him. "What's wrong with you, Martín Cortés? Why have you turned into a clumsy oaf, half asleep on your feet? Do you want to be expelled from the Court?"

"Please don't expel me, Don José. My father would be angry."

"Come on then, boy, what is it?" He was a good-hearted man despite his gruff exterior.

"I . . . I have bad dreams . . . about my Mamá . . . people laughing at her. And they call me *bastardo.*"

"Ah," he'd nodded and scratched his grizzled head. "You'll bear the burden of it, boy, so you may as well know the truth. Your mother's an Indian, a traitor to her people, some say. And you're her bastard son. Your father has a Spanish wife now and a legitimate son."

"I have a brother?" Martín's face had lit up.

"A half-brother."

"What's his name?"

"Another Martín, like you. But he's the son and heir and you, my boy," he'd clamped his hand on Martín's shoulder, "you must know what you're fighting, Martín, then you can fight back."

"I will fight for the king when I'm a man," he'd said.

He lay awake in the darkness trying to remember how his Mamá looked. At his uncle's house in Estremadura he had waited every day for her to come, and had chewed on the *ruda* to keep her memory alive on his tongue, until the pouch was empty and he could no longer see her face. His cheeks burned and his throat was sore and swollen. He longed for something he could not name, his body burning with circles of unspoken desire. He tried to imagine what his brother looked like, then he fell asleep and dreamed of running along the canals of Mexico-Tenochtitlan, the air hot and prickly on his skin, his brother's hand clasped in his. When he woke in the night his neck and throat were so swollen that his breath came in rasping heaves and he couldn't swallow.

Don José wrote to Cortés of his son's illness.

. . . *Lamparones, a wretched and disfiguring condition by which the boy's neck is swelled with burning ulcers which suppurate and, God willing, will empty out and leave but a scar. He calls for you, Don Cortés, and for his mother* . . .

By the time Cortés received the letter Martín had survived a raging fever in which he had seen the face of his mother leaning over him, felt her cool cheek pressed against his burning face. He had smelled the sweet spice of her breath, and the taste of *ruda* had burst in his mouth, bringing him the comfort he needed. When the boy returned to his duties Don José saw that he was changed in some essential manner by his delirium.

Martín the firstborn grew in the desert of his parents' absence, his resentment of all things Spanish growing with him. It is Spain that keeps my father from me, my father who loves me and knows I am special. Papá has another wife, a new family. I am responsible for my mother now. He vowed to drive the Spanish out of her land, to find his brother and make his family whole.

"I will set it all to rights."

Chewing on his secret, he survived the cruel jibes and gossip of the court.

∾

Paméla sat at a window table, looking by turns at her watch and the doorway. Ten forty-five. She sipped the dregs of her hot chocolate and looked anxiously up and down the street. Rows of leather boots with pointed toes and intricate patterning hung from a *zapatería* across the street. The city was full of shoestores with fetishistic displays of leather footware. But the broad feet of the indigenous people were either bare or were thonged with plastic sandals, as though they were walking to the beach, back to the shores of some ancient land where their lives had been different.

The waitress eyed her questioningly. Paméla smiled and ordered *la plata típica: huevos fritos, frijoles, plátanos con crema, aguacate, tortillas y arroz.* An hour later she paid her bill and left the plate untouched. She walked the short distance to the Palacio Nacional and presented herself to the now familiar guard. "Please, take me to Señora Fabiana's apartment."

"No visitors."

"But I was there two days ago. I have an appointment."

"No visitors."

"Is Miguel here?"

The guard, a Mayan with a face as stony and beautiful as the sculptures of the Popol Vuh, shook his head. It was hopeless. She turned and walked back to her hotel. She felt very tired.

"You have reached the office of Dónde Están. I'm away from the office for one week. Please leave a message and I'll call you when I return June 21st." Anna-María's warm voice.

Paméla put the phone card in her wallet and left the lobby of Chalet Suizo. She walked out onto the street and headed towards Casa Central, where Sister Rosa recognized her immediately and opened the door.

"*Buenos tardes, niña.* You've come to see Sister María-Teresa?"

"No, Sister Guadalupe."

The little nun folded her hands and cocked her head like a brown-eyed bird. "That is not possible. Sister Guadalupe is resting."

A voice echoed in Paméla's head. 'If you need help later you can come to me.' She was desperate. "Alright. Sister María-Teresa."

"Come with me."

∽

After he'd gotten rid of Paméla, Ernesto had taken Fabiana out to dinner, a rare event intended as a celebration of their triumph over the intrusion of the past into their lives. He was determined to protect Fabiana against the crushing knowledge that Paméla had brought back. He owed it to her. After all, hadn't Fabiana protected him from his own dreadful knowledge, given him a haven in which to redeem himself? They sat in the dark limousine with its smoked windows, both wearing dark glasses even though it was night-time. When the driver opened the door for Fabiana, Ernesto, already on the sidewalk, immediately took her arm. The maitre d' led them to a secluded area and seated them at a table by a dribbling fountain. The pool was murky with algae and Fabiana watched as two slow turtles circled the pool, disturbed by an occasional flash of gold. She picked at her food, her face pale and drawn. They rarely left the Palacio, because she felt conspicuous on the arm of the famous Generalísimo. She wanted above all to avoid drawing attention to herself. Ernesto had suggested they go dancing after the meal, but she insisted they return to the apartment and once there she clung to him, pressing her body into him as though she would merge with his flesh. Her bones bruised him and he was gentle, so gentle with her as she pushed against him like an enemy.

When he woke in the night and heard water running in the bathroom, he lay vigilant until it stopped and everything was silent, then he crept through the apartment. The light from the bathroom shone across the dim hallway. As he passed the darkened kitchen he sensed something and, turning his head quickly, saw Fabiana, her mouth filled with stale tortillas, little pieces falling to the floor as she began to sob, still chewing. Ernesto stood naked in the hallway staring at her. She bowed her head, gulping, trying to swallow.

"Don't be angry with me," she said. "Please, please, don't be angry with me."

He moved then, released by her words and wrapped himself around her naked body. She was damp and warm from the shower, sweet-smelling. "*Mi amor,* what is this? Come to bed," he said softly.

"I'm sorry, I'm sorry," she sobbed. "I can't help it. My head is filled with . . . terrible things."

He brought her a glass of water and sat her up, propped between his legs, and massaged her head and temples until she finally slept, leaning against his chest, her head flung back under his chin. When they were woken by the ringing of his cell phone, Ernesto cancelled his engagements for the day and they slept till noon and lazed in bed all afternoon making love; it was the only way to calm her. He ordered food and drinks from the Palacio kitchen and spread a cloth on their big bed and they picknicked there, tethered by their senses to keep Fabiana from flying away. But he couldn't keep hold of her. She slipped away again in the night and he found her curled on the tiles of the shower stall, hot water beating down on her thin body.

"*Sangre, sangre, sangre,*" she murmured, rubbing at her feet with a little piece of soap.

Ernesto didn't want to take her to the hospital, so he held her all night while she wept as though there could be no end to her grief. "Don't leave me, Ernesto. Never leave me."

"Never," he whispered, his voice gruff with emotion, and he held her tighter until he felt her ribs contract and her breath grow shallow. Then he got out of bed and padded to the kitchen for a glass of water and a sleeping draught. They lay together through the second day until she emerged finally from her dark place. Fabiana didn't know what day it was. Each moment had been a cluster of all the moments, past and future, a tower of time. At the end of the second day the tower had fallen and the hours returned, divided into minutes, seconds, ticking away; the eternal moment lost.

∾

"So you found her?"

Paméla nodded.

"And now you wish you hadn't. What did you expect, an open-armed welcome?" María-Teresa smiled wearily, then her eyes narrowed. "How did you find her?"

"Through an agency. And she did welcome me."

"Really?"

"But the next day she was different, as though something had happened. You said you'd help me."

"I warned you, Paméla, it's better not to disturb the past. It's possible that seeing you was very painful for your mother, did you think of that?"

"How could she live with an army man?"

"In Guatemala we're all caught in this web together, victims and victimizers, army and civilians. Since the conquest of our country 500 years ago our blood has been mixed. We no longer know who are the conquered and who are the conquerors. Whose people are we talking about? Whose side are we on with our mixed blood?"

"You too?"

She nodded. "My grandmother was Mayan. In the Guatemalan army Mayan boys are trained to kill their mothers, their brothers, their sisters. The *kaibiles* are taught to eat the enemy, to tear out the heart, still beating, and sink their teeth into it. The *kaibiles* are a special corps, like the green berets, trained to kill like animals, by instinct. You know from your dream, Paméla, how great is the horror, but you haven't lived it and you have no right to stand in judgement on people who've survived such horror in the best way they can. We can't go on living with hatred. We must surrender our pain or we die. Your mother has found something to live for with her general. She's found a place, away from the street, to belong."

"But he's a murderer. He put his hand on me and I felt . . . contaminated."

"His hands are clean, my dear. He only gave the orders. Now he's harmless. He guards the president like a dog."

"Why is everything so complicated here? I can't go and see my own mother because she lives in a secret apartment. You wouldn't tell me about her because she's a secret. Every time I try to do something people tell me, 'No, no, you can't, it's forbidden, it's secret, it's dangerous!' "

"Welcome to Guatemala. That is what it's like here. We've lived so long with war, with danger and secrecy, that our lives have become infected with it. But we do our best to live and to care for each other. You must have compassion for your mother. As you grow older you'll learn the complexities that can lead a woman to love her jailer, but you'll never know what it is to be Guatemalan."

"What do you mean?"

"Your mother made the choice for you, to become a Canadian."

"No! You're a liar! The Sisters took me from her. She told me."

María-Teresa reached out her hand to Paméla across the desk. "Paméla, your mother was a child herself when you were born. She could not have looked after you."

"Was she raped?"

"I don't know." She shook her head. "Guatemalans are not the only people who suffer. It is the same in Salvador, Chile, Nicaragua, in Colombia and Argentina . . . There is a curse on Latin America, and on any place where people try to live close to the earth. It is the way of the world now to destroy this earth. We must do what we can to resist, Paméla, even if it is hopeless." A smile spread slowly on her face, a smile of such warmth that Paméla didn't know if she was being dismissed or encouraged when María-Teresa said gently, "You will find your way."

She walked down the cool corridor and sat for a few minutes in the courtyard, the nun's words echoing in her mind. Of course she thought of Guadalupe and how they'd sat there together only weeks ago, but it seemed like months. So much had happened. The convent was still and silent as though everyone were sleeping. She had seen a staircase leading off the corridor and now she retraced her steps, tip-toeing past María-Teresa's door, and started up the stone steps. When she reached the top she continued down another long corridor, which smelled of disinfectant. She imagined the nuns on their knees scrubbing the flagstones. A chink of light sliced through the dimness; a door to her right, not quite closed. She listened. No sound. She pushed the door gently then she smelled her, the lemon scent. She thought of Fabiana, her smell obscured by powders and perfumes, and she felt a stab of longing. Guadalupe lay on a narrow bed, eyes closed, hair loose on the pillow. She had removed her cardigan and the top buttons of her blouse were undone, revealing the swell of her breast. Paméla had a ridiculous urge to tiptoe in and wake her with a kiss, to touch her fan of shocking hair. She was about to leave when Guadalupe opened her eyes. She sat up immediately, hands covering her breast.

"I'm sorry."

"It's all right. Come in. Please, come."

"I shouldn't have . . . "

"Yes, yes, you must come." Guadalupe moved very quickly, swinging her legs over the edge of the bed, buttoning her blouse, pulling her cardigan from the chair and slipping her arms into it. Then she stood quite still. "You surprised me. A wonderful surprise," she said. "I didn't expect . . . "

They stood awkwardly by the open door until Paméla turned and closed it gently. As she did this Guadalupe took the haircomb from her bedside table and swiftly pulled her hair back and secured it.

"Please," she gestured to the bed and quickly smoothed the bedcover, "Sit."

Paméla nodded and sat on the warm bed.

"You found her?"

"Yes." She told Guadalupe everything that had happened in the brief time since they'd met Miguel in the park. She was so involved with her story that she didn't notice the sadness in Guadalupe's face.

"Now that you've found your mother you will leave Guatemala."

"Not until I can persuade her to come with me. And now I can't even see her. The general *is* a guard-dog."

"You broke your promise."

"What?"

"You went to Sister María-Teresa. You told her."

"No, I lied. I said I'd found her through an agency. I wouldn't even have seen her, but Sister Rosa said you were resting. I was desperate. I'm sorry. I would never betray your trust."

"It's all right. I forgive you."

"There's nothing to forgive!"

"Shh. Please keep your voice down. You're in my private room. It's forbidden, don't you understand?"

"Everything is forbidden in this country," Paméla whispered vehemently. "I understand it very well. Don't you understand? I love Fabiana. She's my real mother. When I'm away from her I see her everywhere, I think about her all the time and . . . " She stopped suddenly as though she'd said too much. "Lupe?" They sat, thighs almost touching, held in the silence of the massive convent building. The air they breathed was like a question. "I have something for you." She brought the replica of Ixchel out of her pocket. It fit exactly into the palm of her hand. She reached for Guadalupe's hand and dropped the figure into her open palm.

Guadalupe looked at Ixchel, then back at Paméla. "I cannot." She dropped the little sculpture on the bed as though she'd been burned. She jumped up and walked over to the window.

"Why not? What's wrong?"

Guadalupe stood at the window staring at the purple jacaranda, her eyes filling with it. "I cannot accept your gift." She spun around. "I'm Catholic. I'm married to Christ," she whispered.

"And you pray to his mother who fixes everything," Paméla said bitterly. "It's only a gift, Lupe. I apologize for intruding on your privacy. I'll go."

"What are you going to do?"

"I'm going to wait every day at Peñalba until she comes."

"And if she doesn't?"

"She will. I have faith too, in human love."

Guadalupe turned back to the window, stung. She was still staring at the jacaranda blossom when she heard the door close. Then she allowed herself to cry. Loss upon loss. She had not allowed herself to feel the loss for so many years, the loss of her mother, her brothers, her little sister, the loss of her father and everyone in her village, the loss of baby Flor.

"Now it's my decision." She sat on the bed and blew her nose. "That's the difference now."

∾

Cortés had returned to Mexico with his pure-blooded bride, Doña Juana Ramírez de Arellano y Zuñiga, daughter to the Count of Aguilar, and had taken up his own title as Marqués del Valle de Oaxaca and built a palace at Cuernavaca, close to the capital, with the smashed remains of the Aztec pyramid which had stood there. The young adventurer who had fled his plantation in Cuba found himself burdened with acres of land inhabited by poor Indians, a second wife, a second son and a growing family, prospering amidst his broken dreams.

"What is it, Hernándo?" Juana said, her voice husky with sleep. She held out her arms to her husband, who sat on the edge of the bed, head in hands. "Come, come to me."

Cortés rose abruptly. "It's my old wounds," he said and left their bedchamber, slamming the heavy door. He paced the corridors of his labyrinthine palace remembering the days of starvation, fever, sleeplessness, weeks of marching with blood in his nostrils. Like a dog he paced the shrinking borders of his life, the years of privation twisting his bones as he began to realize that he would never rule the land he'd conquered. He was still stinging from an encounter in the city.

"Ah, Don Hernándo, what brings you to the capital?" Don Antonio de Mendoza had inquired, "The management of your estates?"

The Viceroy of New Spain never failed to infuriate Cortés with his subtle sarcasm. He was angered too by the treatment of the Indians. Under Mendoza's governance certain structures had been set in place to benefit the Spanish crown, such as the *encomienda,* a system whereby land was given to the conquistadors and Indians were required to work it in exchange for the protection and salvation of their souls by their Catholic masters. This ensured conversion and their loyalty as slaves. Cortés himself was a beneficiary of the *encomienda*, an uncomfortable fact which had moved him to action.

"I have come to mediate in the disputes with the Indians. Their land is taken and they're branded as slaves in great numbers, all in the name of the Church."

"Don't trouble yourself, Marqués," Mendoza had replied. "You've tamed them quite effectively. Now let us govern them. Much has changed since your day."

"I've suffered for this land," growled Cortés, "The earth of Mexico has drunk our blood. It has claimed us, and our blood is mixed with the blood of the Indians now. A fatherless generation of mestizos is growing which I fear will one day rebel and . . . " He had been unable to continue as he'd remembered his firstborn son in Spain, and a shiver of premonition shook him. "It is the land that matters, not the blood," he had told himself, "the land that I have conquered with my men, for our progeny, not for Spain."

The sun rose, flooding the hills with a gentle light and he remembered Malintzín, returned, he'd heard, to her homeland on the Gulf. "*Mi lengua,*" he whispered, "*Mi lengua bonita.*" He would make a journey, yes, he would find her and expose that bigamist, Jaramillo. He would not believe that she was dead as her husband claimed.

∾

"Blessed Virgin, give me command over my heart, help me to keep my vows of service and chastity. In this my hour of need show me the way to regain my equilibrium."

Guadalupe had gone late to the chapel, wanting to make confession, but when she reached the booth she realized that she didn't know what to confess. She returned to her pew and knelt for more than an hour gazing up at the illuminated Virgin.

"Oh, Blessed Mother, you smile your eternal smile. A hundred rivers run through my body and I am lost in their current. What does it mean? Help me, Mother, to rise above this, to rise on the moon with you and live eternally pure, beyond time . . . "

It was the Gods of her village who answered her finally, in Mam, the language of her people, and Guadalupe began to weep as the words entered her and found places to burrow and nestle, disturbing memory. She remembered the clay figure of Ixchel on her father's altar propped beside Itzámná, God of all creation. Why had she refused the gift? She was filled with regret and begged forgiveness. But it had seemed to her that the gift signified more than it appeared to. Was it the pain of her past, or a promise of something unthinkable that disturbed her? Her head spun for a moment as she stood, then she left the chapel through the side entrance and walked along a colonnade to the convent. She was at the foot of the stairs, about to begin her ascent to the sanctuary of her bedroom, where Ixchel stood propped on her writing table, when she heard Sister María-Teresa's voice.

"Sister Lupe! I hope I haven't hurt your feelings, my dear, by assigning Sister Rosa in your place."

"Of course not."

"You seem upset."

"No."

María-Teresa looked into her eyes. "You are duplicitous. Tell the truth, Guadalupe. I can help you."

"You can't."

María-Teresa took her hand and led her into the courtyard. "Now tell me the truth," she said, sitting on the bench, "Is it the doctor?"

"No, no, no," Guadalupe shook her head back and forth. "I'm so tired of saying no to my life, always no!"

María-Teresa's eyes glittered with a strange mixture of hope and vigilance. She took Guadalupe's face in her hands and held her there, forcing her to look into her eyes. "You can trust me, Guadalupe, I know you like my own self."

"Oh, Sister, it's the Canadian girl, Paméla. Her coming has brought back all the memories that have lain buried since before I became a *novicia*. The dedication of my life to our Lord allowed me to put it all behind me. I pushed it into the darkness and vowed never to think of it. I shouldn't say this, Sister, but you'll understand, won't you? It's as though our faith were a way of denying what has happened to us."

María-Teresa pulled back in shock.

"Forgive me, I didn't mean . . . It's only . . . the destruction of my village, the loss of my family . . . everyone . . . " She broke down and wept and María-Teresa held her, an expression of bliss creeping into her face like a blush.

"You told her, didn't you?"

"I couldn't deny her. I loved her as a baby."

"You broke your word to me."

"Forgive me."

"Only Our Lady can forgive our sins."

"It doesn't seem like a sin to allow love where there's been loss and suffering."

María-Teresa leaned back, holding Guadalupe at arm's length. She looked at her quizzically. "I didn't know you had moved so far from us, Sister. There are many kinds of love: eros, agape, carnal, divine . . . "

"But the love for a child — "

"Is the love for our Lord."

"So how can it be a sin to — "

"Paméla is not a child. You cannot live in the past, Sister. You have responsibilities. The girl will suffer for what you've done. And you've broken our trust. You have much to answer for."

"I'm sorry, Sister. I'll do penance."

"And I thought you *were* doing penance." María-Teresa shook her clenched hands nervously. They were tingling with an old feeling, her legs too, tingling with pins and needles. She got up from the bench and paced back and forth. As blood flowed through her limbs anger bloomed. "I was foolish enough to feel sorry for you. You've made a fool of me, Guadalupe." She kicked suddenly at the lilies clustered in the corner. A blossom snapped and fell to the earth, the curled petals weeping drops of moisture as they bruised and turned brown. "Perhaps an extended work period in the country, under supervision, to remind you of your duties."

Guadalupe shuddered and bowed her head. "Whatever you say, Sister."

∾

It was exactly ten o'clock when Fabiana arrived at Peñalba.

"Mamá! Where were you?" Paméla tried to hug her but Fabiana shied away.

"We must sit in the back. Come, there's a table in the corner."

"What happened yesterday? I waited and waited."

Fabiana shrugged. "One day is as good as another." Paméla felt foolish for the turmoil she'd gone through and tried to put it aside as they settled themselves and ordered breakfast. There was an awkward silence.

"Mamá? Take off your sunglasses. I can't see you."

"My eyes are sore . . . the sunlight."

"It's dark back here." She leaned across and removed the glasses, and for a moment they looked into each other's eyes, then Fabiana bowed her head. "I'm sorry," Paméla said and she put the glasses into Fabiana's hands. "What happened?"

"A bad night. I couldn't sleep."

"Did he hurt you?"

"Ernesto never hurts me," she said fiercely. "It's the memories . . . terrible pictures in my head." She took a package of cigarettes from her purse. Paméla wondered what else she kept in that private woman's domain; lipstick, love letters, photographs? Did Ernesto give her money? The cigarette quivered between her lips as she flicked a small gold lighter and sucked on the flame.

"*Rubios. Lo mejor cigarro de todo Guatemala,*" Paméla said, exaggerating the rolled R's like the commercial she'd heard on the radios that blared from the street stalls. She felt stupid when Fabiana stared blankly at her, unresponsive.

"I don't know what to do, *niña.* You've upset my life and there's no way to go back."

"Back to what?"

"To the peace of forgetting."

"I'm sorry for upsetting your life, but what about my life? Don't you think I have feelings too!" Immediately the words were out of her mouth Paméla regretted them. A war waged within her. She wanted desperately to be held in her mother's arms and gobble up the love she had missed, but she wanted to scream at Fabiana for all their lost years. She wanted to cause a scene and tell everyone in the restaurant how she had suffered.

"*Disculpeme,*" Fabiana whispered, reaching across the table for Paméla's hand, clasping it. "I can take you to your father if that's what you want." Her nails pressed a row of half moons into the fleshy side of the girl's palm. "I remember where he lives, but I don't know if — "

"No! I've only just found you. How can I handle meeting him as well?" She pulled her hand away, rubbing her palm. "I'd probably hate him anyway. He abandoned you, didn't he, then you had to go with Ernesto — "

"No, no, it's not true, you don't understand — "

"Then explain to me. I don't know anything about you after the massacre. What happened after you left the village?"

Fabiana was silent for a minute, then she leaned back in her chair and dragged on her cigarette, inhaling deeply. "I came to the capital. I don't know how I got here, but I remember the woman in the Banco de Guatemala and the sisters at Casa Central. They taught me Spanish and Sister Rosa took me to the house of Señora Méndez. That is where your life began, inside my body, and I gave thanks to Madre Maria for the peace you brought me, because I did not understand."

"What d'you mean, Mamá?" Paméla's voice was soft now as she leaned forward with her elbows on the table, intent on her mother's story.

"I was very young. No one had explained to me how life is created."

"Were you raped?"

"No. The Señor was kind to me, but I didn't understand what we were doing."

"The bastard. You were just a child."

Fabiana shook her head. "Please help me," she said urgently. "Tell me again . . . your dream. Tell me I'm not crazy. I can't believe that everything I remember is true, because I've never told anyone."

Their food came — thick white plates loaded with eggs, rice, beans and fried plantain; a pot of salsa roja and a basket of steaming tortillas — but they barely touched it as Paméla talked and Fabiana listened, smoking cigarette after cigarette, disappearing behind glazed eyes, returning slowly as Paméla touched her, insisting, "Come back, Mamá, come back."

When Fabiana began to talk her speech was rapid, confirming every detail of Paméla's dream — the empty blackboard, the burnt cornstalks in the fields around the village, the white bone splintered at Mamá's shoulder, the open mouths of the Papás . . . "I couldn't see Papá's face, but I knew it was him sticking out of the mountain, because I saw his belt. He used to beat me with that belt. It was brown with a silver buckle and his name was burned into the underside of it. In front there were five notches for his children. I wanted to pull that belt out of his trousers and hit him with it, but he was already dead. All the Papás were dead." Her eyes were bright and she was alive with an energy that Paméla hadn't seen in her before.

People were crowding into the restaurant, filling the tables. It was lunchtime. Fabiana began to eat her food ravenously, shovelling congealed eggs into her mouth, scooping up cold beans and salsa with a furled tortilla. As she ate Paméla told her about Canada, about her life there, her studies, about Hannah and Fern's house, the giant maple shading the front of the house, the chestnut in the backyard. "Come to Canada with me, Mamá!" she said.

Fabiana stopped chewing and looked up, her mouth full, her eyes questioning. Paméla leapt into that moment of uncertainty.

"I've been to the Canadian Consulate and to the Immigration office. We have to get you a passport. I'll come with you. I know where to go."

"No, no, my life is here."

"Just for a visit, to see if you like it. If you decide to stay I can sponsor you and we can be together finally."

But Fabiana had resumed her eating and, like an animal, she was completely absorbed.

By one o'clock they were out on the street. "Where shall we go?" Paméla asked as people pushed past.

"I must go home and rest. I'm tired, Paméla."

"Can I see you tomorrow?" She felt like a lover. She thought of Guadalupe standing at her window, the little Ixchel lying on her bed. I should have brought it for Fabiana.

"I'll meet you at Catedral Metropolitana."

"Ten o'clock?"

"*Mas o menos.* Who knows what can happen?"

Paméla scribbled on a scrap of paper. "Here — the phone number of my hotel, just in case."

Fabiana put the paper carefully into her purse. "I'll be inside the cathedral. You'll find me."

Paméla hugged Fabiana. She smelled her expensive perfume, heady and intoxicating, so different from Guadalupe's clean lemon smell. "Can I walk with you to the Palacio?"

"No, it's better that we say goodbye here." She kissed her and turned to join the slow crush of people.

"Mamá?" Paméla held her arm and pulled her back. "Will you come with me tomorrow to the passport office?

"I have no papers, no birth certificate, nothing."

"There are lots of people like you who've lost everything. There are ways around it. I talked to Immigration."

Fabiana looked at Paméla for a moment as though she were a complete stranger, then turned and disappeared into the crowd, her stiletto heels clicking on the sidewalk.

Paméla walked back to Chalet Suizo, collapsed into fresh sheets and slept deep and dreamless. When she woke it was already dusk; she could hear birds swarming in the trees. She showered and washed the morning smoke from her hair, trying to forget Fabiana's blank look as she'd turned to leave. She went to eat at Café Rey Sol, then spent the evening at the internet café e-mailing her friends in Toronto, telling them she'd soon be coming home, bringing her mother, sending the story over and over to make it real. She started writing to Hannah and Fern, a long involved message about her feelings for Fabiana, about Guadalupe's refusal of her gift, about her growing prejudice against Catholicism, but she erased it without sending because she didn't know what she was trying to say. Her feelings were like a tangle of coloured threads, impossible to extricate one from the other. "Grow up," she told herself. "You must figure this out for yourself." She looked up at the clock, which was always accurate in the internet café. Way past five. She imagined Guadalupe kneeling in the Capilla Medalla Milagrosa and she felt the little medallion still pressed against her breast. If it had been earlier she would have run there and put her hand on Guadalupe's shoulder and watched her turn in surprise, just to see her radiant smile.

When she got back to her room she took the postcard of the Palacio Nacional down from the wall and wrote on the back:

Hi Talya, Here's a picture of my mother's house.
Isn't it grand? I found her. She's beautiful.
I'm bringing her home. Saludos, Paméla.

∽

The general sat brooding in his leather chair, a vein beating in his forehead from the centre of his hairline across his furrowed brow. When Fabiana's crisis had passed and he had finally gone home yesterday Alicia had screamed at him in front of the servant, "Go back to your whore! You think I care? It's your children who will punish you for this. You missed Nineth's *quinze años!*"

His daughter's fifteenth birthday. The biggest day in a girl's life, her entry to womanhood, how could he have forgotten?

"I'll make it up to her. I had duties to perform for the president."

"Liar! The president is in Mexico. You think I'm stupid? Three nights you've been gone, like a filthy tomcat. I could divorce you for this, Ernesto!"

He sprung from his chair and paced the room. He usually covered his tracks; back before dawn, breakfast with the family, regular appearances at mealtimes, then out again, late at night, a phone call from the President, his cell phone the perfect alibi. Alicia knew, but she didn't care so long as he kept up appearances. Ernesto had boundless energy, too much for one woman, and he had juggled his affairs expertly until now.

He placed a cushion on the floor and knelt to pray. He remembered the early days with Fabiana, how she'd healed him of the things he'd had to do, how she'd forgiven him and absolved him with her body. He remembered the first time they had knelt together in the Pentecostal Church of the Word, how the past had flown from his mouth in words he didn't understand, how they had raised their voices together in prayer, singing and shouting in many tongues, everyone taken out of themselves with the glory of the Word. Strange, he thought, that the great Generalísimo, Rios Montt, told us Evangelicalism would save the Indians from themselves when it is we who are saved. The girl's face floated behind his closed eyes. She looks as Fabiana looked twenty years ago, but looks are deceiving. She's a gringa, one of those earnest, well-meaning gringas who thinks she can come to Guatemala and interfere in our lives. The girl is dangerous.

He sat back on his haunches and dropped his head into his hands. He couldn't pray without Fabiana. She was like a limb and without her he was not himself. Ernesto lumbered to his feet, his knee joints stiff and painful, and slumped in his chair. Yesterday when he'd arrived at the apartment stinging from Alicia's insults, he had found Fabiana sleeping, so small in their big bed. She had lain in the centre, her hair spread like a dark aura, her face peaceful finally with a slight smile twitching her mouth. All his anger had melted away in a flood of tenderness. He had bent to kiss her forehead and listen to her breath, feel its steady push and suck on his cheek, warm and cool. She had stirred and half opened her eyes, smiling, reaching her arms around his neck.

"My love, I want always to wake to your handsome face."

He had kissed her, a long slow kiss, her mouth so soft and yielding. "Where have you been today?"

"Nowhere, Ernesto. I've been waiting for you." She had begun to unbutton his shirt.

"The guard told me you went out in the morning."

"Oh, yes . . . to meet my daughter." Nonchalant, as though she'd forgotten for a moment.

"Where did you meet her?"

"In a restaurant." Casual, a throwaway. She had pulled at his shirt, freed it from his trousers and begun to trace patterns on his chest with her fingertips.

"Maybe you have a plan?"

"No." Sleepy, languid. "Only to speak with her, Ernesto. She's my child. Soon she'll leave Guatemala."

"August 1st."

"Mmm." Her hands on his belt, unbuckling it, gripping the zipper of his fly.

"She'd like to take you with her." The vein had beaten his forehead as she'd grasped his penis, silencing him. Her hands were strong, her body lithe. With a cat-like leap she was above him and he'd felt her sliding onto him until he was buried deep within her body. They had soared and swooped like mating eagles, clasped together, falling, falling, breaking apart an inch from the earth, swooping upward on the current of their own pleasure.

After what seemed an eternity Fabiana had spoken from the hollow of his shoulder. "It's true. She wants me to make a passport."

"For a visit to Canada? What an idea! You must go, *mi amor.*"

She had looked up then, her eyes wild and dark. She had grasped his arms and laid her head on his chest. "I don't want to leave you, Ernesto!"

Slowly he had encircled her with his arms. "You are free, *mi corazón.* I trust you." His heart pounded with fear now as he remembered his words. "I'll help you with the passport." A risk, a test.

"Maybe . . . "

"What, my love?"

"Maybe you're right, Ernesto. You think I should go? Just for a visit?"

He'd always been a winner at the gaming tables. He'd have to continue his bluff and take another tack.

He cursed the girl for forcing him into duplicity against the woman he loved, for interfering in his life, making trouble in his marriage, causing him to forget his daughter's birthday. Ernesto was afraid, but he'd been trained in overcoming fear. He was a soldier. He knew what to do.

∾

María-Teresa knelt by her bed. Angry welts criss-crossed her naked back, but she hardly felt them. Her back was numb and her hand, clenched on a leather thong, prickled with pins and needles. She bit her lip till blood drizzled down her chin, but she felt nothing. She pressed her elbows into the mattress and bounced her knees on the hard floor until she almost cried out in pain and gratitude. Tears poured down her face finally and she collapsed onto the bed.

"Forgive me, forgive me, Holy Virgin, for I have sinned and failed in my duty. I have had forbidden thoughts and feelings, save me from myself, from the sin of my anger, my jealousy, my evil nature. I am not fit to live, so help me, Mother, temper my passion, humble me before Your Son, Our Lord Jesus Christ!"

She paced through the night on her knees and in the morning her flesh stung as though it had been scrubbed with salt. The pain sustained her through the day as she limped down the colonnade to prayers, to the dining hall, to her office. She dared not look at Guadalupe.

∾

The long procession was led by Hernán Cortés and his wife, Doña Juana Zuñiga. There was music and dancing, feasting and revelry as throngs of converts clogged the streets, falling down under the power of the Virgin of Guadalupe. Some were crushed underfoot as they worshipped. Juan de Zumarraga, first Archbishop of Mexico City, smiled as he remembered the moment of his inspiration. He remembered it exactly; the golden rim of the cup upon his lower lip, the bite of red wine, his smack of satisfaction, behind him the Virgin spreading her eternal wings, her foot firmly on the serpent's head as its body encircled the earth. On her shoulder the baby Christ, his arms reaching to heaven. Zumarraga remembered turning to raise his cup to her and at that very moment receiving his brilliant idea, thereafter attributed to the inspiration of the Holy Virgin.

It had taken some time to find the right man; Juan Diego, a humble Indian bearer whose family was in great need. They chose the place; Tepeyac Hill, a site dedicated to the Aztec Mother Goddess Tonantzin, conveniently close to the capital. During that year of 1531 there had been three appearances, but no one had believed Juan Diego. The one who appeared to him did not resemble Tonantzin, according to his description, although she did speak to him in his native Nahuatl and said her name was Santa María de Guadalupe, Juan Diego had reported. The Archbishop was pleased to hear this. He had himself visited the 200 year old shrine of Guadalupe in the province of Estremadura, birthplace of Cortés, the former governor.

Finally, in December, shortly before the celebration of Christ's birth, the Virgin had appeared yet again to Juan Diego, in the form of Guadalupe as before, but this time she bore roses in winter and presented them to the

Indian as proof of his vision. The people were impressed. They said the cloak that Juan Diego carried the roses in was imprinted, petals embroidering themselves on the material. They said the Archbishop gasped when Juan Diego laid the fresh roses at his feet, letting his patterned cloak fall open, sucking his thumb where a thorn had pierced him. "Finally the Spanish Fathers will listen to us," they said. "They listened to Juan Diego, an Indian like us." The people flocked to Tepeyac Hill. A chapel was built on the site of Juan Diego's vision, a shrine to Guadalupe.

On December 26, 1531 Juan Diego's cloak was taken from Tenochtitlan to Tepeyac Hill, a long procession, winding up the hill, throbbing with the power of conversion.

"At last we have transformed the mestizos from the bastards of violated Indians into children of the pure Virgin," declaimed the Archbishop. "And our Lord Jesus Christ, who has suffered and died for them, is their surrogate father," he added, keeping pace with Cortés and Doña Juana.

∾

A small woman, devoutly Catholic, advanced on her knees up the nave of Catedral Metropolitana, her skin rubbing on the worn stones. Spangles of light splashed gold and scarlet on the stones and on her withered cheek. She advanced in an ecstasy of mystery, muttering.

"*María, madre de Cristo, no hay solución a este dolor. Devuélveme a Clara Luz, mi niña llevada por los militares hace veinte años. O que me lleve la muerte.*"

Banks of candles sputtered and flared in their oceans of wax, illuminating the woman's grief-goldened body. Fresh-cut flowers trembled and put forth their scent all over the cathedral. Cries and sighs and shuffling sounds filled the air, thick with prayer.

Paméla dipped her fingers in the font of holy water and touched her forehead as she'd learned from Guadalupe. The cathedral was filled with people, praying in the pews and side chapels, milling about in the aisles, lighting candles and making offerings. She started down the left-hand aisle, looking around eagerly for Fabiana. She saw the old woman, still advancing on her knees, tears runnelling her cheeks. She saw three women kneeling at the altar rail, heads bowed, their scarves flaming with light reflected through the stained glass scenes of Christ's humiliation. She gazed at the sculpted figures as she passed, every Virgin and Saint with a different face; the face of the sculptor, of his wife or child. Images of ourselves, she thought, that we invest with power, then we worship them. Some were festooned with *milagros* — tiny replicas of limbs, hearts, hands, hanging by ribbons and permeated with prayers for the miraculous intercession of the Virgin in some illness or misfortune. Paméla remembered her prayer to Saint Jude Thaddeus, patron saint of the impossible, and she smiled at the irony. Perhaps her mother had been kneeling in the cathedral even then. She moved on towards the end of the aisle, where a small group was clustered at the feet of the crucified black Jesus, but something pulled her attention. She turned and saw Fabiana kneeling on the altar steps of a side chapel, her hands clasped high in front of her, head tilted, praying to a small figure of the Virgin. A shaft of light pierced her mother's back, thrown from a window in the larger body of the cathedral. Light spread like blood in a circle over her spine where her ribs flared, caging her heart. Paméla felt the beating of her own heart, the pulsing of life in her wrists, behind her knees, at her throat, and in the petalled fold of her genitals. "Mamá," she whispered.

Fabiana turned quickly. Her face lit up and she rose from her knees and opened her arms to embrace Paméla. "Come," she said, taking her by the hand, "I was giving thanks to the Holy Mother for returning you to me." They knelt together on the altar steps in the small sanctuary. "She is La Virgen del Socorro. She's answered my prayers."

Paméla looked up at the Virgin. She was only three feet high, flanked by gold pillars and dressed in deep red with a dark cloak, and a large, domed crown. The paint was darkened with age and her face was framed with blonde hair, giving her a doll-like quality, at once banal and haunting as though, over the years, she had been invested with great power. Fabiana put some coins into the alms box and lit two candles, one for each of them. Then they walked out into bright sunlight and stood on the steps of the cathedral looking at the stalls on Parque Central.

"You're better today."

"Yes, I slept and I dreamed of your birth. But it was now and I kept you with me."

"Oh, Mamá." She stroked Fabiana's face. "Does my father even know of my existence?"

Fabiana shrugged, lifting her hands in a helpless gesture. "I never saw him again after the Señora turned me out of her house." She met Paméla's steady gaze. "He was a good man. He was kind to me. He had a library with many books and he taught me to speak Spanish. I knew nothing. I worked in his house. There was no one but him to protect me."

Paméla stared at the sidewalk, which was covered with bird shit. "I can look after you now."

"I have Ernesto."

"No. Don't you see, Mamá? It's the same thing. You're grown up now and you're doing the same thing, letting a Ladino man have control over you."

"You have no right. Ernesto loves me. I am free to do as I wish."

"Then come to Canada with me."

Fabiana drew herself up, a small woman clutching her purse for security. "We will go for my passport."

Paméla gasped. "You mean . . . you'll come!"

"Why not?" she replied bravely. "Ernesto wants me to go. And he will help with the passport. I can give his name as a reference." She laughed as Paméla hugged her. "You see, you misjudge him."

"I'm sorry."

Museo Ixchel, the textile museum named for the Mayan Goddess of weaving, was a bright building with light flooding through many windows, a relief after the dingy passport office where they had waited more than an hour before being ushered into an even smaller office. Paméla had slipped an American $50 bill across the desk with Fabiana's application, which she'd filled out herself, because Fabiana could neither read nor write. They had given the general's name as reference and the clerk had grinned and promised that the passport would be ready within three weeks. "That means six," Fabiana had whispered, "Maybe five if we're lucky. Ernesto told me."

The museum was filled with beautiful fabrics, all hand-woven in brilliant colours. "Mamá, have you seen this before?" Paméla pointed to a backstrap loom with a half-completed weaving strung on its faded threads. One end was slung around the hips of a stiff model, the other end attached to a pole. Fabiana stared, her eyes faraway, her face expressionless. "Did your mother weave with a loom like that tied to a tree?"

"I don't remember much before the massacre, except . . . my mother grinding the corn on a piece of stone. She made tortillas, slapping her hands, like this." Fabiana clapped her hands together slowly, from side to side. "Me and Dolores sat on the ground shelling beans from the dry pods, watching Mamá."

Fabiana stood a long time before a small figurine of Ixchel, like the copy Paméla had given to Guadalupe. Paméla asked her if she wanted a copy of Ixchel for herself from the museum shop, but she shook her head, so Paméla bought her instead a piece of brightly woven fabric. "This is for your apartment," she said, "to brighten that place and make it yours."

"*Gracias, gracias*," she said, bundling the rolled cloth under her arm.

"Don't you want a bag?" the assistant asked and Fabiana shook her head.

They walked through the campus of Marroquin University, past the Popol Vuh Museum and through streets dappled with sunlight filtering through a bright canopy of leaves. They passed a hibiscus hedge loaded with scarlet flowers and as Paméla plucked one and put it behind Fabiana's ear she thought of Guadalupe. She wanted to see her again, to apologize for her intrusion. When they reached the busy thoroughfare of La Reforma, where buses barrelled along every few minutes belching black exhuast, Fabiana turned to Paméla suddenly. "I don't want to leave you, but I'm nervous. It's not safe for you to be seen with me."

"But you're my mother."

"Please, you must listen to me. In Guatemala many things happen; people disappear for no reason. You must trust me and go back to Canada."

"No! What are you talking about? I'm not leaving this country without you."

"You don't understand, because your life is different from mine."

"But you agreed to come. What about your passport?"

"Shhh, I'm content now that I've found you. I prayed for you to come, now I have my wish and it's enough."

"But this is just the beginning, Mamá."

"No, no," she touched Paméla's face, fear in her eyes, "I mustn't ask for more."

A bus had stopped and people were crowding on. Fabiana kissed Paméla and jumped onto the bus as it started moving. As she grabbed the railing her weaving dropped and rolled into the gutter. For a moment her eyes were wild, but she couldn't move. Paméla picked up the dusty cloth and started running. She caught up with the bus at the next stop and thrust the weaving into Fabiana's arms just before it took off again.

"Phone me!" she screamed as the bus disappeared in a cloud of dust and exhaust, leaving her on the sidewalk with tears pouring down her contorted face. "I hate her, I hate her, I hate her!" she sobbed, trying to keep her panic at bay.

∾

"Bless this food to our bodies and us to thy everlasting service."

"Amen," the Sisters chanted in unison.

Guadalupe picked up her fork and ate in silence. She was in the centre of the long table, filled with silent Sisters eating. Baskets of warm tortillas were passed to and fro, each Sister keeping watch over her neighbours' needs. Guadalupe felt María-Teresa's eyes on her. It will be good for me to go away, she thought, while part of her screamed, Don't send me, please! She bit into her tortilla. It tasted like sawdust. She remembered Flor tasting banana for the first time, her little mouth smacking and sucking, tastebuds exploding with pleasure, fists clenched as she waved her arms up and down. Sister Angelina tensed at her side and Guadalupe felt a tap on her ankle. She reached for the tortillas and passed them to Angelina, then she saw that she already had two tortillas on her plate. Angelina coughed politely, covering her mouth. Ah, the water jug. Guadalupe reached again and poured. A slice of lemon floated on the surface. She felt the warm nuzzling of baby Flor's nose on her neck and without warning the water jug slopped and spilled over onto the table. She covered her mouth with her napkin to stifle a scream, then her chair scraped on the flagstones and tipped over, crashing as she ran from the dining-room. María-Teresa limped after her and found her huddled against a pillar jutting from the wall, supporting an arch in the colonnade.

"Guadalupe!"

She whirled around. "Oh Sister, forgive me."

"Are you ill?"

"I am . . . " she gasped for breath, "I am overcome."

María-Teresa reached out hesitantly and patted Guadalupe's shoulder, shifting her own weight to relieve the pain in her knees. Guadalupe noticed immediately.

"Sister, your leg, what have you done?"

"A fall, it's nothing. Sister Rosa will rub it for me." She pursed her mouth tight to hide her scarred lip, but the movement pulled the scab and it began to bleed again, trickling from her mouth.

"Oh Sister, what is happening to us?" Guadalupe cried.

María-Teresa turned away and after a moment Guadalupe saw her shoulders shuddering. She reached out her hand, hovering, unable to touch her, as though there were an invisible barrier around her body. When María-Teresa turned back she'd gathered herself and wiped her mouth. She licked her lips nervously to lap the still oozing blood and spoke sternly, avoiding Guadalupe's eyes.

"The sooner you go the better it will be for you, Sister. I will telephone Mother Superior at the convent in Huehuetenango and arrange accommodation for you, until you are . . . better. The Sisters will look after you."

Guadalupe felt a shaft of sunlight warming her face. Her lips parted slightly. "What about my work in the village?"

"It will resume of course." María-Teresa stood like a stone, holding herself immobile as she spoke. "I'll tell Sister Rosa that there is no longer need for her to replace you. You may return when Mother Superior deems you fit. You are not well, Guadalupe. You must rest."

Despite her stillness María-Teresa seemed to move beyond her form, a ghostly entity, and for a moment Guadalupe thought she was embracing her. She felt enveloped, even though María-Teresa had not moved, and she felt suddenly afraid of this woman who had been her closest friend and advisor.

"Goodnight, Sister," she said quickly, and she bowed and hurried down the colonnade, relieved to escape.

જ

Zaachila had heard the wailing night after night, filling the darkness until she knew she must return to the city to look after María. The mournful sound had followed her on her journey back over Mount Orizaba; Zaachila knew it was Malintzín she'd heard, speaking in the voice of Cihuacoatl. Now she calls her La Llorona, the Weeping One, and she goes to Tepeyac Hill to give thanks to Tonantzin for her safe return, but she calls her Guadalupe. Everyone has a new name.

જ

"Telephone for Señorita Paméla!"

She jumped up from the table, almost tipping the chair in her eagerness as she hurried into the lobby of Chalet Suizo and picked up the receiver.

"Mamá?"

"Paméla? It's me. I'm sorry about yesterday."

"Can I see you?" There was a pause. "Mamá? Are you there?"

"It's better we don't meet for a while."

"Please, I must see you. I don't understand . . . "

"I can't explain now. The cathedral . . . in half an hour."

"Yes."

"Be careful."

The phone clicked and Paméla was left with the dialling tone. What does she mean, 'be careful,' when everything's finally falling into place? Last night she'd dreamed of walking down Bloor Street towards the OISE building. There was a woman at her side and she'd felt so happy she could almost float away. The woman's identity wasn't clear. She was Fabiana, but it was Hannah who talked to her and Fern's quick gestures slicing the air, and all through her dream the smell of lemons and a sweet, sad feeling inside her happiness.

Paméla fought her way down Avenida 6, dodging between stalls, walking in the road when the sidewalk became too crowded. As she ran up the cathedral steps she saw a man leaning against the grey stone wall as though he were part of it. She noticed him because she'd seen him before, as she'd turned the corner outside Chalet Suizo, standing outside the gothic structure of the police headquarters. He was a small man with a neat mustache and he wore jeans and a dirty yellow T-shirt. Nothing remarkable about him really, except that Paméla wondered how he'd gotten ahead of her.

Fabiana was waiting in the back pew. She took Paméla's hand and led her to their side chapel. There were only two souls there, each intent on their prayers. "Kneel with me," Fabiana whispered. They knelt before La Virgen del Socorro and Fabiana began whispering without looking at Paméla. "You must leave the capital for a while."

"But, Mamá, we've already been through this."

"Listen to me. I'll come with you when my passport is ready. Until then I can't see you. It's too dangerous. I know that if you leave the capital you'll be safe. You must trust me."

"How will I find you again? Can I come to the Palacio?"

"No. We'll meet at Peñalba, five weeks from today."

"Oh Mamá, it's such a long time. I thought we could do so many things together, everything we've missed; going to the park, shopping, the cinema . . . "

"We'll have time in your country."

"You'll come for sure, you promise?"

"Yes, I promise."

"Don't let me down again."

"I won't."

"I'll book your ticket and arrange for your visa."

"Yes, now go, please, quickly. *Que le vaya bien.*" She closed her eyes tightly as tears rolled down her cheeks. "Go!" she hissed. As Paméla walked down the aisle a yellow shirt caught her eye. It was the same man. He was praying. This is ridiculous. I'm getting as paranoid as everyone else in this country.

∽

Her bag was packed. She would take the bus to Huehuetenango the next day, accompanied by Sister Angelina, who would return the day after. Angelina had requested this duty, because of her concern for Guadalupe since the incident in the dining room.

Huehuetenango was a city too, but smaller than the capital, easier, and it was close to the village where Guadalupe worked with Doctor Ramírez. The thought of seeing Chavela brought her comfort, but María-Teresa's green eyes haunted her. "We cannot afford to give away the heart, Guadalupe," she'd said. "The heart is our power and we must use it for the good of the world. These personal affections pass, but the love of our Lord endures. We have chosen to sacrifice our lives to a higher calling; it is a great privilege and we must be worthy of it."

Guadalupe walked across the street to the park, wondering how long it would be until she returned. It's my choice, she thought. I can be sad or I can embrace this opportunity to renew my vows and strengthen my heart. Sister María-Teresa is right, of course she's right. Her shoes kicked up little clouds of dust. It was five thirty in the afternoon. She had avoided the Chapel, choosing instead the solitude of her own thoughts. Where would I be now if my family had lived, if our village had survived? I'd be married with many children. I would perhaps be a grandmother by now. She held all the promise and loss of her life balanced within her. She felt young, and sometimes so old.

. When she looked up she saw Paméla crossing the street. She started running when she saw Guadalupe, and the soldier on guard turned to watch her, her hair bouncing on her shoulders, leaves scattering as she ran.

"I'm sorry. I'm so sorry for invading on your privacy. I should never have gone to your room, but . . . " She stopped abruptly. Guadalupe's surprise had dissolved into a brilliant smile.

"I'm going away tomorrow."

"To the village?"

"Sister María-Teresa is sending me to our sister convent in Huehuetenango. I've been . . . ill."

"I'll come with you."

"What about your mother?"

"She wants me to leave the capital while her passport's being made. She's coming home with me, Lupe!"

Guadalupe's face was wiped of expression, as though a curtain had dropped.

"What's the matter?" Paméla asked.

"I don't know. Everything is confused."

"I feel the same. All this paranoia and secrecy."

"Are you in danger?"

"No, but I had to see you, Lupe, to apologize. I'll stay away if that's what you want. But I have to go somewhere for a few weeks, and how wonderful that you're going away too. Could we go together? What's Huehuetenango like? Could you take me to the village?"

Guadalupe began to laugh. The soldier was watching them.

"What's so funny? Am I babbling?"

Guadalupe took her arm and walked her down the path out of earshot. "Don't take the early bus," she said. "Come in the afternoon. There's a bus at two o'clock with the Los Halcones line. The journey to Huehuetenango is five hours and your ticket will cost 30 quetzales. Go to Todos Santos Inn on Calle Dos, it's in the centre near the bus station. I'll find you there, Paméla. I'll come as soon as I can."

Oh Blessed Mother, what have I done? My heart is alive again. I'll go to the village and serve my people.

∾

"What is this?" Ernesto picked up the weaving from the centre of the table where Fabiana had spread it.

"It was a gift from my daughter."

"Ah, the tourists like to buy our Indian folkloric wares," he said, throwing the cloth over his arm, dancing around the room, teasing her.

"I like it, Ernesto!" Fabiana ran after him and grabbed the weaving. "I want to keep it in our apartment as a memento." She spread the cloth on the table again and smoothed it.

"Of course, my love, of course," he said brusquely. "So your daughter has left?"

Fabiana turned quickly and met his questioning eyes. "She's left the capital."

"And she will return?" He leaned over the table, his face close to hers.

"Of course, when my passport is ready. It's only for a visit, Ernesto."

"How long?"

Fabiana shrugged. "Two weeks, maybe three?"

"You've never been outside Guatemala. I'm afraid for you."

"But you said — "

"I didn't think you would — "

"You go to the United States with the president." she said accusingly. "Why can't I go, just once, only once, Ernesto?"

He took her in his arms and held her tightly, stroking her hair nervously. "I'll miss you, Fabiana. You've never been away from me."

"But you've been away from me, Ernesto, and what could I do? It's your turn to trust me."

"I do."

"Then why did you have Paméla followed?"

He pulled back from her. "You sent her away?"

"Yes. I don't want you to be jealous, my love." She reached up and touched his cheek. The skin was beginning to sag around the tired lines of his handsome face. "Promise me you won't let them touch her, Ernesto. Promise me."

He took hold of her hands and knelt on the carpet, tugging at her to join him. When they were both kneeling, facing each other, he spoke. "In the name of the Lord, I promise, on my heart I promise," he slammed his fist against his chest, "Your daughter will not be harmed, Fabiana." His eyes burned into hers, demanding that she speak. But Fabiana did not speak. She wound her arms around Ernesto's neck and leaned back, her face relaxing into a languid smile. He watched her eyes, caught the switch of mood, and his body was infused with her as she slowly pulled herself closer, bending and bracing her arms for strength as, with a slow unfolding, she wound her legs around his kneeling hips, swaying from side to side, rubbing against him like a cat. Ernesto began to pray and Fabiana joined him, entwined in one skin, neither knowing which was holding and which was held, trembling with one voice.

PART FOUR

Culture has taken over from nature as the primary factor in evolutionary selection.

—Arthur Koestler

Paméla walked past the police headquarters at noon to see if the man was there, but there was no one. The ominous grey building was deserted. By the time she reached the bus station she was preoccupied with buying her ticket and lining up to get a window seat, so she missed him as he leaned against the peeling wall, munching on a cone of freshly roasted peanuts, and watched her climb the steps of the bus bound for Huehuetenango. As they rumbled out of the city in a cloud of dust and fumes Paméla peered through her smudged window at the garbage-pickers scavenging through piles of steaming débris. They were children mostly and old people with bent backs, their cardboard homes dwarfed by mountains of waste. Here and there dogs rooted like pigs, and vultures flocked, their great black wings blurring the shimmering air.

It was dusk when she arrived and checked into the Todos Santos Inn. There was no message from Guadalupe, so she went out and walked a block to the plaza. It was strung with fairy lights and people crowded in the doorways of brightly lit cafés. What am I doing here, waiting for my mother in another city when we've just met? This is another crazy nightmare. She was lonely and homesick, so she walked into the Mi Tierra internet café and sat down at the only vacant screen.

Dearest Hannah and Fern: It's just a matter of time now. I can't wait to get home, although part of me feels like I'll never leave Guatemala. (Did I tell you about Guadalupe? She's the one who handed me over to you). I can't quite believe I'll actually be sitting on that plane with Fabiana, bringing her home to meet you. My whole life has become a series of unbelievable happenings. Did you have a good time at the lake? Don't rent my room out. I really am coming home. Just cooling my heels in Huehuetenango for a while. August 1st, AC 241, arriving 3:50 pm, OK?

All my love, Paméla.

She slept fitfully in the noisy Inn with buses driving through her dreams. Fabiana stood on the steps of each bus, a brightly-coloured cloth unfurling from her arms into Paméla's outstretched arms. She woke weeping from a final dream where Guadalupe was driving away, waving to her, shouting "Goodbye, goodbye," and María-Teresa held her arms so that she couldn't wave back.

She stayed in her room all morning, waiting for Guadalupe, then she went out for lunch and when she returned there was a message at the front desk. *I missed you. I'll come tomorrow at two.* She threw herself onto the bed and punched the pillow with her fist. Then she lay, listening to all the sounds: voices in the corridor, buses rumbling by, music on the street, *Girls just wanna, girls just wanna have fun* . . . Images skittered behind her eyes, all the craziness of the past weeks, creeping forward like children playing grandmother's footsteps, shape-shifting across her retina kaleidoscopically: Fabiana's shocked face as she stepped out of the shadows, Ernesto's booted foot pulsing, Sister Rosa's hand darting out to grab her, Guadalupe's smile, a burst of purple bougain-villea . . . She plunged into it, burying her face in the papery petals, wait till tomorrow, everything melting, senses jumbled, heart pumping, dirty yellow flash at the corner of her eye, Fabiana kneeling, her lips moving, 'We'll meet at Peñalba five weeks from today,' Ernesto's hand heavy on her shoulder, an explosion of *fuego del bosque*, burning, burning, big orange flowers, the aroma of lemons filling her eyes, head melting, trickling into her body . . .

Guadalupe was waiting in the lobby of the hotel. It was two thirty.

"I thought you weren't coming," she said.

"I'm sorry. I forgot the time."

"Can we go to your room?"

Paméla nodded. Her room was on the ground floor close to the lobby. She opened the shutters and afternoon sunlight flooded in, washing over Guadalupe's face. As she moved into shadow, sitting on the bed, Paméla pulled up a chair and sat opposite, watching her. She was smooth like a deep river with a hidden current.

"Are you comfortable here?"

"Yes. Are you better?"

Guadalupe smiled and looked down into her lap, hands twisting her rosary. "In a few days they'll send me to the village."

"How far is it?"

"Not far, fifty kilometres. I'll work in the clinic with Doctor Ramírez." She hesitated a moment. "Will you come with me?"

Paméla leaned forward. "Oh yes. Can I? Can I help?"

Guadalupe reached out for Paméla's hands. "We always need help. There's so much work to do in Huixoc."

"What's it like? Does it remind you of your village?"

"Sometimes. When I hold the children at the clinic I remember my baby sister. I held her when the soldiers came. We were hiding under the table."

"What happened?"

"My mother was so brave. She faced them with her hands on her hips. 'There are no rebels here,' she said. 'We're honest people. Let us live!' But the soldiers kept shouting, 'You're protecting the rebels! Look at all these tortillas. You're feeding them.' I heard her scream as they forced themselves on her. They stuffed tortillas in her mouth to stop her screaming, and they made my father watch, then they shot him. I saw it all, but I couldn't move. My hand was over Isabella's mouth, my other hand covered her eyes, and I held her with my body so they wouldn't see her. But she was so still I thought I'd suffocated her. Then they found us and they kicked Isabella out of my arms. I ran, I ran like a coward. I'll never forgive myself for running away."

Guadalupe's face was rigid. Paméla, still holding her hands, moved onto the bed beside her.

"If you hadn't run you'd be dead. Your mother said, 'Let us live.' She wanted you to live, Lupe. You must forgive yourself. It wasn't your fault."

"Only God can forgive me."

"What kind of God allows such things to happen, a whole village destroyed, a little girl left all alone? What kind of God is that? Not a forgiving God. No, Lupe, only you can forgive yourself."

"The Spanish came to destroy our people, but we survived; all these centuries our people have survived. In our time the war of genocide starts again, as though it had been underground, a wild animal sleeping all this time, but it's impossible now to tell who is the enemy. It was our own people who came to the village, Paméla. They spoke our language, our Mam."

"Extinguish the fires, break the vessels, abandon the cities, the pyramids, the hearth. Everything must change in time."

Guadalupe bowed her head, and Paméla was silent. Every gesture, every contact of their bodies seemed exaggerated like circus clowns and figures on stilts. She swung from a trapeze and, in slow, slow motion, reached out until her arm lay on Guadalupe's shoulders, the veins of her inner elbow pulsing at her neck. White horses circled her belly, their hooves thundering as Guadalupe turned to her. They inhaled each other and their breath changed rhythm in the heady uncertainty of the afternoon. Paméla couldn't imagine how they would ever disengage until Guadalupe finally stirred and she was released into the air, holding her breath, reaching again for her trapeze.

"Sometimes I wish I could leave this country." Guadalupe was surprised by her own voice, by the shocking words that splashed in her ears.

"You could. Fabiana's leaving."

"Ah yes?"

"Of course."

"We will see."

"I told you, her passport's being made."

"The general won't let her leave."

"He told her she's free to go, for a vacation. It's her choice, whether to stay with me in Canada — "

"Or return to everything that's familiar."

"Don't tell me it's about tortillas. That's what Señor Ruiz at the Consulate said."

"It is about tortillas, Paméla. It's about the corn, the earth, our bodies, our land, our food. There's no way to escape the circle. You'll come to the village with me and you'll see."

"What will I see?"

"The life you've forgotten because you were torn away from it when you were a baby."

"Extinguish the fires, break the vessels . . . Everything must change in time."

∾

Guadalupe was late returning and Mother Superior had questioned her. Now, in the privacy of her room she closed her eyes and smiled. She couldn't stop smiling and hugging herself. This must be wrong, she thought. She wanted to laugh out loud, to hear her own voice shouting, to taste the sounds in her mouth. She threw her arms up in the air and twirled around like a dancer. She had never danced, not since she was a child, bobbing with Mamá and her brothers to the sound of the marimbas. In her village there had been many festivals and celebrations, always with marimba music, and people wearing the masks of the Spanish as they danced the history of their conquest, making fun of the conquerors. She remembered the figure of Maximón, slumped in the corner of the communal house, an old straw hat on his head, a cigar sticking out of his wooden mouth. Maximón was the twin brother of Jesus, created by the Tz'utjiles people of Santiago Atitlan, to share his passion, but Maximón was always ready for a party, with his beer bottle and cigar, even though he shared Christ's destiny, working constantly to seek balance in a world of illness, wrongdoing, sorcery and death. This is what her father had told her and she remembered it now as she twirled around the room. "This can't be wrong. I feel alive!" She stopped suddenly as she heard María-Teresa's voice, saw the look in her eyes, and recognized now what she had denied for so many years. She knew María-Teresa would never permit herself the expression of such feelings. Guadalupe looked up at the crucifix hanging above her bed, almost ready to fall on her knees when, with a quick movement she turned and took the statue of Ixchel from the drawer of her desk. It was so small. It fit perfectly into her hand and took warmth from her flesh. She held it a moment with closed eyes, then brought it to her lips. "Mother Ixchel, I'm learning to love," and she wept, muffling the sounds with her cardigan, pulling it over her head like a chicken settling into the feathers of its wing. "Who can I love? I am a nun." This was her suffering, the uncertainty, the certainty.

∞

May 1539: The cortege moved like a slow serpent, snaking its way from Toledo to the royal tombs at Granada, and Martín was one of the bearers. During the first lap of the eighteen-day journey his nostrils were filled with the pungent scents of myrrh, aloe and musk, but as they advanced through the warmth of a Spanish spring the poorly embalmed body of the Empress Isabel, defeated by childbirth, matched the slow procession with an equally slow but sure decomposition. The pages bearing the casket on their shoulders tied strips of scarlet cloth across their mouths and noses.

After the Empress was interred Martín entered the household of her bereaved son Felipe, eleven years old and five years his junior.

∞

The first days in Huixoc were difficult. Some of the people spoke Spanish and welcomed Paméla, but many, including the elders, spoke only Mam. They nodded and smiled at her and the old women gave gifts of eggs, coffee, avocados, for her and Guadalupe, and for Doctor Ramírez. Of course the village setting was beautiful, high in the mountains, overlooking a coffee finca. Paméla could barely believe her eyes each morning as she watched the sun rise through the mist, turning the valley into a sparkling trough of gold. She felt at one with the village then, as though she were part of it and not thousands of miles from home. But by nine the gentle sun was a burning white fireball blinding her and she was locked inside her body, tight and edgy. Living conditions were difficult. Every time she dropped off to sleep she was woken by the infuriating whine of mosquitoes and by morning she was covered in bites. There was nowhere to shower, the outdoor toilet was a hellhole, and the single dirt road that ran through the village turned into a rut-puddled mud track every time it rained, which was generally each afternoon. When the village children got over their shyness they began to follow her everywhere, asking questions, giggling at her answers, almost ridiculing her. When a small boy threw a stone and ran away laughing Paméla had difficulty holding back her tears.

The people had clamoured around Guadalupe when she arrived, glad to see her back. From the first day she had been occupied at the clinic, often into the evening, and Paméla was lonely, so she asked if she could help. Doctor Ramírez shrugged his shoulders and said there was nothing for her to do, but when Guadalupe interceded she was allowed to assist, calling in patients, reaching for supplies on the shelves, holding babies while their mothers were examined, all the time watching Guadalupe, waiting for a few words with her. She gave up all pretence of control over her life. She watched the people in the village and slowly surrendered to the rhythm of their lives, rising at dawn to eat tortillas and drink coffee, standing by the stove with the women while the men ate, sitting on rickety chairs at an oil-clothed table. Everything happened very slowly and mysteriously. Even when people spoke Spanish for her benefit, in the house where she and Guadalupe stayed, Paméla could not understand the logic of their lives. Her questions received no direct answers, but slid sideways into the mud, like the wheels of the rare vehicles that braved the dirt road. Her anger and frustration rebounded on her, because there was no one who would play a part in it, and so eventually she had to surrender and become like a child. Then she met Chavela, and she fell in love, with her people, with the land.

Chavela had been in Huehuetenango to buy more thread at the *mercado*. She was expecting Guadalupe and the Doctor, but somehow she must have missed them there. When she returned to Huixoc after a few days, having visited the ancient site of Zaculeu and the village of San Pedro Necta for ceremonies with the elders, she heard that Guadalupe had arrived and she went to the clinic to see her and to get medicine for her husband, although the clean mountain air of the village was the best medicine. Antonio's lungs had been weakened by torture and he suffered from bronchitis. She saw Paméla sitting in the corner and greeted her in Mam. Paméla responded without understanding, but was unable to continue.

"She's from Canada, like you, Chavela, and she speaks Spanish, but no Mam," Guadalupe told her.

In the afternoon Paméla climbed the steep grassy bank to Chavela's house and found her on her knees, weaving. Her shyness dissolved as Chavela greeted her in English, the first she'd heard in two months, and showed her the weaving, explaining the significance of the colours and patterns. She replied in Spanish, exclaiming at the beauty of the half-woven cloth, at the wonder of finding herself in this village, her own story emerging like a long red thread drawn from her mouth by this gentle woman. When she was finished Chavela said something in Mam which felt to Paméla like a prayer or a blessing and she let the sounds wash over her.

"I will teach you your language if you want, Paméla." Chavela left her weaving lying on the ground and took her hand. "Come with me. I'll show you my garden and we'll begin there."

She taught her the names of the flowers, fruits, vegetables and herbs growing around the borders of her house: *tse bech* — *hibisco* — hibiscus, *laa* — *ortiga* — a nettle-like leaf used for pain relief. She named them in three languages — Mam, Spanish and English, so that Paméla learned the difference by feeling the vibration of each set of sounds, and began to understand more than Mam, but what language itself meant, the music of it, the response in her body. *Saq xi'n* — white corn, *xq'an xi'n* — yellow corn, *chaq chenq'* — red beans, *eq' chenq'* — black beans, *k'um* — squash, *poo ich* — hot green peppers, *chaq lo'j* — bananas, *oj* — avacado. She learned the names of trees, grasses, earth and sky. A new world opened in her, a part of herself which had been dormant, and she felt limitless, expanding into this place, Huixoc, on the edge of the world, joined with all the forces of nature.

Chavela pulled a leaf from a small plant and handed it to Paméla. "Taste this."

She put it on her tongue and rolled the leaf in her mouth, then she bit into it, absorbing the taste, bitter and intoxicating. She smiled at Chavela. "It tastes like coconut, but sharp and bitter."

"It is called *ruda*, a herb to help with pain. In English they call it rue. Do you have a garden in Canada, Paméla?"

"At my mothers' house, yes."

"When you leave Huixoc I will give you a cutting from this *ruda*. If it grows in your garden it's a good sign. You can make tea from it and you will be healthy."

Chavela took her to visit Manuela and her new baby, and as Paméla held the little boy against her heart, a throb of new life, Chavela said, "My kids are coming soon from Canada; my two sons, my daughter Julia and her husband, with my grandson. We will all be together again, and for my eldest son it will be his first time in Guatemala since he was a baby, just like you, Paméla. Everyone is coming home."

∾

Cortés owned estates and palaces in the capital, in Cuernavaca, in the valley of Oaxaca and in Coyoacan, but he wanted governance. He was determined to gain control of his ebbing life and to rule the land he'd conquered. He marshalled his men and made another expedition, to the north this time, to the lower reaches of California. He sought a strait that might link the Pacific with the Caribbean. Failing to find it, he sailed far into the Pacific seeking China and suffered terrible storms, a mutiny, and finally a shipwreck. Bad food, aching bones and insomnia plagued him, but Cortés revelled in his privations, believing they would cleanse his soul. He had financed the expeditions himself, mortgaging his lands and pawning his goods until he had nothing left. Repeated petitions to the king went unanswered while his tailors presented him with sheaves of overdue bills and his servants sued him for salaries due. Even his luck at the gaming tables ran out. He was drowning in a sea of debt.

By the year 1540 Cortés had no choice but to return to Spain. Forty-two days on the water in his fifty-sixth year. Again, a small boy accompanied him, his legitimate son, Martín, of pure Spanish blood. But time had defeated Cortés. As he stood at the prow of the ship a wall of bureaucrats rose with the waves, quill pens in hand, crashing against the hull, pushing him backwards into the ashpile of the past. The nation he had conquered, many times the size of Spain, the woman he had loved, whose body had disappeared without trace, taking with it his power over the land and all his good fortune . . . *I've grown old like my father who died in my absence. I wanted him to be proud of me. I dreamed of conquering the world like Alexander the Great. In Marina's arms I thought myself immortal; she enchanted me with her forked tongue.*

He stepped ashore unheralded, the man who had mapped the New World, named rivers and islands, cities and mountains, his achievements forgotten in Spain. But Martín his firtborn, now well established in the household of the future king, Felipe, greeted his beloved father like a hero and fought by his side, an exemplary Knight, under the banner of the Holy Roman Emperor, Carlos V, against the Infidel, Suleyman. When their fleet was battered by a storm off the coast of Algiers and Carlos gave the order to retreat, Cortés pressed to take Algiers with a reduced army, but the Europeans didn't know his powers of conquest, nor the impulse still alive in the old soldier, so Cortés was forced into retreat with 12,000 men lost in that storm.

∾

"Today there's a market in the next village. Everyone's going so there'll be no clinic. We can go if you like," her quick words tripping.

"With everyone else?"

"Yes, the bus will be crowded."

"Don't you want to rest?" Paméla asked. "You've been working so hard, Lupe."

"There's a special place I want to show you."

"Where is it?"

"You'll see. Chavela will come too. It's a long walk."

"I don't mind. I'd rather walk than ride in a crowded bus. We'll take our raincoats and some food for a picnic."

Guadalupe laughed. "You like to plan things, don't you?"

"What's wrong with that?"

"Nothing. But sometimes things don't turn out the way you plan."

"You think Fabiana won't come, don't you?"

An expression of pain crossed Guadalupe's face. It was only an instant, but Paméla caught it and she reacted immediately.

"Let's not talk about her, Lupe. How long have we been here anyway?"

"Six days."

"It feels like weeks. I've lost track of time."

"It's difficult for you, isn't it?"

"Did you speak Mam to me when I was a baby?"

"Of course. It was our secret language. No one at the convent understood."

"Chavela is teaching me. Just a few words, but . . . it's like remembering another life."

Paméla spoke with such intensity that Guadalupe remembered her as a baby, the freshness and vitality washing over her, recalling her.

It was a long walk out of the village before they began their ascent into the pine forest. When Chavela decided to stay home and work on her weaving Paméla felt glad. She wanted Guadalupe to herself, but even though she'd longed for Guadalupe's attention in the past week now that she had her alone she was silent. They walked arm in arm and Guadalupe laid her head on Paméla's shoulder in that affectionate gesture she'd seen amongst the village women. This place was so different from the capital, different from anywhere Paméla had been and yet she felt completely at home. As they entered the forest she remembered Iximché and the hot pine smell. She'd been fresh from travelling then and full of confidence, determined to find her own way. Now she felt humbled and hesitant, yet stronger than before, like a different person, but more herself than she'd ever been. She couldn't imagine ever leaving this place. When she thought of going back to the capital, meeting Fabiana, arriving with her in Toronto, it seemed impossible, like another world that she couldn't inhabit, even in her imagination, so she anchored herself in the forest, step by step, immediate and full.

"We're nearly there," Guadalupe said and she took Paméla's hand and started running, pulling her along the pine-covered pathway, which ended suddenly in a clearing inside a circle of tall pine trees, interspersed with red and yellow cedar. She sensed Guadalupe's excitement, but she saw nothing unusual, only a stone, barely visible against the dark background of the tree trunks. Guadalupe ran and knelt before the stone, and Paméla followed her and saw that there was a circle of smaller stones around the large one, which seemed to be growing as she gazed at it. There were fresh flowers and candles, some half-burned, some melted onto the stones.

Guadalupe turned and looked up at Paméla. "This is where my father brought me," she said. Paméla knelt on the ground where so many had knelt before her, and Guadalupe took her hand and placed a pine cone in it. "My village was not far from here. My father came to this shrine to pray and to make offerings to Itzámná. This is his shrine, the God of all creation. Do you see his face?"

Paméla peered at the charred stone, darkened by the smoke of candles and copal incense. She half closed her eyes and the face began to appear, dark eye sockets joined by a crack in the stone, pitted nose and broad cheeks. It was a subtle face, a face that merged with its surroundings. God of all creation; no body, only a head which held the world inside, a stone head which was everywhere you looked if only you could see it, in the forest all around, in the rivers, features worn smooth by the water, under the earth, working towards the surface, in the air, meteors hurtling through the sky. Paméla placed the pine cone in the circle and touched the rock face. It was cool and porous, releasing a memory in her skin of the funeral parlour, Hannah's father lying in an open coffin. She'd touched his waxy face, felt the emptiness of death, and wondered where Zaideh had gone. Bubby had wanted her to kiss him, but she couldn't. She had cried and run away. She leaned forward now and kissed the stone. It seemed to warm under her touch, as though it drew life from her body.

Guadalupe leaned back on her heels and turned to Paméla. "I've never brought anyone else here. For years I couldn't come, it was too painful. This is the most special place." She bowed her head and murmured a few words in Mam, then she turned and said the words again, and Paméla repeated them, beginning to sense the meaning behind the sounds. After a while Guadalupe stood and stretched her arms to the sky. A patch of light glanced through the trees onto her face. "I know where we can swim. Come."

They ran through the woods, back the way they'd come and Guadalupe veered off onto a narrow trail, looking behind her to check that Paméla was following. It was mid-day and the air was thick and warm. She heard the stream before she saw it, a rapid bubbling and trickling of water over stones. Guadalupe was already paddling in the shallow part of the stream by the time she caught up. Paméla saw a deep pool in the centre of the stream, Guadalupe lifting her skirt, wading in.

"Can I take my clothes off?"

"Of course," Guadalupe replied.

"Nobody will come?"

"Sometimes they come to the river, but another place, further downstream."

Paméla pulled off her jeans and shirt and waded into the water. Guadalupe watched her dive into the deep pool, and she stood there unsure what to do, then she turned her back and quickly removed her blouse and skirt, throwing them on the shore, and plunged into the water with Paméla. She felt the shock of cold water on her nakedness as she flipped under, eyes open, and came up with face and hair streaming, to the sound of Paméla's voice.

"Lupe, this is wonderful!"

"I learned to swim here, with my father."

Guadalupe dove under and swam in the green depths, her belly brushing the muddy bed. After a long while Paméla heard her surface behind her, then they swam in circles, the water like layers of filmy cloth, concealing them. Guadalupe was the first to emerge from the stream. She shook herself, her hair splattering drops of water on the stones, and dressed quickly. She was lying in a patch of sun, savouring the warmth, when Paméla came out shivering. She dressed and sat by Guadalupe, huddling into herself for warmth.

"Are you cold? Let me warm you." Guadalupe sat up and took Paméla in her arms, rubbing her body, cradling her into the sunlight, letting the sun fall on her head, then they were still, listening to the air fill with the buzzing of insects, their whirring wings. Paméla felt the river water drying on her skin, patterning her with its journey through the forest bed. Her teeth were moist, her tongue floating in her mouth, weightless. She watched Guadalupe's lips, slightly parted, the line of her nose. Their eyes met and the forest enclosed them in a cocoon of sound, filling their blood with a hot, sweet thickness and the aroma of pine sap.

"Soon you will return to your other life."

The words jolted Paméla. "Not yet. Don't talk about it, Lupe. I'm not ready."

In the ensuing silence they retreated, each into her own corner. Paméla stood and walked over to a ceiba. She ran her hands over the smooth trunk; the tree of life, muscled with growth. It felt like cool flesh under her fingers, like tendons and ligaments hidden within the tree. She turned to Guadalupe and caught the sadness in her eyes, then immediately Lupe was on her feet, laughing, brushing pine needles from her skirt.

"Are you hungry? Let's eat our picnic."

Returning them, as though in the silence they had been dreaming.

❧

In 1542 Malintzín's daughter, María, aged sixteen, married Luis de Quesada of the Mendoza family. Within eighteen months she gave birth to a child.

I dwell by the river, a stone embedded in soft earth, but I am everywhere for my spirit wanders the land and I see everything. They call me La Llorona, the Weeping One, because I cry for my lost children. When they hear me in the night they close the shutters and bolt the doors; they say I will steal my children back.

I see my child, María, in the courtyard of her husband's house. She kneels on the earth, tugging at the weeds around the roots of her maíz. It is growing well. There will be a fine harvest with many cobs to hang in the rafters of her house,

*where they will dry for the making of tortillas, atole, tamales,
to feed her family over the winter. She is my daughter,
unmistakably. Now Zaachila comes with a baby in her arms.
She is older, plumper, her face still sweet and willing. The
little one punches the air with her fists and wobbles inside the
circle of Zaachila's arms, then she turns her head and laughs,
reaching for her mother, and I know, unmistakably, that both
my children are his; they are the children of Quetzalcoatl who
returned to sire them, as it was predicted. My heart fills with
love for María whom I could never love as I loved Martín,
not knowing if she came from Jaramillo. Now my spirit could
enter the earth in peace, but for my firstborn, my Martín. I
want him home in the land of his birth.*

∾

The countryside sped by, giving way to garages
and automechanic yards as the bus rattled into
Huehuetenango, coughing exhaust fumes. The driver
cracked his gum and shifted gears sleepily as the
conductor leapt on and off the steps, shouting destin-
ations, waving his arms and signalling with an ear-
splitting whistle.

"Here we go again," Paméla said, smiling at
Guadalupe. "I miss the village already." She carried a
small cutting of Chavela's *ruda* plant in a plastic bag,
rooted in the earth of Huixoc.

"It will seem strange without you next time I go to
the village."

"We still have a few days. I wish you could come and
stay with me at the Todos Santos Inn."

"They expect me at the convent. But I'll come whenever I can . . . until you leave for the capital."

"Lupe, I have an idea," Paméla said eagerly. "We'll go to Mi Tierra and open an e-mail account for you."

"I don't know how to use a computer."

"I'll show you. It's easy. We can write to each other when I go back to Canada."

"You drag me into your strange world and then you leave me here, alone."

"Oh, Lupe, please."

"What will you do if Fabiana lets you down?"

"She won't. I know she won't. She promised."

"I hope I'm wrong. I was wrong before. You found her, didn't you? You did so much more than I thought you could."

"I'll e-mail you as soon as I get back to Canada and tell you what's happened," she said confidently. "I have a computer in my bedroom."

"You're crazy! I love you, Paméla but leaving Guatemala made you crazy."

Paméla grinned and shrugged. "Fabiana may come back. It's only a vacation as far as she's concerned. And maybe . . . well, now I think that might be for the best. I understand her better since I've been in the village, although I didn't realize it until just now. If she comes back, Lupe, then I'll come here to visit, maybe every year."

"We will see what happens." Guadalupe saw herself in Fabiana's place, climbing the steps of a huge aeroplane, flying across the border into the United States, flying for hours and hours to Canada, stepping into a new world.

She smiled at her own foolishness. She hoped Fabiana was courageous enough.

༄

December 2nd, 1547: He was sixty-two years old. He must have known that death was near, because he was on his way south to take ship for Mexico, going home, when he fell ill near the city of Seville. Hernándo Cortés made his final will, requesting his bones be returned to the New World to rest in the earth he had unwittingly ravaged by his very existence. He died as he had lived, surrounded by men, this man who had loved so many women, but who as Malintzín had understood, knew nothing about love. As life ebbed from his body his vision left him and in the embrace of darkness he listened and heard her voice far away, heard her soft tongue skillfully turning the words, closer now, her throat gushing, words tumbling one from another into his lap. He heard her voice rising with a piercing cry, then silence. Hearing is the last sense to go. He knew in that eternal silence all his desire; Malintzín with her conquering tongue, in his service, the word of God. He knew himself scalpel of the king, scourge of the Gods, his greed and passion for power used to effect an inevitable evolution in which culture supplants nature. *My governance was a dream. I was a pawn.* Hernándo left his body willingly, freed at last from his desires, and he rose above the town of Castilleja de la Cuesta where his corpse lay in a small room of a humble house. As he rose above the earth, above the ocean, he saw the small part he had played in a great design, and he knew himself finally as essential and expendable. He was forgiven.

∾

"Did you bring your weaving, Mamá?"

"Ernesto wanted me to leave it." Fabiana sat close to Paméla, stroking her hand, her body rocking almost imperceptibly.

"You don't have much luggage."

"I have everything I need. And my passport." She held it up proudly. The taxi dropped them off at the main entrance and they checked in at the Continental counter downstairs.

"You can take your bag on the plane, Mamá. It's small enough."

Fabiana shifted the zippered cloth bag from one arm to the other.

"Do you want me to carry it for you?"

Fabiana shook her head.

"It's hard for you to leave, isn't it?"

"Everything is so new."

"You'll be all right, Mamá. If you decide to stay with me in Canada we'll come back to Guatemala together and apply from here, then you'll be a legal immigrant."

Fabiana stayed close to Paméla as they walked down the concourse and took the escalator up to the next floor to have coffee. When their flight was called finally Paméla took a deep breath. "Here we go." Fabiana stood up. Her hands were trembling. They started walking towards departure gate number 27. Paméla went first as they passed through security, throwing her daypack onto the moving conveyor belt. She walked through the sensor frame and stood with raised arms while the female guard frisked her, then she beckoned to Fabiana.

At the departure gate she showed their passports and boarding passes, and glanced at Fabiana who was smiling with that faraway look. Paméla had kept her mind occupied with the necessary steps towards their departure, but now that they were poised for flight, she was flooded with the memory of Guadalupe, of their time in the village with Chavela, and their final days together in Huehuetenango. She was going home with her mother as she'd planned, but at what cost? Her mind raced ahead onto the plane, into the clouds, breaking through the blue brightness. If she hadn't already been half way to Toronto she would have felt Fabiana's fear.

"Rows 21 to 35, now ready for boarding."

But there would have been nothing she could have done. She handed their boarding passes to the Continental hostess, who tore them and handed the stubs back with a tired smile. She was already walking towards the hatch when something registered and she spun around. Fabiana was not there. She ran back and searched the blurred faces in a crowd of waiting passengers. She was jostled and pushed by people passing through the gate. The hostess said something, but she couldn't hear for the rush of blood in her ears.

"It's too late. You can't go back," a woman's voice said, a hand on her arm.

"I've lost my mother," she said breathlessly, "I've lost my mother!" She wrenched free and pushed through the crowd, out into the lounge. It was empty; the remaining passengers were standing in line. She ran down the corridor, almost blind with panic. Then she saw Fabiana's small figure flanked by two men, hurrying away into the distance. "Mamá!" she screamed and Fabiana spun around, her hands covering her mouth. She raised her arms and gestured Paméla to go. Paméla ran towards her, but the two men came at her and grabbed her by each arm and started dragging her towards the gate. They dragged her backwards, away from Fabiana, who stood in the empty corridor, her body a knot of anguish. That image of a woman filled with desire, unable to take a step, was to stay with Paméla forever.

"*Que le vaya bien,*" she heard whispering in her ears, "*Que le vaya bien, mi niña,* I am with you always."

"We'll escort her onto the plane," one of the men said to the hostess at the gate. She nodded and told them to pass quickly, the plane was about to leave. Paméla looked around in desperation, but the place was deserted and the men's hands were like iron clamps on her upper arms as they walked her rapidly down the covered ramp to the plane.

"Why?" she screamed. "Why are you doing this?"

"You're lucky to get away," the second man said, "You're not welcome in Guatemala. She saved your life."

Paméla saw every detail of his face; his thin mustache, the gaunt face, eyes narrowed with watching. He wasn't wearing the yellow shirt today.

"Don't ever try to come back," he said, "You're marked."

∾

Fabiana curled into Ernesto's arms as the limousine carried them from the airport. He held her as she sobbed and after a while her weeping subsided and she relaxed against him, staring vacantly at the darkened bulletproof windows. The driver turned to ask something and Ernesto barked at him, but his whole demeanor changed as he bent his head to Fabiana.

"*Mi corazón*," he murmured, stroking her hair, "*Gracias, Fabiana, disculpe, mi amor, perdóneme,*" a chant of apology and gratitude from a man who had gambled up to the last minute, then lost his nerve. "Forgive me, Fabiana, I couldn't risk losing you."

She looked up at him then, deep into his old, wrinkled eyes, bloodshot from lack of sleep. She raised her hand to his face and stroked his tired cheek. "I know," she said, "It's enough. I can't ask for more."

When they arrived home he undressed her with great tenderness and put her to bed, and he lay with her, fully clothed, his arm cradling her head, until she slept, then he crept from the room. When she woke, Fabiana found him slouched in a deep chair in their reception room, his mouth gaping. She unpacked her small bag and tiptoed past him to take a shower. She washed her hair and perfumed her body, dressed in a fresh blouse and skirt, then she made coffee and woke him. Her bright weaving illuminated the room.

∾

In 1540 the two Martíns, then seven and seventeen, had met for the first time, but their paths had soon divided as Martín the elder had married Bernaldina de Porras, daughter of a Spanish *hidalgo,* and resumed his service to the Spanish Crown. His heart had burned with the desire to return to Mexico as he had accompanied the Prince to England in 1555 for Mary Tudor's wedding, as he had fought for the Spanish in France, Algiers and

Germany, but his father's words had echoed, the words that shaped his life: "To fight the enemy you must learn to be like them. We must protect ourselves against the Spanish. They would be lords over us." Martín was well conditioned to endure one place while desiring another.

In 1556 when Carlos V abdicated in favour of his son, Felipe II, it was the end of an era and Europe, joined now to the Americas, shrank on its bones and tightened its hold. In 1560 when Felipe proclaimed that lands conquered in the Americas could not be held in perpetuity, but must revert to the Crown after the second generation, the path was laid for rebellion.

After Cortés' death Martín had received the promise of his bones together with a small annual pension, while his young brother had inherited all the estates and the title of Marqués del Valle in perpetuity, exempted from the king's proclamation. In September 1562, at the age of forty, Martín sailed home with his brother, the Marqués, carrying their father's bones, to be buried in the earth of Mexico according to Cortés' wishes. His bones shone in the hold of the ship, radiant with knowledge, sailing home to the land of his love, completing the circle. But it would be 385 years, seven interments and exhumations, before his bones came to rest in the wall of Iglesia de Jesus Nazarene, the old Jesus Hospital built by Cortés after the conquest and later converted into a church. A descendant would place his ancestor's bones in the wall to the left of the altar, where they would be sealed, with a plaque on the stone, as the serpent opened its gentle mouth and swallowed its tail.

The Cortés brothers' ship, battered by a storm, was at first mistaken for a pirate vessel as it lurched into the port of San Francisco de Campeche on the Gulf. As Martín stepped onto dry land, pale and weary from the long voyage, he heard a strangely familiar language. At first he did not recognize the Nahuatl words, then his face flushed with a sudden warmth as the soft guttural sounds stirred within him. Everywhere he looked there were people like himself, mestizos with golden skin and almond-shaped eyes, not quite Spanish, not quite Indian. Martín Cortés was not a man given to exuberance, but a new sense of belonging grew in him and in February of 1563, when he reached the city of his birth, all his senses came alive to the familiarity of the place and to his forgotten self, the small child abandoned before he'd had a chance to know who he was, or to understand the world he had entered.

He has come, my child, he is home and now he remembers. He sees my face, feels the warmth of my body against his, he hears me call to him in the night, xochitl xolotl. *He embraces his sister, his full-blooded sister, and asks her about me, but María remembers less than you, Martí. I left her with Jaramillo and his new wife. Oh, my children, you must find each other and hold tight. I am the ground you walk on, the air you breathe, I am the river and the fire, my tears consumed by my flaming heart. I am a spectre in the land, and I will watch over you, my lost children.*

∾

A sudden summer rain fell, causing a rainbow to arc across the sky as Paméla landed on runway number 9 at Pearson International.

"Oh, darling, you're home." Hannah held Paméla in her arms while Fern hovered behind her holding a huge bouquet of pink roses. She thrust them into Hannah's arms as she embraced Paméla.

"Don't cry, Pam, don't cry, it's all right. You found her, that's what matters."

Paméla had wept all the way to Houston, where she'd sat catatonic in the airport during her three hour layover pondering her double loss and the ban on her return to Guatemala. She felt she'd been cruelly tricked, leaving Guatemala for the second time in her young life, and now barred from the country, at least until the general was dead. Just as her connecting flight was called, she remembered Hannah and Fern and called collect to tell them what had happened. She'd slept fitfully on the last lap, roused by the steward to return her seat to an upright position just in time for the sickening jolt of wheels hitting tarmac.

"Darling, I can't believe you're actually here. I'm so proud of you and all you've achieved. Your trip was a huge success even if it didn't end quite the way you expected." Hannah sat close to Paméla in the back seat as Fern drove them home along the MacDonald-Cartier Freeway, onto Queen Elizabeth Way, and down the Gardiner Expressway. All the way Paméla talked rapidly about Guadalupe, the massacre of her village, her work at Casa Central, about Chavela and the village of Huixoc. When Hannah asked about her birth mother all she would say was that her nightmare had belonged to Fabiana and she had returned it to her, as a gift.

"How can that terrible story be a gift? Isn't it best forgotten?" Hannah asked.

"No," Paméla said emphatically. "Without it she wouldn't have been able to make a choice."

By the time they turned north onto the Don Valley Parkway Paméla was asleep, her head resting on Hannah's shoulder.

"Where am I? Are we home?" Paméla woke abruptly as Fern swerved into the exit lane and the driver behind her honked his horn.

"Almost. We're at the Gerrard Street exit. Soon be there." She swerved again as a transport truck overtook the little car, creating a windstream. "Sorry about that. Are you OK, Pam?"

"I just want to crawl into bed and sleep for days."

"Everyone wants to see you, darling," Hannah said. "We planned a party for the weekend, but under the circumstances . . . we can reschedule when you're feeling up to it."

"By the way, you got straight A's in all your courses."

"I did?"

"Except Latin American history. Your grade is pending that paper you were researching. Congratulations, babe!"

"It's good to see you smile again," Hannah beamed.

They pulled into the curb in front of their house on Albemarle, and Paméla turned to look at the three storey structure rising like a strange pyramid out of an ascending rockery dotted with shrubs and Japanese maples. The giant maple was in thick leaf, dwarfing the house. Is this really where I live, she wondered.

"Let me help you with your pack," Fern said, opening the trunk.

"It's okay, I can manage." Paméla leaned in and hoisted her backpack, much lighter now than on her journey out. She'd given most of her clothing and her sandals to Lupe, and the rest of her things she had distributed in the village. Hannah and Fern turned to each other, their eyes speaking all that had passed during their daughter's absence. They watched her walk slowly up the steps to the front door, heave her pack onto the door step and reach for the key hidden under a plantpot in the smoke bush. She let herself into the silent house as though they weren't there, and walked down the hallway to the kitchen. Everything was sparkling. The house smelled of her childhood, of cleanliness and neutrality, a faint smell of musky incense somewhere in the background. She had a sudden longing for tortillas. She opened the fridge and saw a sealed plastic packet lying there. She could have cried, but she laughed as she remembered Señor Ruiz at the Canadian consulate, his sage words, her own naiveté. She dropped her pack on the floor and walked into the living room where rows of books and CDs stared back at her, an archive of contemporary, woman-centred culture lovingly arranged. There was Fern's pile of papers on the coffee table, waiting to be marked, Hannah's knitting spilling from a cloth bag on the floor beside her chair, the piano with its shining keys bared, welcoming her. She felt lost in limbo between the quickly-receding world of

Guatemala and this clean, sharply defined place where she'd grown up, dotted with details that should have comforted her, but which she now saw with an alien eye. It's like a dream, she thought, as though I was never there and Fabiana and Lupe didn't really exist. She wanted to weep as she relived yet again that wrenching moment of loss as the plane took off, but she had no tears left. In the background she heard Hannah's voice, smelled the pink roses as Fern plunked them in a vase and filled it with water, felt a hand on her shoulder, but she was almost asleep on her feet and was unable to respond. She heard herself mumble something as she moved slowly through the hallway and up the stairs, two flights to her bedroom. It was a long, low-ceilinged room, with a balcony overlooking the garden. She sat at her desk, switched on the computer and opened her e-mail account. Several messages came in, none of them from Lupe. She didn't bother opening them.

You were right, Lupe, she didn't come. Of course, Fabiana loves Ernesto, yes, I discounted her life. I miss you all the time.

She walked over to her bed, lay stomach down on the brightly-patterned cover and lost consciousness.

She stood in the doorway of the schoolhouse. Rows of children sat with their backs to her. One little girl, sucking thoughtfully on her pencil, turned and stared. She turned back to her desk and began writing on a black slate with the wet end of the pencil. Paméla turned and walked away from the schoolhouse, across the square. There was a green mound where the Papás had lain; bones under the earth pushed at the green skin, shaping it, like the mounds of Kumarca'aj. Paméla was a grown woman in her dream and she saw everything as she walked through the village. She saw the imprint of her shoes on the dry red earth, she saw the milpa in the distance, bright corn patterning the fields as broad leaves sprung from the centre of the plants, filling the air with a pale green scent. She entered a small hut. It was dark inside. The mud-brick walls were patterned with handprints and as she looked up she saw that the roof was made of dried corn leaves lashed together in thick bunches. She walked through the coolness of the abandoned kitchen, touched the empty comal, stuck her finger in the cold ashes congealed under a metal grid and wiped it across her forehead. There was no sound, nothing. It was as though she were watching herself in a silent movie. Then she saw herself standing in another doorway, watching Fabiana, who sat on the bed, her back against the wall, holding Ernesto between her legs, a tiny man, his back supported by her belly. Her arms, one hand in each of his, were wrapped around him, wrapping his own arms like a double straitjacket. He stared down at the blanket with glassy eyes, and Fabiana was in her faraway place, her eyes glazed over. As Paméla turned she heard whispered words breaking the silence of the ghost village. "Que le vaya bien, I am with you always . . . always . . . with you always." When she turned back they were gone and in their place lay Guadalupe holding out her arms. Her lips were parted, her face radiant with desire. Paméla stepped forward into the room and as she stepped she began to fall, down and down through the darkness . . .

She woke with a shock as she heard the front door slam.

∽

"Hannah?" Fern was washing salad in the kitchen, and she turned sharply as the door slammed.

"I got a couple of videos, a bottle of wine and some mangoes." Hannah plunked them down on the counter and kissed Fern. "Is she awake yet?"

"Not a sound." She dried her hands on her apron, and followed Hannah to the kitchen table.

"D'you think she seems different?"

"Hard to say. She's still in shock, poor kid."

"I feel terrible saying this, Fern, but . . . " Hannah's voice was low, conspiratorial, "I was almost glad."

"Me too. At least we can be honest with each other. I hate to see her so sad, but underneath it I can see she's changed."

"Yes, she's grown up, and now that it's happened I feel so silly. That's all I was afraid of really."

"Always beating yourself up."

"Not any more, I promise. I've changed too. Thank you for rocking our boat," she laughed.

"It had to be done. I want you forever. Pam will go away again, eventually."

"Maybe sooner than we think. She seems somehow, more independent, preoccupied with her own life. She didn't even ask about us."

"Well, look what she's been through. It must have been terrifying when those thugs dragged her onto the plane."

"I know, I can't even think about it. But even if it had gone according to plan and Fabiana had arrived with her, Paméla's different, Fern. I can't quite put it into words yet."

"She's not the girl who left us with such high hopes, is she?"

"She's carrying something now, the weight of her own culture, her own parentage, although she hasn't mentioned a father. I wonder if Fabiana told her anything."

"D'you think it was wrong of us to adopt her?"

Hannah laughed. "I think your question is ridiculous!"

"I remember you asking me something like that yourself a few months ago."

"You're such a gadfly. You pushed me, didn't you?"

"What d'you mean?"

"You prodded me into facing my greatest fear, that my baby's grown up. Now there's nothing to be afraid of."

"Not even when she leaves for good?"

Hannah shook her head. "We have post-menopausal zest to look forward to, darling. People start new lives when their kids leave home. Early retirement, travel, new careers . . . "

"Let's open up that bottle and drink to Paméla's homecoming."

Fern watched a smile playing on Hannah's lips as she opened the wine and poured it. Their eyes met as they clinked glasses.

"To all our homecomings," Hannah said, and they drank. Hannah laughed and wiped Fern's chin where a drop of wine dribbled, then she kissed her lips softly. "There's something I want to tell you," she whispered, "but I'm scared."

"What is it?"

"An idea I've had, but it only came clear today when Pam was talking on our way back from the airport."

"So? What is it? Don't keep me in suspense."

"I want to take my mom back to Germany . . . to Dachau."

"Oh my God, whatever for? She's sick, Hannah."

"I think it might help her. You can come too if you want. When Pam was talking about the massacre I kept seeing images of the camp. It's always been a vivid place for me even though Mom would never speak of it. She'd say, 'I don't remember. I don't remember anything.' Pam described her dream as a gift to her mother, and when I said surely it was best forgotten she said . . . "

" . . . 'Without it Fabiana wouldn't have been able to make a choice.' Yes, I heard, she was so emphatic."

"Fern, I think my mom left a big part of herself in Germany. I believe I have to take her back to find herself. People can live their whole lives without knowing who they are."

Fern was shaking her head, incredulous. "Here it is, another layer. How come you never told me any of this?"

"I took it for granted because it's always been there; Mom and her distance, as though she weren't really there, and me trying to fill the gap. You know how it is when you live with something. You just accept it as normal. But last week when I called, Mom was in the tub and her nurse answered, so we talked a bit, and she told me that Mom's started talking about her life in Germany, about when her parents were still alive. Fern, she keeps on saying, 'I want to go home.' I've got to take her. It's for both of us. There are tours from Munich. Dachau is a suburb with brand new condos just meters from the wall of the camp and the *Arbeit macht Frei* gate." She grasped Fern's hands. "I know it sounds crazy, but I'm so excited!"

There was a moment in which Fern simply stared at Hannah, expressionless, then she burst out laughing. "My crazy lover! A whole new can of worms. And you call *me* a gadfly!" She hugged Hannah and danced her around the kitchen, twirling her until they careened into the corner, dizzy from their spinning.

"Crazy, crazy!" Hannah gasped, "The whole world is crazy!"

"What's up?" Paméla stood in the doorway rubbing her sleepy eyes. In her hand she held a cutting in a plastic bag, its roots wrapped in damp paper. "I'm going to plant this in the yard," she said. "It's from the village." She nibbled at a leaf, savouring the bitter taste as she padded across the kitchen floor in her bare feet. "It helps with pain," she said, glancing back at her mothers with a big smile.

∼

"Guadalupe!" María-Teresa held out her arms and they joined hands, observing each other. A blush of colour suffused María-Teresa's cheeks and she couldn't prevent herself from smiling. "You are better, my dear. You look radiant."

"Yes, Sister. The mountain air has revived me."

"We've missed you at the convent. But you could have stayed longer. Why did you come?"

"It was long enough. And you, Sister, you've recovered?"

"I am well, Guadalupe, extremely well," she beamed, then her brow furrowed with concern. "Doctor Ramírez told me there was a foreigner in the village helping at the clinic. Who was it?"

Guadalupe paused a moment, her mouth open, "A girl who was travelling."

"Not Paméla?"

"Yes."

"Did you plan this?"

For a moment Guadalupe could not answer. A reluctance rankled inside her, something angry and rebellious. She was unsure of what María-Teresa's question implied; whether it was an accusation, a reprimand or a simple question of curiosity.

"Why do I always feel guilty in your presence, Sister?"

"Is there something to be guilty about?"

"It was a simple thing, a holiday, she wanted to help, she's searching for herself. Being in the village was very good for her. If you'd only seen how she blossomed," Guadalupe burst out, her own face flushed now as María-Teresa paled.

"We are not on this earth to provide vacations for tourists, Guadalupe. We are here to engage in God's work, to go amongst the people and represent Him."

"Paméla is one of our people, Sister. Why do you denigrate her? She deserves God's love as well as another."

"God's love?"

"What are you saying?"

"What are you feeling, with your bright eyes and flushed cheeks?"

Guadalupe spun around and ran from the courtyard, the bougainvillea a blur of red as she ran past it and up the stairs, two at a time, to her room. She slammed the door and threw herself on the bed. When she stopped crying an eerie silence surrounded her and she held her breath, listening, convinced that Sister María-Teresa was on the other side of the door. She rose from the bed and crept slowly towards the door. Her hand shot out sudddenly, grabbed the door-handle and wrenched it open on a spectral emptiness which frightened her more than if the nun had been there, spying on her.

∾

Chavela knelt on the hard-packed earth in front of her house. Dawn had barely broken and Antonio still slept. When he woke she would make the tortillas and coffee for breakfast, and in the afternoon they would go down to La Democracia, and from her mother's house there she would telephone to Canada and speak with her sons, her daughter, her grandchild, to make the final arrangements. She wondered what Paméla was doing, whether she had carried her words of Mam back to Canada. Chavela knew what it was to be in one place and long for another, to feel her body tugged and pulled. She knew that once you move about in the world you are always uprooted, never content once you have divided your heart. It was not my choice, she thought, but now

I live in more than one place. There are many worlds in this world.

She passed her shuttle through the open shed; one more thin strand pressed into the long stream of colour stretching between her body and the trunk of the tree at the corner of her house. Her weaving was almost done. Shots of red through the yellowed moon, the dark night patterned with stars, red, red, running through, pathways through the Heavens. She heard the bed creaking as Antonio rolled over and sat up. She heard the wheezing and coughing as his lungs awoke from the nightmare of their damage, gasping for air. How many times had they dunked his head, held it under until his lungs were bursting with emptiness, begging him to inhale the filthy water?

∾

A burning torch flared, its flames licking the stone wall of the palace. Logs were piled high in the grate, glowing on young Martín's pulsing jaw. The Marqués had grown, curved like a horn, in the shadow of his father's humiliation and had inherited his ambition to rule. He harboured a hatred of Spanish rule and plotted for the freedom of Mexico.

"Our father was broken by the king's neglect, brother. We must avenge him and seek autonomy for our country. He sought to have his governorship reinstated, but more than that he would have been king of Mexico, and I his heir."

"Avenge a dead man? Let him rest, brother. We are home. Isn't that enough?"

"Remember that you are Mexican, like me! Born on this earth, in a palace built with the stones of a Culhua-Mexica temple."

"What of your Spanish blood?"

"It matters not, brother."

"It gives you privilege."

"Swear your allegiance."

Martín clasped the Marqués' hand. "I will serve you, brother," he said solemnly, "I will join your retinue and wear your livery."

"Even though I am a full-blooded Spaniard?" he asked, his mouth twisted with irony.

"We are Mexican!" Martín declared. The firelight flickered on his face, warming his skin, accentuating the slope of his eyes. His young brother's face was hidden in shadow.

Martín lived in his brother's house on the western side of the plaza, with his children and his wife, Bernaldina, come from Spain. When the whispers started again he recognized the movement of leaves swirling in the courtyard, the dust around his feet, and he wrapped a cloak around his body and kept to himself. But his brother sought him out.

"There are thousands will join us in an insurrection."

"I cannot."

"To avenge our father."

"You have his lands."

"You wear my livery. Arm yourself, brother."

The disinherited nobility clustered around the Marqués, plotting their rebellion against the king's proclamation, until the echoes of their whispering rattled the shutters of the Viceroy's palace and burst them open. Men were arrested, imprisoned, interrogated and tortured. The Avila brothers were executed in the plaza before a crowd shocked into silence, and many more followed. The Marqués, with much to lose, paled with regret and knelt before the Viceroy to swear his oath of allegiance. He was sent to Spain to make his appeal before the Royal Court. The man who would be king of Mexico settled for his father's title and the retainment of his lands, while his brother remained in prison.

As he was led in chains, tied backwards on a donkey, through the Plaza de Santo Domingo, Martín the firstborn kept his silence. Seeing the son of Cortés treated like a common criminal, the people were silent. Martín was silent as they entered the Palacio de la Inquisición, silent as they tied him on the rack, silent as they turned the wheel. Silence, silence, all was silent save the tearing of his flesh, the cracking and popping of his bones as they left their sockets. The only sound in the city was the wailing of La Llorona through the long night. Not a word of betrayal passed his lips, son of *Los Malinches*, and on the third turn of the wheel his faithful soul whispered, "I will never speak. I will set it all to rights."

Martín Cortés, born under the sign of sacrifice and endurance, to right the wrongs of others, survived the rack and was sentenced to perpetual exile from his homeland in March of 1568. In addition he was banned from the Royal Court of Spain where he had grown up and served for thirty-three years. He set sail from Villa Rica de la Veracruz and returned to the only life he knew; war. Martín fought for Spain in the War of Granada, against the Islamic Moors in their last stand — the Morisco rebellion. He died fighting in the spring of 1569.

"His life will be lived astride the ocean, in perpetual exile, wandering, rootless . . . "

Malintzín sinks into the earth, her heart fractured, her song of grief holding the centre, her heart's desire, her children. She is a broken stone gone to ground and the land trembles with her cries, which fill the limestone caverns, rise through the sinkholes, echo in the night . . .

∾

María-Teresa saw her reflection in the darkened window of her room, the curve of her breast, the jut of her nipple, the rippled line of her ribcage. She couldn't sleep. Her narrow bed had become a rack. She dressed and slipped down the corridor silently, keys dangling at her waist, across the courtyard and down the long colonnade. She opened the door to the chapel and entered. She stood in darkness until her eyes discerned the pillars and arches, the stony saints and stained-glass scenes of the Passion. She advanced up the aisle towards the Holy Virgin and knelt before her on the cold stone. There she wept through the night, her body loosening with surrender, her heart exulting in the first grief she had allowed it. Sister Rosa found her at first light, slumped on the floor, an expression of bliss upon her face.

∾

Guadalupe climbed the steps of the bus. She carried a small suitcase and wore dark glasses. She sat by the window, her head covered, and pulled her cardigan tight. Her bus travelled north for five hours. In the city of Huehuetenango she took another bus, travelling west. They passed the turning for Huixoc and drove through La Democracia on the way to La Frontera. There she left the bus and shared a taxi with a young couple to Ciudad Cuauhtemoc. From there she walked across the border into Mexico. She changed her money into Mexican pesos, bought a bus ticket on the Cristóbal Colón line heading for San Cristóbal de Las Casas, and sat by the dusty road waiting. Makeshift buildings shimmered in the afternoon heat; a dog lay in the road panting; mariachi music blared from a transistor radio on the café counter where the young couple drank Coca-Cola.

The bus came finally and she took a window seat, her suitcase in the rack above her head. She leaned back as the bus jerked forward in a cloud of dust, disturbing the dog. Guadalupe stared out of her window at an avenue of pines bordering a field of yellow flowers. Donkeys grazed at the roadside. Everything was the same, but somehow different, darker, more distinct. It was the first time she had crossed the border. Paméla pulled her north, but part of her was still at the convent. She felt María-Teresa's eyes on her as she sat with the Sisters, eating silently. She smelled the earth surrounding the courtyard, felt the crumbling of it between her fingers, the lilies trembling. A blue light floated before her eyes, the aura surrounding Our Lady of the Medalla Milagrosa, and her knees bruised the wooden pew as she rose, pressing the memories. She didn't know how to leave. The wealth of her heart, the passion of her life, the love of God; could she live without these? Could she carry all that with her or did it exist only in the objects around her at the convent, echoing back to her, feeding her with the years of prayer, gilding her leaden heart with repetition? Her fingers curled around the small figure of Ixchel nestled in her pocket. She smelled smoke rising from the places where her fingers pressed and saw the coming days in the swirling patterns of her mind. Smiling, she lay back, her head rolling from side to side with the motion of the bus.

∾

Paméla heard the clip and squeak of wet stems as an old woman in a brightly-coloured scarf cut white gladiolas and arranged them in a vase in front of the altar. She turned to look down the aisle of the Iglesia de Jesus Nazarene. It had been a hospital, the first on the continent, built by Cortés after the conquest. Across the street was the palace he'd built for himself, which his descendants had inherited, and where the Museo de la Ciudad de Mexico was now housed. Bursts of red gladiolas lined the aisle, and Orozco's murals swept overhead on the high vaulted ceiling. She inhaled the sweet freshness of flowers mixed with the musty smell of history, layers of it; men lying in bloody rows, people kneeling in prayer, bones carried and interred in the walls of this ancient place, built on an Aztec site. She'd spent the morning in the National Palace looking at Diego Rivera's murals, meticulous works documenting the history of Mexico since the conquest. The Palace bordered the eastern side of the zócalo, the central plaza of Mexico City, where once the ancient city of Tenochtitlan had flourished. Walking south on Pino Suárez, hunting for the bones of Hernán Cortés, Paméla had found the place where

Moctezuma and Cortés first met, marked by a large stone plaque: *el dia 8 noviembre de 1519*.

She'd searched the church without success. There were plaques and memorials to other conquistadors, but she had to ask a young boy to show her where Hernándo's bones were sequestered. He took her up the steps to the left of the altar and pointed to a plaque embedded in the wall. *1485 – 1547 Hernándo Cortés*, and above was a crest with a cross in the centre and a crown. His bones had been sealed behind the stone wall, the boy said, in 1947 by a descendant of one of the four powerful branches of the Cortés family. Paméla placed her hand on the cold stone. There had been no fathers in her life, only mothers — Hannah, Fern, Fabiana, Guadalupe. One day perhaps she would see Fabiana again and she would ask her to take her to her real father, but it was a passing thought, lacking the emotion which might prompt her to pursue it. Maybe there was a middle-aged man at a desk somewhere, bent over his books in a pool of lamplight, shelves of books towering behind him. What did he have to do with her? Did he even suspect or care about her existence? Fabiana had been waiting for her, dreaming about her, before she'd arrived in Guatemala. How could her father be other than a disappointment at this stage in her life? Her heritage seemed to have more to do with history than biology.

Paméla turned and walked down the flaming aisle, out into the warmth of the Mexican winter. It was early December and already the vendors were hawking their Christmas wares on the streets. She tried to imagine Moctezuma greeting Cortés, tried to reclaim that moment on this busy street with people teeming by, jostling each other in their hurry. Had Tenochtitlan been like this? Were the Aztec line dancers in the zócalo something more than a tourist joke with their plumed head-dresses and their ankles rattling with conch shells? Did Cortés leave Malintzín in Coyoacan to visit this hospital, to supervise the building of his palace, to take the dead Emperor's daughters under his wing? She'd been to Cuernavaca to see the palace where he'd lived with his wife, Juana de Zuñiga, but there'd been nothing of him there. The palace was like a museum. Curled in the sunken entry, an archeological curiosity, was the skeleton of a man, a servant of the Cortés family, unnamed and unremarkable.

She turned and started walking south towards the Pino Suárez subway. She would travel to Coyoacan and find the Casa Colorado. She had asked everyone she met about Malinche. Was she a traitor? Did the Mexicans hate her? What does it mean, *Malinchista?*

"We call it *Malinchista* if someone speaks out against Mexico, or if they are susceptible to foreign influence," a street vendor told her. "But we don't hate Malinche," he said, laughing, "She is our mother."

Everyone's face softened when they spoke of her. There was a lightness, a warmth, a feeling of compassion and perhaps even gratitude for the woman who had changed history and given birth to Mexico.

∾

Paméla's face was elusive. Guadalupe couldn't picture her even though it had only been four months since she had waved goodbye to her, never expecting this, another chance. She stood before the altar in Iglesia San

Francisco de Assisi and gazed up at a massive wall of oval medallions depicting the saints, flanking the central figures of the Virgin and Saint Francis. Excitement and sadness churned inside her and suddenly she felt very, very tired. She turned and walked out of the church into bright sunlight. People passed through the forecourt of the church, a few tourists dwarfing the small people from outlying villages, who wore hand-woven cloth, the men in dark trousers with hats and creamy shirts, the women like bright birds in their skirts and *huipiles*.

Guadalupe walked across the cobbled yard and sat on a bench in Parque Fray Bartolomé de Las Casas. It was a formal park with hedges topiaried into the shapes of birds and animals. The tree trunks were whitewashed. Red and yellow flowers covered the ground inside wrought-iron fences low to the ground, and tall red gladiolas disturbed the orderly nature of the park like raucous birds with frilled plumage. Guadalupe sat facing a row of cafés on one side of the park where a few people lingered over breakfast at the outdoor tables, drinking coffee, eating *pan dulce*. She inhaled the crisp mountain air and felt the sun on her face. Her hair was loose, but she'd covered it with a scarf, which she removed now and shook her head until her hair was spread all around her shoulders. She still wore her plain blue skirt with a white blouse under her cardigan, although folded carefully in her suitcase were the jeans and bright blouses Paméla had given her. Her face was drawn with the strain of the past weeks, the pain of her loss, her guilty longing, the many e-mails back and forth, the impossible choice. At the entrance to the café stood a shrine to Guadalupe edged with the familiar, caterpillar-like aura of striated light, but this one seemed different. Guadalupe walked over and stood before it, taking in every detail of her namesake. Her altar was banked with candles burning steadily in the sunlight. Big red roses echoed the patterning of Juan Diego's cloak, and there were Guadalupe's beloved lilies with pale gladiolas and orange balls of fiery dahlias. The fierce flowers guarded and reflected the Virgin, whose head was inclined slightly to the right, her hands held together in eternal prayer. She was held by her sculptured aura with its scalloped edges. This evocation seemed almost muscular, as though the Virgin could step out of her cradle of light onto the cobbled stones of the street and step right into Guadalupe's body. She breathed in and held her hands to her breast. She looked down at the angel boy, his little wings spread, open arms holding the tails of the Virgin's gown, draped across the new moon which rested on its back, as it does in that part of the world. Guadalupe imagined the Virgin cradled in the moon and she thought of Ixchel, the Old Moon Goddess, Mother of all the Gods, with her husband Itzámná. Then she knew in a flash of fire through her heart that Ixchel and Guadalupe were one and that she was one with them and that she carried all the colour and fragrance and beauty of this shrine within her. The sweetness of her childhood in the village, her years in the convent, her future in Canada with Paméla burst through her like a swollen river breaking its banks, forming new tributaries. She was free and her freedom was not the leaving she had imagined. It was a coming, a belonging. Guadalupe smiled her brilliant smile and turned blindly, the shrine swimming before her eyes as she walked towards Avenida Insurgentes. Every few steps she turned to look again at Guadalupe, turning in circles like a little girl, with light springy steps. She felt twelve years old again, before the devastation, before any of it. She heard her mother's voice, warm in the sunlight, "Let us live," the smell of tortillas, she felt Isabella's arms around her neck, the rough and tumble of Mynor and Felipe. I am Calixta, her soul exulted, on and on, always, and she knew that she had left the convent and that she carried it with her. There was no need to go back.

She saw Paméla step down from the bus, and her heart filled with gratitude as she watched her looking around anxiously, waiting for the driver to unload her pack. Guadalupe savoured that moment of voyeurism, watching her, knowing before *she* knew. It was to stay with her all her life.

"You look different," Paméla said when they finally pulled back from a long embrace. Guadalupe wore a yellow silk blouse with faded jeans and red sandals.

"My clothes?"

"No, you. Your face, your eyes," Paméla said.

Guadalupe nodded. "Everything is changed. You can call me Calixta now."

"You won't go back?"

Guadalupe smiled and shook her head. "I've left my country. I've left everything behind. We're on our way, Flor de Maya. We will celebrate the end and the beginning here in San Cristóbal."

∽

Her weaving was done. Chavela took it off the loom, cut the threads and tied the ends. She was just beginning to knot the threads when she heard her children's voices. Hearing is the first and the last sense. She jumped up and saw them in the distance, walking up the muddy road in their running shoes and jeans. Her daughter held the little boy's hand. He'd grown. He was walking. Chavela left her weaving lying on the earth in front of the house and ran down the hill to meet them, her great heart overflowing. They greeted each other in Spanish, the language they'd spoken together in Canada. She lifted her grandson into her arms, and when she spoke to him in Mam his face broke into a smile; he remembered her.

At night she lay with him in the hammock, swinging above the earth, her weaving draped across their bodies, and when the little boy slept he dreamed himself inside the moon where he lay with Grandmother Ixchel.

EPILOGUE

●

Suspended in my hammock, I see everything repeated over and over; victory and loss, ecstasy and despair, creation and devastation merging like balls of mercury into a single sphere, then shattering, reforming, changed. The Earth is my kaleidoscope; I gaze on it, jiggling the patterns, playing with the diaphanous layers and configurations of the universe. History is a palimpsest of the eternal moment in which I exist.

GLOSSARY

alcalde	mayor
maíz	corn
masa	dough
cenote	deep natural limestone well
comedor	café
novicia	novice
oreja	spy, eavesdropper
comida	dinner
mercado	market
comal	skillet
pan dulce	sweet bread
hidalgo	spanish nobleman
caballero	knight, gentleman
pila	basin, trough
zapatería	shoe store
niña	girl
milagros	miracles
huipiles	blouses
cha'x a'jan	jade fly
q'ab q'anup	ceiba branch

The glyph on the title pages and at the beginning and end of each section is from the Mayan calendar. This glyph is named Ajmaq; it signifies the wisdom of the Grandmothers and Grandfathers, the spiritual leaders who fortify our souls.

PHOTO CREDIT: VICTOR PÉREZ RODRÍGUEZ

ABOUT THE AUTHOR

AMANDA HALE's first book, *Sounding The Blood* was a Fiction finalist for the BC Relit Awards and was voted one of the top ten novels of 2001 by *Now Magazine*. Her work has appeared in numerous publications, including: *A Room of One's Own*, *The New Quarterly* and *Fiddlehead*. Hale lives on Hornby Island in British Columbia.